Cradock Nowell

A Tale Of The New Forest

Vol. II

by

R. D. Blackmore

Double9 BOOKS

Cradock Nowell

A Tale Of The New Forest

Vol. II

by R. D. Blackmore

ISBN: 978-93-71467-37-7

Published by

DOUBLE 9 BOOKS

2/13-B, Ansari Road
Daryaganj, New Delhi – 110002
info@double9books.com
www.double9books.com
Tel. 011-40042856

ABOUT THE AUTHOR

Richard Doddridge Blackmore, who wrote under the name R. D. Blackmore and was born on June 7, 1825, and died January 20, 1900, was one of the most famous English writers of the 1800s. He was praised for vividly describing and giving people in the countryside personalities. Like Thomas Hardy, he was born in Western England and his works have a strong sense of where they are set. A poster for R. D. Blackmore's book Perly-Cross. Blackmore, who is sometimes called the Last Victorian, was one of the first literary writers of the period that other writers like Robert Louis Stevenson followed. People have said that he is proud, shy, quiet, strong-willed, sweet-tempered, and self-centered. His other books are no longer in print, except for Lorna Doone, his novel, which has stayed famous. In Berkshire (now Oxfordshire), Richard Doddridge Blackmore was born on June 7, 1825, at Longworth. He was born a year after his older brother Henry (1824–1875). His father, John Blackmore, was Curate-in-Charge of the church. His mother died a few months after he was born. She had typhus, which had spread through the town.

CONTENTS

CHAPTER I

It was a Tuesday evening when Cradock Nowell and Amy Rosedew signed and sealed, with the moon's approval, their bond to one another. On the following day, Dr. Hutton and wife were to dine at Kettledrum Hall; and the distance being considerable, and the roads so shockingly bad—"even dangerous, I am told, to gentlemen who have dined *with me*, sir," said Kettledrum, in his proudest manner—they had accepted his offer, and that of Mrs. Kettledrum, which she herself came over to make, that they should not think of returning until after breakfast on Thursday. In consequence of her husband's hints, Rosa felt the keenest interest in "that Mrs. Kettledrum. Leave her to me, dear Rufus. You need not be afraid, indeed. Trust me to get to the bottom of it." And so she exerted her probing skill upon her to the uttermost, more even than ladies usually do, when they first meet one another. Of course, there was no appearance of it, nothing so ill–bred as that; it was all the sweetest refinement, and the kindest neighbourly interest. They even became affectionate in the course of half an hour, and mutual confidence proved how strangely their tastes were in unison. Nevertheless, each said good–bye with a firm conviction that she had outwitted the other. "Poor thing, she was so stupid. What a bungler, to be sure! And to think I could not see through her!"

But the return–match between these ladies, which was to have come off at Kettledrum Hall—where, by–the–by, there appeared a far greater performer than either of them—this interesting display of skill was deferred for the present; inasmuch as Rosa was taken ill during the mysteries of her toilet. It was nothing more serious, however, than the "flying spasms," as she always called them, to which she had long been subject, and which (as she often told her husband) induced her to marry a doctor.

Rufus administered essence of peppermint, and then a dose of magnesia; but he would not hear of her coming with him, and he wanted to stop at home with her, and see that she sat by the fire. She in turn would have her way, and insisted that Rue should go, "for he had made himself such a very smart boy, that she was really quite proud of him, and they would all be so disappointed, and he was taller than Mr. Kettledrum, she felt quite sure he was." The bearing of that last argument I do not quite perceive, but dare not say that she erred therein, and to Rue it was quite conclusive. So Ralph Mohorn was sent for, the pony–carriage countermanded, and Rufus set forth upon Polly, whose oats were now restricted.

Kettledrum Hall stood forth on a rise, and made the very most of itself. Expansive, and free, and obtrusively honest, it seemed to strike itself on the breast (as its master did) with both gables. A parochial assessment committee, or a surveyor for the property–tax, would have stuck on something considerable, if they had only seen the outside of it. Look at the balustrade that went (for it was too heavy to run) all along the front of it, over the basement windows. No stucco, either; but stone, genuine stone, that bellied out like a row of Roman amphoræ, or the calves of a first–rate footman. After that, to see the portico, "decempedis metata," which "excipiebat Eurum"—not Arcton in this climate. No wonder—although it was rotten inside, and the whole of it mortgaged ten fathom deep—that Bailey Kettledrum hit his breast, and said, "Our little home, sir!"

"Your great home, you mean," said Rufus; "what a noble situation! You can see all over the county."

They had come to meet him down the hill, in the kindest country fashion, Mr. and Mrs. Kettledrum, like Jack and Jill going for water.

"Not quite that," replied Kettledrum; "but we saw you with my binocular, between two and three miles off, and became so anxious about Mrs. Hutton, that I said to my wife, 'Put your bonnet on;' and she only said, 'Bailey, put your hat on;' nothing more, sir, I assure you; nothing more, sir, upon my honour."

Rufus could not see exactly why there should have been anything more, but he could not help thanking them for their kindness, and saying to himself, "What nice people! Quite an agricultural life, I see, in spite of that grand mansion."

"Now," said Mr. Kettledrum, when Polly had been committed to one of the stable–boys—but Rufus still wanted to look at her, for he never grew tired of admiring anything that belonged to him, and he knew they wouldn't do her legs right—"now, Dr. Hutton, you have come most kindly, according to your promise, so as to give us an hour or two to spare before the dinner–time. Shall we take a turn with the guns? I can put my hand on a covey; or shall we walk round the garden, and have the benefit of your advice?"

Rufus looked in dismay at his "choice black kerseymeres;" he had taken his "antigropelos" off, and was proud to find not a flake on them. But to think of going out shooting! He ought not to have dressed before he left home, but he hated many skinnings. And he could only guess the distance from the lodge to this place. So he voted very decidedly for a walk in the kitchen–garden.

Into this he was solemnly instituted, and the beauties all pointed out to him. What a scene of weeds and rubbish! How different from Bull Garnet's dainty and trim quarters, or from his own new style of work at Geopharmacy Lodge! Rotten beansticks crackling about, the scum of last summer's cabbages, toad–stools cropping up like warts or arums rubbed with caustic, a fine smell of potato–disease, and a general sense of mildew; the wall–trees curled and frizzled up with aphis, coccus, and honeydew; and the standards scraggy, and full of stubs, canker, and American blight, sprawling, slouching, hump–backed, and stag–headed, like the sick ward of a workhouse fighting with tattered umbrellas.

"Ah," said Rufus, at his wits' end for anything to praise, "what a perfect paradise—for the songsters of the grove."

"Oh," replied Mr. Kettledrum, "you should hear the Dook admire it. 'Kettledrum, my boy,' he said, when he dined with me last Friday, 'there is one thing I do envy you—no, sir, neither your most lady–like wife, nor yet your clever children, although I admit that neither of them can be paralleled in England—but, Kettledrum, it is—forgive me—it is your kitchen–garden.' 'My kitchen–garden, your grace,' I replied, for I hate to brag of anything, 'it is a poor thing, my lord Dook, compared to your own at Lionshill.' 'May I be d—d,' his grace replied, for I never shall break him of swearing, 'if I ever saw anything like it, dear Kettledrum, and so I told the Duchess.' And after all, you know, Dr. Hutton, a man may think too little of what it has pleased God to give him."

"Well," said Rufus to himself, "I'm blessed if *you* do. But I don't like you any the worse for a bit of brag. I have met great brags in India, and most of them honest fellows. But I must peg him down a bit. I must, I fear; it is my duty as an enlightened gardener."

"But you see, now," said Bailey Kettledrum, smacking his lips, and gazing into profundity, "you see, my dear sir, there is nothing 'ab omni parte beatum;' perhaps you remember the passage in the heroic epistles of—ah, Cicero it was, I believe, who wrote all those epistles to somebody."

"No doubt of it," said Rufus Hutton, who knew more of Hindustani than of Latin and Greek combined; "and yet St. Paul wrote some."

"Not in Latin, my dear sir; all St. Paul's were Greek. 'Nihil est,' I now remember, 'ab omni parte beatum.' I don't know how it scans, which I suppose it ought to do, but that isn't my look–out. Perhaps, however, you can tell me?"

"I'm blowed if I can," said Rufus Hutton, in the honesty of his mind; "and I am not quite sure that it has any right to scan."

"Well, I can't say; but I *think* it ought,"—he was in the mists of memory, where most of the trees have sensitive roots, though the branches are not distinguishable. "However, that can't matter at all; I see you are a classical scholar. And, Hutton, I like a classical scholar, because he can understand me. But you see that these trees are rather—ah, what is the expression for it——?"

"Cankered, and scabby, and scrubs."

"That is to say—yes, I suppose, they would crop the better, if that be possible, for a little root–pruning."

"You have gathered the fruit for this year, I presume?"

"Well, no, not quite that. The children have had some, of course. But we are very particular not to store too early."

"I really don't think you need be."

"Why, many people say, 'let well alone;' but my gardener talks of making——"

"A jolly good bonfire of them, if he knows anything of his business. Then drain the ground, trench, and plant new ones."

Mr. Kettledrum looked quite thunderstruck; he caught hold of a tree to help him, and a great cake of rotten bark, bearded with moss, came away like the mask of a mummer. It was slimy on the under side, and two of his fingers went through it.

"Nice state of things," said Rufus, laughing. "I suppose the Dook likes lepers?"

"Why, my dear sir, you don't mean to say——"

"That I would leave only one of them, and I would hang the head–gardener upon it."

That worthy was just coming round the corner, to obtain the applause of a gentleman well known to the *Gardener's Chronicle*; but now he turned round abruptly, and scratched his head, and thought of his family.

When Rufus came down and entered the drawing–room, he was perfectly gorgeous; for although he had been in full dress for the main, he knew better than to ride with his Alumbaggah waistcoat on. There was nothing in all the three presidencies to come up to that waistcoat. It would hold Dr. Hutton and Rosa too, for they had stood back to back and tried it. And Rufus vainly sighed for the day when his front should come out and exhaust it. He stole it, they say, from a petty rajah, who came to a great durbar with it, worn like an Oxford hood. At any rate, there it was, and the back of Cashmere stuff would fit either baby or giant. But the front, the front—oh, bangles and jiminy! it is miles beyond me to describe it.

All simple writers, from Job and Hesiod downwards, convey an impression of some grand marvel, not by direct description of it, which would be feeble and achromatic, but by the rebound, recoil, and redouble, from the judgment of some eye–witness. If that eye–witness be self–possessed, wide–awake, experienced, and undemonstrative, the effect upon the reader's mind is as of a shell which has struck the granite, burst there, and scattered back on him. So will I, mistrusting the value of my own impressions, give a faint idea of Rufus his waistcoat, by the dount of it on that assembly.

The host was away for the moment somewhere, perhaps blowing up the butler, for his wife was telling her sister how nervous and even fidgety her beloved Bailey was growing; but Mr. Corklemore was there, and came forth to salute the great Rufus, when his heavy eyes settled upon the waistcoat, and all his emotions exploded in a "haw" of incredulous wonder. Mrs. Kettledrum rose at the same instant, and introduced her sister.

"My sister, Dr. Hutton, whom I have so earnestly longed to make acquainted with dear Mrs. Hutton, Mrs. Nowell Corklemore; Mr. Corklemore, I know, has had the pleasure of meeting you. Georgie, dear, you will like her so—oh, goodness gracious me!"

"I don't wonder you are surprised at me, Anna," exclaimed Mrs. Corklemore, with wonderful presence of mind. "How stupid I am, to be sure! Oh, Nowell, why didn't you tell me? How shameful of you! But you never look at me now, I think." And she swept from the room in the cleverest manner, as if something wrong in her own dress had caused her sister's ejaculation.

"Excuse me one moment," said Mrs. Kettledrum, taking her cue very aptly; and she ran out, as if to aid her sister, but in reality to laugh herself into hysterics.

After all there was nothing absurd, *per se*, in Rufus Hutton's waistcoat, only it is not the fashion, just at present, to wear pictorial raiment; but the worthy doctor could not perceive any reason why it should not be. He was pleased with the prospect of creating a genuine sensation, and possibly leading the mode; and having lost all chance of realizing these modest hopes at Nowelhurst, why, he must content himself with a narrower stage for his triumphs. He had smuggled it from home, however, without his wife's permission: he had often threatened her with its appearance, but she always thought he was joking. And truly it required some strength of mind to present it to modern society, although it was a work of considerable art, and no little value.

The material of it was Indian silk of the very richest quality. It had no buttons, but golden eyelets and tags of golden cowries. The background of the whole was yellow, the foreground of a brilliant green, portraying the plants of the jungle. On the left bosom leaped and roared an enormous royal tiger, with two splendid jewels, called "cat's–eyes," flashing, and a pearl for every fang. Upon the right side a hulking elephant was turning tail ignominiously; while two officers in the howdah poked their guns at the eyes of the tiger. The eyes of the officers in their terror had turned to brilliant emeralds, and the blood of the tramping elephant was represented by seed rubies. The mahout was cutting away in the distance, looking back with eyes of diamonds.

Beyond a doubt, it required uncommonly fine breeding, especially in a lady, to meet that waistcoat at a dinner–party, and be entirely unconscious of it. And perhaps there are but few women in England who would not contrive to lead up to the subject, quite accidentally, of course, before the evening was over.

The ladies came back as grave as judges; and somehow it was managed (as if by the merest oversight) that Dr. Hutton should lead to dinner, not the lady of the house, whom, of course, he ought to have taken, but Mrs. Nowell Corklemore. He felt, as he crossed the hall with her, that the beauty of his waistcoat had raised some artistic emotion in a bosom as beautiful as its own. Oh, Rufus, think of Rosa!

Let none be alarmed at those ominous words. The tale of Cradock Nowell's life shall be pure as that life itself was. The historian may be rough, and blunt, and sometimes too intense, in the opinion of those who look at life from a different point of view. But be that as it will, his other defects (I trust and pray) will chiefly be deficiencies. We will have no poetical seduction, no fascinating adultery, condemned and yet reprieved by the writer, and infectious from his sympathy. Georgiana Corklemore was an uncommonly clever woman, and was never known to go far enough to involve her reputation. She loved her child, and liked her husband, and had all the respect for herself which may abide with vanity. Nevertheless she flirted awfully, and all married women hated her. "Bold thing," they called her, "sly good–for–nothing; and did you see how she ogled? Well, if I only carried on so! Oh, if I were only her husband! But, poor man, he knows no better. Such a poor dear stick, you know. Perhaps that is what makes her do it. And nothing in her at all, when you come to think of it. No taste, no style, no elegance! When *will* she put her back hair up? And her child fit to put into long–clothes! Did you observe her odious way of putting her lips up, as if to be kissed? My dear, I don't know how *you* felt; but I could scarcely stay in the room with her."

Nevertheless the ladies did stay, and took good care to watch her, and used to say to her afterwards, "Oh, if I were only like you, dear! Then I need not be afraid of you; but you are—now don't tell stories—*so* clever, and *so* attractive. As if you did not know it, dear! Well, you *are* so simple–minded. I am always telling my Looey and Maggie to take you for their model, dear!"

On the present occasion, "Georgie Corklemore," as she called herself, set about flirting with Rufus Hutton, not from her usual love of power, nor even for the sake of his waistcoat, but because she had an especial purpose, and a very important one. The Kettledrum–cum–Corklemore conspiracy was this—to creep in once more at Nowelhurst Hall through the interest of Dr. Hutton. They all felt perfectly certain that Cradock Nowell had murdered his brother, and that the crime had been hushed up through the influence of the family. They believed that the head of that family, in his passionate sorrow and anger, might be brought to their view of the subject, if he could only be handled properly; and who could manage that more adroitly than his first cousin once removed, the beautiful Mrs. Corklemore? Only let her get once invited, once inducted there, and the main difficulty after that would be to apportion the prey between them. They knew well enough that the old entail expired with the present baronet; and that he (before his marriage) held in fee pure and simple all that noble property. His marriage–settlement, and its effects, they could only inkle of; but their heart was inditing of a good matter, and Mr. Chope would soon pump Brockwood. Not quite so fast, my Amphictyonics; a solicitor thirty years admitted (though his original craft may not be equal) is not to be sucked dry, on the surprise, even by spongy young Chope. However, that was a question for later consideration; and blood being thicker than water, and cleaving more fast to the ground, they felt that it would be a frightful injustice if they were done out of the property.

Only two things need be added: one that Sir Cradock had always disliked, and invited them but for appearance' sake; the other, that they fairly believed in the righteousness of their cause, and that Rufus Hutton could prove it for them, as the principal witness tampered with.

Mrs. Corklemore was now, perhaps, twenty–five years old, possibly turning thirty; for that lustrum of a lady's life is a hard one to beat the bounds of; at any rate, she had never looked better than she did at the present moment. She was just at the age to spread open, with the memory of shyness upon them (like the dew when the sun is up), the curving petals of beauty. Who understands the magnetic current? Who can analyze ozone? Is there one of us able to formularize the polarity of light? Will there ever be an age when chemists metaphysical will weigh—no more by troy weight, and carat, as now the mode is, but by subtle heart–gas—our liking for a woman? Let us hope there never will be.

That soft Georgiana Corklemore, so lively, lovely, and gushing, focussed all her fascinations upon Rufus Hutton. She knew that she had to deal with a man of much inborn acuteness, and who must have seen a hundred ladies quite as fair as Georgie. But had he seen one with her—well, she knew not what to call it, though she thoroughly knew how to use it? So she magnetized him with all her skill; and Rufus, shrewdly suspecting her object, and confiding in a certain triarian charge, a certain thrust Jarnacian, which he would deliver at the proper moment, allowed her to smile, and to show her white teeth and dimples of volatile velvet (so natural, so inevitable, at his playful, delightful humour), and to loose whole quiverfuls of light shafts from the arch flash under her eyelids. What sweet simplicity she was, what innocent desire to learn, what universal charity. "How dreadful, Dr. Hutton! Oh, please not to tell me of it! How could any ladies do it? I should have fainted at once, and died half an hour afterwards." She turned up her large mild eyes, deeply beaming with centralized light, in a way that said, "If I died, is there any one who would think it a very, very great pity?"

Rufus had been describing historically, not dramatically, the trials of the ladies, when following their regiment during a sudden movement in the perils of the mutiny. With a man's far stiffer identity, he did not expect or even imagine that his delicate listener would be there, and go through every hour of it. But so it was, and without any sham; although she was misusing her strange sympathetic power. Mrs. Nowell Corklemore would have made a very great actress; she had so much self–abandonment, such warm introjection, and hot indignant sympathy; and yet enough of self–reservation to hoop them all in with judgment. Meanwhile Mrs. Kettledrum, a lady of ordinary sharpness, like a good pudding–apple—Georgie being a peach of the very finest quality—she, I say, at the top of the table was watching them very intently—delighted, amused, indignant; glad that none of her children were there to store up Auntie's doings. As for Mr. Corklemore, he was quite accustomed to it; and looking down complacently upon the little doctor, thought to himself, "How beautifully my Georgie will cold–shoulder him, when we have got all we want out of the conceited chattering jackanapes."

When the ladies were gone, Mr. Bailey Kettledrum, who had no idea of playing dummy even to Mrs. Corklemore, made a trick or two from his own hand.

"Corklemore, my dear fellow, you think we are all tee–totallers. On with the port, if you please, 'cessantem Bibuli Consulis amphoram,' never shall forget that line. The bibulous consul, eh! Capital idea. Corklemore, you can construe that?"

"Haw! Perhaps I can't. Really don't know; they beat a heap of stuff into me when I was a very small boy; and it was like whipping—ha, haw, something like whipping——"

"Eggs," said Rufus Hutton, "all came to bubbles, eh?"

"Not at all, sir, not at all; you entirely misunderstand me. I mean that it was similar to—to the result produced by the whipping of a top."

"Only made your head go round," said Mr. Kettledrum, winking at Rufus; and thenceforth had established a community of interest in the baiting of "long Corklemore." "Well, at any rate," he continued, "Hutton is a scholar—excuse my freedom, my dear sir; we are such rustics here, that I seldom come across a man who appreciates my quotations. You are a great acquisition, sir, the very greatest, to this neighbourhood. How can we have let you remain so long without unearthing you?"

"Because," said Rufus to himself, "you did not happen to want me; when are you going to offer to introduce me to 'the Dook?'"

"And now, gentlemen," continued Mr. Kettledrum, rising, swelling his chest out, and thumping it athletically, "it is possible that I may be wrong; I have never been deaf to conviction; but if I am wrong, gentlemen, the fault is in yourselves. Mark me now, I am ready, such is the force of truth, I am ready here at my own board (humble as it is) once for all to admit that the fault is in yourselves. But the utterance I swell with, the great thought that is within me, is strife—no, I beg your pardon—is—is—rife and strongly inditing of a certain lady, who is an honour to her sex. I rise to the occasion, friends; I say an honour to her sex, and a blessing to the other one. Gentlemen, no peroration of mine is equal in any way to the greatness of the occasion; could I say, with Cicero, 'Veni, vidi, vici,' where would be my self–approval? I mean—you understand me. It is the privilege of a man in this blessed country, the first gem of the ocean—no, I don't mean that; it applies, I believe, to Scotland, and the immortal Burns—but this, sir, I will say, and challenge contradiction, a Briton, sir, a Briton, never, never, never will be free! And now, sir, in conclusion, is there one of you, let me ask, who will not charge his eyes, gentlemen, and let his glass run over——"

"Haw," cried Mr. Corklemore, "charge his glass, come, Kettledrum, and let his eyes run over—haw—I think that is the way we read it, Dr. Hutton."

"Gentlemen, I sit down; finding it impossible to obtain an adequate bearing, I close my poor attempt at cleansing my bosom of the perilous stuff, sir—you know the rest—the health of Mrs. Hutton, that most remarkable children—excuse me, most remarkable woman, whose children, I am quite convinced, will be an honour to their age and sex. Port of '51, gentlemen; a finer vintage than '47."

He had told them that it was '34, but both knew better; and now "in vino veritas."

At last Mr. Bailey Kettledrum had hit the weak point of Rufus, and, what was more, he perceived it. Himself you might butter and soap for a month, and he would take it at all its value; but magnify his Rosa, exalt the name of his Rosa, and you had him at discretion.

"Remarkable, sir," he inquired, with a twinkle of fruity port stealing out from his keen little eyes, "you really do injustice; so many ladies are remarkable——"

"Haw, well, I never heard——"

"Confound you, Corklemore," said Kettledrum to him aside, "can you never hold your tongue? Sir,"—to Rufus—"I beg your pardon, if I said 'remarkable;' I meant to say, sir, '*most* remarkable!' The most remarkable lady"—this to Corklemore, in confidence—"I have ever been privileged to meet. 'What children,' I said to my wife, but yesterday, 'what children they will be blest with!' Oh, he's a lucky dog. The luckiest dog in the world, my boy."

However, they were not so very far from the sloping shores of sobriety when they rejoined the ladies, and made much of the small Misses Kettledrum, tidy children, rather pretty, and all of the pink ribbon pattern. After some melting melodies from soft Georgie's lips and fingers, Mrs. Kettledrum said,

"Oh, Dr. Hutton, do you ever play chess? We are such players here; all except my poor self; I am a great deal too stupid."

"I used to play a little when I was in India. We are obliged to play all sorts of games in India." Dr. Hutton piqued himself not a little on his skill in the one true game. At a sign from their mother, the small Kettledrums rushed for the board most zealously, and knocked their soft heads together. Mrs. Corklemore was declared by all to be the only antagonist worthy of an Indian player, and she sat down most gracefully, protesting against her presumption. "Just to take a lesson, you know; only to take a lesson, dear. Oh, please, don't let any one look at me." Rufus, however, soon perceived that he had found his match, if not his superior, in the sweet impulsive artless creature, who threw away the game so neatly when she was quite sure of it.

"Oh, poor me! Now, I do declare—Isn't it most heartbreaking? I am such a foolish thing. Oh, can you be so cruel?"

Thrilling eyes of the richest grey trembled with dewy radiance, as Rufus coolly marched off the queen, and planted his knight instead of her.

"Mrs. Corklemore, can I relent? You are far too good a player." The loveliest eyes, the most snowy surge, in the "mare magnum" of ladies, would never have made that dry Rue Hutton, well content with his Rosa, give away so much as the right to capture a pawn in passing.

Now observe the contrariety, the want of pure reason, the confusion of principle—I am sorry and ashamed, but I can't express these things in English, for the language is rich in emotion, but a pauper in philosophy—the distress upon the premises of the cleverest woman's mind. She had purposely thrown her queen in his way; but she never forgave him for taking it.

A glance shot from those soft bright eyes, when Rufus could not see them, as if the gentle evening star, Venus herself, all tremulous, rushed, like a meteor, up the heavens, and came hissing down on a poor man's head.

She took good care to win the next game, for policy allowed it; and then, of course, it was too late to try the decisive contest.

"Early hours. Liberty Hall, Liberty Hall at Kettledrum! Gentlemen stay up, and smoke if they like. But early hours, sir, for the ladies. We value their complexions. They don't. That I know. Do you now, my dearest? No, of course you don't." This was Mr. Kettledrum.

"Except for your sake, darling," said Mrs. Kettledrum, curtseying, for the children were all gone to bed ever so long ago.

"Well," said Georgie, coming forward, because she knew her figure would look well with three lamps upon it; such a figure of eight! "my opinion is never worth having, I know, because I feel so much; but I pronounce— —" here she stood up like Portia, with a very low–necked dress on—"gentlemen, and ladies, I pronounce that one is quite as bad as the other."

"Haw!" said Nowell Corklemore. And so they went to bed. And Rufus Hutton wondered whether they ever had family prayers.

When all the rest were at breakfast, in came Mrs. Corklemore, looking as fresh as daybreak.

"Oh, I am so ashamed of myself. What a sluggard you will think me! What is it in the divine song of that great divine, Dr. Watts? Nowell, dear, you must not scold me. I cannot bear being scolded, because I never have tit for tat. Good morning, dearest Anna; how is your headache, darling? Oh, Dr. Hutton, I forgot! No wonder I overlooked you. I shall never think much of you again, because I beat you at chess so."

"Game and game," said Rufus, solemnly, "and I ought to have won that last one, Mrs. Corklemore; you know I ought."

"To be sure, to be sure. Oh, of course I do. But—a little thing perwented him—his antagonist was too good, sir. Ah, we'll play the conqueror some day; and then the tug of war comes. Oh, Anna, I am so conceited! To think of my beating Dr. Hutton, the best player in all India."

"Well, darling, we know all that. And we must not blame you therefore for lying in bed till ten o'clock."

"Oh," said Rufus, with a groan, "do look at ladies' logic! Mrs. Corklemore gained one game out of two—only because I was—ah–hem, I mean by her very fine play—and now she claims absolute victory; and Mrs. Kettledrum accepts it as a premise for a negative conclusion, which has nothing on earth to do with it."

But Rufus got the worst of that protest. He tilted too hard at the quintain. All came down upon him at once, till he longed for a cigar. Then Mrs. Corklemore sympathized with him, arose, their breakfast being over, and made him a pretty curtsey. She was very proud of her curtseys; she contrived to show her figure so.

"Confound that woman," thought Rufus, "I can never tell when she is acting. I never met her like in India. And thank God for that same."

She saw that her most bewitching curtsey was entirely thrown away upon him; for he was thinking of his Rosa, and looking out for the good mare, Polly.

"Dr. Hutton, I thank you for your condescension, in giving me that lesson. You let me win that last game out of pure good nature. I shall always appreciate it. Meanwhile I shall say to every one—'Oh, do you know, Dr. Hutton and I play even?' taking very good care meanwhile never to play again with you. Shocking morality! Yes, very shocking. But then I know no better, do I, Nowell, dear?"

"Haw! Well, Georgie, I am not so sure of that. My wife is absolute nature, sir, simple, absolute—haw—unartificial nature. But unartificial nature is, in my opinion—haw—yes, a very wise nature, sometimes."

"Haw!" said his wife, exactly like him, while everybody laughed. Then she stood upon tiptoe to kiss him, she was so unartificial, even before the company. All the pretty airs and graces of a fair Parisian, combined with all the domestic snugness of an English wife! What a fine thing it is to have a yoke–mate with a playful, charming manner!

"Good–bye, Dr. Hutton. We are on the wing, as you are. I fear you will never forgive me for tarnishing your laurels so."

Tarnishing laurels! What wonderful fellow so ingeniously mixed metaphors?

"Now or never," thought Rufus Hutton; "she has beaten me at chess, she thinks. Now, I'll have the change out of her. Only let her lead up to it."

"Mrs. Corklemore, we will fight it out, upon some future occasion. I never played with a lady so very hard to beat."

"Ah, you mean at Nowelhurst. But we never go there now. There is—I ought to say, very likely, there are mistakes on both sides—still there seems to exist some *prejudice* against us.—Anna, dear, you put a lump of sugar too much in my tea. I am already too saccharine."

"Well, dear, I put exactly what you always tell me. And you sent your cup for more afterwards."

"Matter of fact animal—how can she be my sister?" Georgie only muttered this. Rufus Hutton did not catch it. Mr. Garnet would have done so.

"Now is the time," thought Rufus again, as she came up to shake hands with him, not a bit afraid of the morning sun upon her smooth rich cheeks, where the colour was not laid on in spots, but seemed to breathe up from below, like a lamp under water. Outside he saw pet Polly scraping great holes in the gravel, and the groom throwing all his weight on the curb to prevent her from bolting homewards. "Hang it, she won't stand that," he cried; "her mouth is like a sea–anemone. Take her by the snaffle–rein. Can't you see, you fool, that she hasn't seven coats to her mouth, like you? Excuse my opening the window," he apologized to Mrs. Corklemore, "and excuse my speaking harshly, for if I had not stopped him, he would have thrown my horse down, and I value my Polly enormously."

"Especially after her behaviour the other night in the forest. It is the same with all you gentlemen; the worse you are treated, the more grateful you are. Oh yes, we heard of it; but we won't tell Mrs. Hutton."

"No, indeed, I hope you won't. I should be very sorry for her to get even a hint of it."

"To be sure," laughed Georgie, "to be sure we will keep the secret, for ever so many reasons; one of them being that Dr. Hutton would be obliged to part with Miss Polly, if her mistress knew of her conduct. But I must not be so rude. I see you want to be off quite as much as fair Polly does. Ah, what a thing it is to have a happy home!"

Here Mrs. Corklemore sighed very deeply. If a woman who always has her own way, and a woman who is always scheming, can be happy, she, Georgie, must be so; but she wanted to stir compassion.

"Come," she said, after turning away, for she had such a jacket on—the most bewitching thing; it was drawn in tight at her round little waist, and seemed made like a horse's body–clothes, on purpose for her to trot out in,—"come, Dr. Hutton, say good–bye, and forgive me for beating you." Simple creature, of course she knew not the "sacra fames" of chess–players.

"We must have our return–match. I won't say 'good–bye' until you have promised me that. Shall it be at my house?"

"No. There is only one place in the world where I would dare to attack you again, and that is Nowelhurst Hall."

"And why there, more than anywhere else?"

"Because there is a set of men there, with which I can beat anybody. I believe I could beat Morphy, with those men at Nowelhurst. Ah! you think me, I see, grossly and stupidly superstitious. Well, perhaps I am. I do sympathise so with everything."

"I hope we may meet at Nowelhurst," replied Rufus, preparing his blow of Jarnac, "when they have recovered a little from their sad distress."

"Ah, poor Sir Cradock!" exclaimed the lady, with her expressive eyes tear–laden, "how I have longed to comfort him! It does seem so hard that he should renounce the sympathy of his relatives at such a time as this.

And all through some little wretched dissensions in the days when he misunderstood us! Of course we know that you cannot do it; that you, a comparative stranger, cannot have sufficient influence where the dearest friends have failed. My husband, too, in his honest pride, is very, very obstinate, and my sister quite as bad. They fear, I suppose,—well, it does seem ridiculous, but you know what vulgar people say in a case of that sort—they actually fear the imputation of being fortune-hunters!" Georgie looked so arrogant in her stern consciousness of right, that Rufus said, and for the moment meant it, "How absurd, to be sure!"

"Yes," said Georgie, confidentially, and in the sweetest of all sweet voices, "between you and me, Dr. Hutton, for I speak to you quite as to an old friend of the family, whom you have known so long"—("Holloa," thought Rufus, "in the last breath I was a 'comparative stranger!'")—"I think it below our dignity to care for such an absurdity; and that now, as good Christians, we are bound to sink all petty enmities, and comfort the poor bereaved one. If you can contribute in any way to this act of Christian charity, may I rely upon your good word? But for the world, don't tell my husband; he would be so angry at the mere idea."

"I will do my best, Mrs. Corklemore; you may rely upon that."

"Oh, thank you, thank you! I felt quite sure that you had a generous heart. I should have been so disappointed—perhaps, after all, we shall play our next game of chess at Christmas with the men I am so lucky with. And then, look to yourself, Dr. Hutton."

"I trust you will find a player there who can give me a pawn and two moves. If you beat him, you may boast indeed."

"What player do you mean?" asked Georgie, feeling rather less triumphant. "Any Indian friend of yours?"

"Yes, one for whom I have the very greatest regard. For whose sake, indeed, I first renewed my acquaintance with Sir Cradock, because I bore a message to him; for the Colonel is a bad correspondent."

"The Colonel! I don't understand you." As she said these words, how those eyes of hers, those expressive eyes, were changing! And her lovely jacket, so smart and well cut, began to "draw" over the chest.

"Did you not know," asked Rufus, watching her in a way that made her hate him worse than when he took her queen, "is it possible that you have not heard, that Colonel Nowell, Clayton Nowell, Sir Cradock's only brother, is coming home this month, and brings his darling child with him?" Now for your acting, Georgie; now for your self–command. We shall admire, henceforth, or laugh at you, according to your present conduct.

She was equal to the emergency. She commanded her eyes, and her lips, and bosom, after that one expansion, even her nerves, to the utmost fibre—everything but her colour. The greatest actor ever seen, when called on to act in real life, can never command colour if the skin has proper spiracles. The springs of our heart will come up and go down, as God orders the human weather. But she turned away, with that lily–whiteness, because she knew she had it, and rushed up enthusiastically to her sister at the end of the room.

"Dear Anna, darling Anna, oh, I am so delighted! We have been so wretched about poor Sir Cradock. And now his brother is coming to mind him, with such delightful children! We thought he was dead, oh, so many years! What a gracious providence!"

"Haw!" said Nowell Corklemore.

"The devil!" said Bailey Kettledrum, and Rufus caught the re–echo, but hoped it might be a mistake.

Then they all came forward, gushing, rushing, rapturous to embrace him.

"Oh, Dr. Hutton, surely this is too good news to be true!"

"I think not," said Rufus Hutton, mystical and projecting, "I really trust it is not. But I thought you must have heard it, from your close affinity, otherwise I should have told you the moment I came in; but now I hope this new arrival will heal over all—make good, I mean, all family misunderstandings."

"Colonel Clayton Nowell," said Mr. Nowell Corklemore, conclusively, and with emphasis, "Colonel Clayton Nowell was shot dead outside the barracks at Mhow, on the 25th day of June, sir, in the year of our Lord one thousand eight hundred and fifty–six. Correct me, sir, if I am wrong."

"Then," said Rufus, "I venture to correct you at once."

"Shot, sir," continued Corklemore, "as I am, I may say—haw,—in a position to prove, by a man called Abdoollah Manjee, believed to be a Mussulman. Colonel Clayton Nowell, sir, commanding officer in command of Her Majesty's Company's native regiment, No· One hundred and sixty–three, who was called,—excuse me, sir, designated, the 'father of his regiment,' because he had so many illegitimate—haw, I beg your pardon, ladies—because of his—ha, yes,—patriarchal manners, sir, and kindly disposition,—he—haw, where was I?"

"I am sure I can't say," said Rufus.

"No, sir, my memory is more tenacious than that of any man I meet with. He, Colonel Clayton Nowell, sir, upon that fatal morning, was remonstrated with by the two—ah, yes, the two executors of his will—upon his rashness in riding forth to face those carnal, I mean to say, those incarnate devils, sir. 'Are you fools enough,' he replied, 'to think that *my* fellows would hurt *me*? Give me a riding–whip, and be ready with plasters, for I shall thrash them before I let them come back.' Now isn't every word of that true?"

"Yes, almost every word of it," replied Rufus, now growing excited.

"Well, sir, he took his favourite half–bred—for he understood cross–breeding thoroughly—and he rode out at the side–gate, where the heap of sand was; 'Coming back,' he cried to the English sentry, 'coming back in half an hour, with all my scamps along of me. Keep the coppers ready.' And with that he spurred his brown and black mare; and no man saw him alive thereafter, except the fellows who shot him. Haw!"

"Yes," said Rufus Hutton, "one man saw him alive, after they shot him in the throat, and one man saved his life; and he is the man before you."

"What you, Dr. Hutton! What you! Oh, how grateful we ought to be to you."

"Thank you. Well, I don't quite see that," Rufus replied, most dryly. Then he corrected himself: "You know I only did my duty."

"And his son?" inquired Georgie, timidly, and with sympathy, but the greatest presence of mind. She had stood with her hands clasped, and every emotion (except the impossible one of selfishness) quivering on her sweet countenance; and now she was so glad, oh, so glad, she could never tell you. "His poor illegitimate son, Dr. Hutton? Will he bring the poor child home with him? How glad we shall be to receive him!"

"The child he brings with him is Eoa, dear natural odd Eoa, his legitimate daughter."

"Then you know her, Dr. Hutton; you could depose to her identity?"

A very odd question; but some women have almost the gift of prophecy.

"Oh, yes! I should rather think so. I have known her since she was ten years old."

"And now they are coming home. How pleasant! How sweet to receive them, as it were from the dead! By the overland route, I suppose, and with a lac of rupees?"

"No," said the badgered Rufus, "you are wrong in both conjectures. They come round the Cape, by the clipper–ship *Aliwal*; and with very few rupees. Colonel Nowell has always been extravagant, a wonderfully fine–hearted man, but a hand that could never hold anything—except, indeed, a friend's."

By the moisture in Rue Hutton's eyes, Georgie saw that her interests would fare ill with him, if brought into competition with those of Colonel Nowell. Meanwhile Polly was raving wild, and it took two grooms to hold her, and the white froth dribbling down her curb was to Rufus Hutton as the foam of the sea to a sailor. He did love a tearing gallop, only not through the thick of the forest.

"Good–bye, good–bye! I shall see you soon. Thank you, I will take a cheroot. But I only smoke my own. Good–bye! I am so much obliged to you. You have been so very kind. Mrs. Hutton will be miserable until you come over to us. Good–bye; once more, good–bye!"

Rufus Hutton, you see, was a man of the world, and could be false "on occasion." John Rosedew could never have made that speech on the back of detected falsehood. Away went Polly, like a gale of wind; and Rufus (who was no rogue by nature, only by the force of circumstances, and then could never keep to it), he going along twenty miles an hour, set his teeth to the breeze, which came down the funnel of his cigar as down a steamer's chimney, stuck his calves well into Polly's sides, and felt himself a happy man, going at a rocket's speed, to a home of happiness. All of us who have a home (and unless we leave our heart there, whenever we go away, we have no home at all), all of us who have a hole in this shifting sandy world—the sand as of an hour–glass—but whence we have spun such a rope as the devil can neither make nor break—I mean to say, we, all who love, without any hems, and haws, and rubbish, those who are only our future tense (formed from the present by adding "so")—all of us who are lucky enough, I believe we may say good enough, to want no temporal augment from the prefix of society, only to cling upon the tree to the second aorist of our children, wherein the root of the man lurks, the grand indefinite so anomalous; all these fellows, if they can anyhow understand this sentence, will be glad to hear that Rufus Hutton had a jolly ride.

Rosa waited at the gate; why do his mare's shoes linger? Rosa ran in, and ran out again, and was sure that she heard something pelting down the hill much too fast, for her sake! but who could blame him when he knew he was coming home at last? Then Rosa snapped poor Jonah's head off, for being too thick to hear it.

Meanwhile, a mighty senate was held at Kettledrum Hall, Mrs. Corklemore herself taking the curule chair. After a glimpse of natural life, and the love of man and woman, we want no love of money; so we lift our laps (like the Roman envoy) and shake out war with the whole of them.

Fools who think that life needs gilding—life, whose flowing blood contains every metal but gold and silver—because they clog and poison it! Blessed is he who earns his money, and spends it all on a Saturday. He looks forward to it throughout the week; and the beacon of life is hope, even as God is its pole–star.

CHAPTER II

Mr. Garnet's house, well away to the west, was embraced more closely and lovingly by the gnarled arms of the Forest than the Hall, or even the Rectory. Just in the scoop of a sunny valley, high enough to despise the water, and low enough to defy the wind, there was nothing to concern it much, but the sighing of the branches. Over the brown thatch hung two oak–trees, whispering leaves of history, offering the acorn cup upon the parlour hearth, chafing their rheumatic knuckles against the stone of the chimneys, wondering when the great storm should come that would give them an inside view of it. For though the cottage lay so snugly, scarcely lifting its thatched eyebrows at the draught which stole up the valley, nevertheless those guardian oaks had wrestled a bout or two with the tempests. In the cyclone on the morning of November 29th, 1836, and again on the 7th of January, 1842, they had gripped the ground, and set hard their knees, and groaned at the thought of salt water. Since then the wind had been less of a lunatic (although there had been some ruffianly work in 1854), and they hoped there was a good time coming, and so spread their branches further and further, and thought less of the price of timber. There was only one wind that frightened them much, and that was two points north of west, the very direction whence, if they fell, crash they must come on the cottage. For they stood above it, the root–head some ten feet above the back–floor of the basement, and the branches towering high enough for a wood–pigeon not to be nervous there.

Now we only get heavy pressure of squalls from the west–north–west after a thorough–going tempest which has begun in the southward, and means to box half the compass. So the two great oaks were regarded by their brethren up the hill as jolly fellows, happy dogs, born with a silver spoon in their mouths, good for another thousand years, although they might be five hundred old; unless, indeed—and here all the trees shuddered—there came such another hurricane as in 1703. But which of us knows his own brother's condition? Those two oaks stood, and each knew it, upon a steep bank, where no room was for casting out stay–roots to east–south–east.

Bull Garnet hated those two trees, with terror added to hatred. Even if they never crushed him, which depended much on the weather, they *would* come in at his bedroom window when the moon was high. Wandering shapes of wavering shadow, with the flickering light between them, walking slowly as a ghost does, and then very likely a rustle and tap, a shivering, a shuddering; it made the ground–floor of his heart shake in the nightmare hours.

Never before had he feared them so much, one quarter so much, as this October; and, during the full and the waning moon after Clayton Nowell's death, he got very little sleep for them. By day he worked harder than ever, did more than three men ought to do, was everywhere on the estates, but never swore at any one—though the men scratched their ears for the want of it—laboured hard, and early, and late, if so he might come home at night (only not in the dark), come home at night thoroughly weary. His energy was amazing. No man anywhere felling wood—Mr. Garnet's especial luxury—no man hedging and ditching, or frithing, or stubbing up fern and brambles, but had better look out what he had in his bag, or "the governor would be there, and no mistake." A workman could scarcely stand and look round, and wonder how his sick wife was, or why he had got to work so hard, could scarcely slap himself on the breast, or wet his hard hands for a better grip, but there was Bull Garnet before him, with sad, fierce, dogged eyes, worse than his strongest oaths had been.

Everybody said it was (and everybody believed it; for the gossip had spread from the household in spite of the maidens' fear of him) the cause of it was, beyond all doubt, the illness of his daughter. Pearl Garnet, that very eccentric girl, as Rufus Hutton concluded, who had startled poor Polly so dreadfully, was prostrate now with a nervous fever, and would not see even the doctor. Our Amy, who pleaded hard to see her, because she was sure she could do her good, received a stern sharp negative, and would have gone away offended, only she was so sorry for her. Not that any fervid friendship, such as young ladies exult in for almost a fortnight incessant, not that any rapturous love exclusive of all *man*kind had ever arisen between them, for they had nothing whatever in common, save beauty and tenacity, which girls do not love in each other: only that she was always sorry for any one deep in trouble. And believing that Pearl had loved Clayton Nowell, and was grieving for him bitterly, how could Amy help contrasting that misery with her own happiness?

For Amy was nice and happy now, in spite of Cradock's departure, and the trouble he had departed in. He loved her almost half as much, she believed, as she loved him; and was not that enough for anybody? His troubles would flow by in time; who on earth could doubt it, unless they doubted God? He was gone to make his way in the world, and her only fear was lest he should make it too grand for Amy to share in. She liked the school–children so, and the pony, and to run out now and then to the kitchen, and dip a bit of crust in the dripping–pan; and she liked to fill her dear father's pipe, and spread a thin handkerchief over his head. Would all these pleasures be out of her sphere, when Cradock came back, with all London crowning him the greatest and best man of the age? Innocent Amy, never fear. "Nemo, nisi ob homicidium, repente fuit clarissimus."

Mr. Garnet would have felled those oaks, in spite of Sir Cradock's most positive orders, if there had not been another who could not command, but could plead for them. Every morning as the steward came out, frowned and shook his fist at them, the being whom he loved most on earth—far beyond himself, his daughter, and the memory of their mother, all multiplied into each other,—that boy Bob came up to him, and said, "Father, don't, *for my sake*."

We have not heard much of Bob Garnet yet; we have scarcely shaped him feebly; by no means was he a negative character, yet described most briefly by negatives. In every main point, except two, he was his father's cardinal opposite. Those two were generosity (which combines the love of truth with a certain warmth of impulse) and persevering energy. Even those two were displayed in ways entirely different, but the staple was very similar.

Bob Garnet was a naturalist. Gentle almost as any girl, and more so than his sister, he took small pleasure in the ways of men, intense delight in those of every other creature. Bob loved all things God had made, even as fair Amy did. All his day, and all his life, he would have spent, if he had the chance, among the ferns and mosses, the desmidiæ of the forest pools, the sun–dew and the fungi, the buff–tips and red underwings, privet–hawks, and emperors. He knew all the children of the spring and handmaids of the summer, all of autumn's laden train and the comforters of winter. The happiest of mankind is he whose stores of life are endless, whose pure delights can never cloy, who sees and feels in every birth, in every growth or motion, his own Almighty Father; and loving Him is loved again, as a child who spreads his arms out.

Mr. Garnet's affection for this boy surpassed the love of women. He petted, and patted, and coaxed him, and talked nonsense to him by the hour; he was jealous even of Bob's attachment to his sister Pearl; in short, all the energy of his goodness, which, like the rest of his energies, transcended the force of other men's, centred and spent itself mainly there. But of late Bob had passed all his time with his mother—I mean, of course, with Nature; for his mother in the flesh was dead many a year ago. He had now concluded, with perfect contentment, that his education was finished; and to have the run of the forest at this unwonted season more than consoled him for the disgrace of his recent expulsion from school.

Scarcely any one would believe that Bob Garnet, the best and gentlest boy that ever cried over Euripides—not from the pathos of the poet certainly, but from his own—Bob Garnet, who sang to snails to come out, and they felt that he could not beat them, should have been expelled disgracefully from a private school, whose master must needs expel his own guineas with every banished pupil. However, so it was, and the crime was characteristic. He *would* sit at night in the lime–trees. Those lime–trees overhung the grey stone wall of the playground near Southampton; and some wanton boys had been caught up there, holding amoibæans with little nursemaids and girls of all work, come out to get lung–and–tongue food. Thereupon a stern ukase was issued that the next boy caught up there would be expelled without trial, as the corrupter of that pure flock. The other boys laughed, I am sorry to say, when "Bob, the natural," as they called him, meaning thereby the naturalist, was the first to be discovered there, crawling upon a branch as cleverly as a looper caterpillar. Even then the capital sentence was commuted that time, for every master knew, as well as every boy, that Bob could never "say bo" to anything of the feminine gender capable of articulating. So Bob had to learn the fourth Georgic by heart, and did most of it (with extreme enjoyment) up in that very same tree. For he kept all his caterpillars there, his beetle–traps, his moth–nets, even some glorious pupæ, which were due at the end of August; and he nursed a snug little fernery, and had sown some mistletoe seeds, and a dozen other delicious things, and the lime–hawks wanted to burrow soon; in a word, it was Bob's hearth and heart–place, for no other boy could scale it. But just when Bob had got to the beginning of Aristæus, and the late bees were buzzing around him, although the linden had berried, an officious usher spied him out—a dirty little fellow, known and despised by all the more respectable *σιωπητέαι* of Southampton. With hottest indignation, that mean low beggar cried out—

"Boy in the tree there! I see you! Your name this moment, you rascal!"

"Garnet, sir, Bob Garnet. And if you please, sir, I am not a rascal."

"Come down, sir, this very instant; or else I'll come up after you."

"I don't think you can, sir," replied Bob, looking down complacently; for, as we shall see by–and–by, he was no coward in an emergency. "If you please, sir, no boy in the school can climb this tree except me, sir, since Brown senior left."

"I can tell you one thing, Garnet: it's the last time you'll ever climb it."

"Oh, then I must collect my things; I am sorry to keep you waiting, sir. But they are such beauties, and I can't see well to pack them."

Bob packed up his treasures deliberately in his red pocket–handkerchief, and descended very cleverly, holding it with his teeth. The next morning he had to pack his box, and became in the school a mere legend.

His father flew into a violent passion, not with the son, but the schoolmaster: however, he was so transported with joy at getting his own Bob home again, that he soon forgave the cause of it. So the boy got the run of the potato–fields, pollard–trees, and rushy pools, and hunted and grubbed and dabbled, and came home sometimes with three handkerchiefs, not to mention his hat, full. One lovely day this October, before the frost set in—a frost of a length and severity most rare at that time of year—Bob Garnet took his basket and trowel, nets, lens, &c., and set out for a sandy patch, not far from the stream by the Rectory, where in his July holidays he had found some Gladiolus Illyricus, a bloom of which he had carried home, and now he wanted some roots of it. He could not think why his father left him so very much to himself now, and had ceased from those little caresses and fondlings, which used to make Bob look quite ashamed sometimes in the presence of strangers. He felt that his father loved him quite as much as ever, and he had found those strong eyes set upon him with an expression, as it appeared to him, of sorrow and compassion. He had a great mind to ask what the matter was; but his love for his father was a strange feeling, mixed with some dread and uncertainty. He would make Pearl tell him all about it, that would be the best way; for she as well had been carrying on very oddly of late. She sat in her own room all day long, and would never come down to dinner, and would never come out for a stroll with him, but slipped out by herself sometimes in the evening; that, at least, he was sure of. And to tell him indeed, him going on now for seventeen years of age, that he was too young to ask questions! He would let her know, he was quite resolved, that because she happened to be two years older—a pretty reason that was for treating him like a baby! She who didn't know a wire–worm from a ring–worm, nor an elater from a tipula, and thought that the tippet–moth was a moth that fed upon tippets! Recalling fifty other instances of poor Pearl's deep ignorance, Bob grew more and more indignant, as he thought of the way she treated him. He would stand it no longer. If she was in trouble, that was only the greater reason—— Holloa!

Helter–skelter, off dashed Bob after a Queen of Spain fritillary, the first he had ever seen on the wing, and a grand prize for any collector, even of ten times his standing. It was one of the second brood, invited by the sun to sport awhile. And rare sport it afforded Bob, who knew it at once from the other fritillaries, for the shape of the wings is quite different, and he had seen it in grand collections. An active little chap it was, greatly preferring life to death, and thoroughly aware that man is the latter's chief agent. Once Bob made quite sure of it, for it had settled on a blackberry–spray, and smack the net came down upon it, but a smack too hard, for the thorns came grinning out at the bottom, and away went the butterfly laughing. Bob made good the net in a moment with some very fine pins that he carried, and off again in still hotter pursuit, having kept his eyes on dear Lathonia. But the prey was now grown wondrous skeary since that narrow shave, and the huntsman saw that his only chance was a clever swoop in mid air. So he raised his net high, and zig–zagged recklessly round the trees, through the bushes, up the banks and down them. At last he got quite close to her, but she flipped round a great beech–trunk; Bob made a cast at hazard, and caught not the Queen, but Amy.

Amy was not frightened much, neither was she hurt, though her pretty round head came out through the net—for she had taken her hat off—and the ring lay upon her shoulders, which the rich hair had shielded from bruises. She would have been frightened terribly, only she knew what was going on, and had stepped behind the tree to avoid the appearance of interfering. For she did not wish—she knew not why—but, by some instinct, she did not wish to have much to do with the Garnets. She regarded poor Bob as a schoolboy, who was very fond of insects, and showed his love by killing them.

But if Amy was not frightened much, Bob, the captor, was. He dropped the handle of his net, and fell back against the beech–tree. Then Amy laughed, and took off the net, or the relics of the gauze at least, and kindly held out her hand to him, and said,

"Oh, how you are grown!"

"And so are you. Oh dear me, have you seen her? Have you seen her?"

"Seen whom?" asked Amy, "my Aunt Eudoxia? She is on there, by the ash–tree."

"The Queen of Spain, Miss Rosedew, the Queen of Spain fritillary! Oh, tell me which way she went! If I lose her, I am done for!"

"Then, I fear, Master Garnet"—["Confound it," thought Bob, "how all the girls do patronize me!"]—"I am very much afraid you must make up your mind to annihilation, if by the 'Queen of Spain' you mean that common brown little butterfly you wanted just now to kill so much."

"Is she gone across the river, then? That is nothing, I assure you. I would go through fire after her. Oh, tell me, only tell me."

Amy could not help laughing; poor Bob looked so ridiculous, fitting a new net all the time upon the ring of the old one, the crown of his hat come to look for his head, his trousers kicked well up over his boots, and his coat an undoubted ventilator.

"I really don't know," said Amy; "how could you expect me to see through your shrimp–net, Master Garnet?"

"Oh, I beg your pardon—how stupid I am, to be sure—I beg your pardon a thousand times; really I might have hurt you. I would not do that for— —"

"Even the Queen of Spain. To tell you the truth, Master Garnet, if I knew where she was gone I would not tell you, because I can't bear to have things killed. In my opinion, it is so cruel."

"Oh!" cried Bob, a very long "oh," drawn out into half an ell; and he looked at Amy all the time he was saying it, which was a wonderful thing for him to do. Then it occurred to his mind, for the first time possibly, what a beautiful creature she was, more softly shaded than a Chalk–hill blue, and richer than a cream–spotted tiger–moth! The moment he felt this Bob was done for; Amy had caught her captor.

Flushed as he was with the long hot chase, his cheeks grew hotter and redder, as he got a dim consciousness of a few of the things which he was feeling. He was like a chrysalis, touched in the winter, when it goes on one side from the crust of the thorax, and sometimes can never get right again. After having said "oh," with emphasis and so much diæresis, Bob did not feel called upon for any further utterance till Amy was gone to her Aunt Eudoxia; and then he contrived to say, "Ah!" He was more put out than he had been even when his pet poplar–hawk caterpillar was devoured alive by ichneumon grubs. He went round the tree ever so many times, and wondered what was the matter with him, how he came there, and what he was doing.

Alas, poor Bob! Nature, who overlooks nothing, was well aware of the difficulties when she cried, "Jump up on my lap, Bob, and never be weaned from me." She knew that things of all sorts would come between herself and her child, some of them drawn from her own mother–milk, but most of them from man's muzzling. Of the latter she had not much fear with Bob; but the former, she knew, were beyond her, and she had none but herself to thank for them. She knew that the lad, so strongly imbued with her own pleasant affluences, was almost sure to be touched with that one which comes from her breast the warmest. And then what would become of zoology, phytology, entomology, and all the other yard–long names which her children spin out of her apron–strings?

While Bob was still fiddling with his fingers, and forgetting all about butterflies, Miss Eudoxia, fetched by Amy, came to hold discourse with him.

"Why, Master Robert, I do declare, Robert, my butterfly boy! I have not seen you for such a time, Robert." And she held out her hand, which Bob took with very little sense of gratitude. To be called a "butterfly boy" before Amy, and Amy to acquiesce in it!

"Ah, you think I have nothing for you, Robert. You school–boys live upon suction. But just wait a moment, my dear."

She drew forth an old horn comfit–box, which had belonged to her grandmother, and was polished up like amber from the chafing of many a lining. This she opened with much ado, poured three crinkled sugar–plums on her gloved palm, and a smooth one as large as a hazel–nut, and offered them all to Robert, with a smile of the finest patronage.

"No, thank you, Miss Rosedew; no, thank you. I am very much obliged to you."

Miss Eudoxia had been wondering at her own generosity, and thought that he was overcome with it. So her smile became one of encouragement and assurance against self–sacrifice.

"Oh, you need not be afraid, Robert. And you can put some under your pillow, and wake up in the night and suck them. How nice that will be, to be sure! You see I know what boys are. And I have plenty left for the infant–school. And they don't deserve them as you do, Robin."

"Miss Rosedew," said Bob, in his loftiest manner, though he was longing for them, only that Amy was there; "you will believe me when I assure you that I never touch sweets of any sort; not even at a late dinner–party."

Miss Eudoxia turned her eyes up, and almost dropped the sugar–plums. But Amy, instead of being impressed, merrily laughed, and said,

"Give them to me, then, auntie, please. Some of the men at the night–school eat sweets after early suppers."

Bob said "good–bye" disconsolately, for he knew that he had affronted Miss Doxy, without rising in Amy's opinion. He forgot all about the gladiolus, and let many great prizes escape him; for the day was the last of the soft and sunny, which tempt forth the forest denizens ere the frosty seal is set on them. In the glimpses of every brown arcade, in the jumbled gleam of the underwood, in the alleys between the upstanding trees, even in the strong light where the golden patches shone, and the wood fell back to look at them, in all of these he seemed to see and then to lose his angel. Her face he could not see clearly yet, hard as he strove to do it; affection is, but love is not, a photographic power. Still he could see her shadowly; her attitude, the fall of her hair, the manner of her gestures; even the ring of her voice would seem to dwell about the image. But he never got them all together; one each time was the leading thing; vague; and yet it went through him.

He made one attempt—for he feared from the first, although he never could feel it so, that his love was a thorough wild-goose chase—the poor boy made one last attempt to catch at some other pursuit.

"Father," he said that very same night, after sitting for hours of wandering, "will you give me a gun and let me take to shooting?"

"A gun!" cried Bull Garnet, starting; "a gun, Bob! What do you mean by it?"

"I meant nothing at all, father. Only I know the way to stuff birds, and there are some rare ones here sometimes, and I want to make a collection."

"Bob Garnet, as long as I am alive, you never shall have a gun."

"Then, will you lend me yours, father? I know very well how to use it. I mean your patent——"

"Never, Bob. My son, if you love me, never speak of it again."

CHAPTER III

When Miss Rosedew and her niece came in to get ready for dinner, Amy cried out suddenly, "Oh, only look at the roses, aunt; how they have opened to-day! What delicious Louise Odier, and just look at General Jacqueminot! and I do declare Jules Margottin is finer than he was at Midsummer. I must cut a few, for I know quite well there will come a great frost if I don't, and then where will all my loves be?"

Amy's prediction about the weather was as random a guess as we may find in great authorities, who are never right, although they give the winds sixteen points of the thirty-two to shuffle in. But it so turned out that the girl was right—a point of the compass never hit till a day too late by our weather-clerks.

That very same night such a frost set in as had not been known in October for very nearly a century. It lasted nine nights and eight days; twice the mercury fell more than half way from the freezing point to zero, and the grass was crisp in the shade all day, though the high sun wiped off the whiteness at noon wherever he found the way to it. Boys rejoiced, and went mitching, to slide on the pools of the open furzery: no boys since the time of their great-grandfathers had done the heel-tap in October. But the birds did not appreciate it. What in the world did it mean? Why, there were the hips not ripe yet, and the hollyberries come to no colour, and half the blackberries still too acid, and, lo! it was freezing hard enough to make a worm cold for the stomach, even if you could get him! Surely there was some stupid mistake of two months in the piper's almanac. All they could say was that, if it were so, those impudent free-and-easy birds who came sponging on them in the winter—and too stuck up, forsooth! to live with them after sucking all the fat of the land, and winning their daughters' affections—those outlandish beggars—be hanged to them—had got the wrong almanac too.

Why, they had not even heard the chatter, the everlasting high-fashion clack, of those jerk-tail fieldfares yet; nor had a missel-thrush come swaggering to bully a decent throstle that had sung hard all the summer, just because his breast and his coarse-shaped spots were bigger. Why, they had not even seen a clumsy short-eared owl flopping out of the dry fern yet—much good might it do him, the fern that belonged to themselves!—nor a single wedge of grey–lag geese, nor a woodcock that knew his business. And those nasty dissolute quacking mallards that floated in bed all day, the sluggards, and then wouldn't let a respectable bird have a chance of a good night's roost—there they were still on the barley–stubble; please God they might only get frozen!

And yet, confound it all, what was the weather coming to? You might dig, and tap, and jump with both feet, and put your head on one side in the most knowing manner possible, and get behind a tuft of grass, and wait there ever so long, and devil a worm would come up! And, as for the slugs, oh, don't let me hear of them! Though the thieves had not all got home yet, they were ten degrees too cold for even an oyster–catcher's stomach: feathers and pip, my dear fellow! it gives me the colic to think of one. Put your head under my wing, Jenny Wren; oh, my darling, how cold your beak is!

Such, so far as I could gather them, were the sentiments of the birds, and their confabulation, when they went to roost, half an hour earlier than usual—for bed is the warmest place after all; besides, what was there to do?—on the 24th of October, 1859. And they felt the cold rime settling down on grey twig, and good brown leaf. Yet some of the older birds, cocks of long experience, buffers beyond all chaff, perked one eye at the eastern heavens, before tucking it under the scapular down—the eastern heavens all barred with murky red. Then they gave a little self–satisfied tweedle, which meant to the ear of Melampus,

"Ah ha! an old bird like me knows something about the weather! Bless my drumsticks and merrythought, I shan't be so cold and hungry, please God, this time to–morrow night."

Oh you little wiseacres, much you know what impendeth! A worse row than all the mallards you grumble at could make in a thousand years will spoil your roost to–morrow night. Think it a mercy if you do not get your very feathers blown off of you—ay, and the tree of your ancestors snapped beneath your feet—before this time to morrow night.

John Rosedew met the prettiest bird that ever had nest in the New Forest, his own little duck of an Amy, in the passage by the parlour–door, at eight o'clock in the morning of that 25th of October. He kissed her white forehead lovingly, according to early usage; then he glanced at the weather–glass, and went nearer, supposing that his short sight had cheated him.

"Why, Amy dear, you must have forgotten to set the glass last night."

"No, indeed, papa. I set it very carefully. You know I can do it as well as you can, since you showed me the way. It was just a little hollow last night, and I moved the Verrier scale just a hundredth part of an inch downwards, and then it was ten o'clock."

"Then may the Lord have mercy on all seafaring men, especially our poor boatmen, and the dredging people off Rushford!"

Mr. Rosedew, as has been said before, was parson of Rushford as well as of Nowelhurst. At the former place he kept a curate, but looked after the poor people none the less, for the distance was only six miles; and now, as his legs were getting stiff, he had bought Coræbus to help him. Rushford lies towards the eastern end of the great Hurst shingle bank, the most dangerous part of Christchurch Bay, being fully exposed to the south–west gales, and just in the run of the double tide; in the eddy of the Needles.

"Why, what is the matter, papa? Even if it rains, it won't hurt them much. And it's as lovely a morning as ever was seen, and the white frost sparkling beautifully. What a magnificent sunrise! Or, at least, a very strange one."

"'Sibi temperat unda carinis.' All is smooth for the present. But I heard the lash of the ground–sea last night, when I lay awake. Fetch my telescope, darling, and come with me to the green room. We can see thence to St. Alban's Head; but the danger is for those beyond it. All the ships on this side of it will have time to work up the Solent. Never before have I known the mercury fall as it has done now. An inch and a tenth in only ten hours!"

When they went to bed on the previous night, the quicksilver stood at 30° 10′. Now it was at 29°, and cupped like the bottom of a champagne bottle, which showed that it still fell rapidly. But as yet the silver of the frost was sparkling on the lawn, and the morning sun looked up the heavens, as if he felt all right. Nevertheless, it was but show: he is bound to make the best of it, and, like all other warm–hearted beings, sometimes has sorry work there.

When they saw that no large craft had rounded St. Alban's Head, only that the poor cement–dredgers were working away at septaria, John and his daughter went to breakfast, hoping that no harm would be, while Miss Eudoxia lay in bed, and reflected on her own good qualities.

Amy came out after breakfast, without any bonnet or hat on, to make her own observations. That girl so loved the open air, the ever glorious concave, the frank palm of the hand of God—for in cities we get His knuckles—that she felt as if she had not bowed before her Friend and Maker, the all–giving, the all–loving One, until she had paid her orisons and sung her morning hymn with His own ceiling over her. So now she walked beneath the branches laden with His jewellery, and over the ground hard–trodden by ministers doing His will, and beside the spear and the flat–grass, chilled with the awe of His breath, and among the wailing flowers, wailing and black and shrivelled up, because His face was cold to them.

For these poor Amy grieved sadly, for she was just beginning to care again for the things whose roots were outside of her. Lo the bright chrysanthemums, plumed, reflex, and fimbriate; lo the gorgeous dahlias, bosses quilled and plaited tight, and wrought with depth of colour; and then the elegant asters, cushioned, cochleate, praying only to have their eyes looked into; most of all, her own sweet roses, chosen flowers of the chosen land—they hung their heads, and stuck together, as brown as a quartered apple. Who could look at them, who could think of them, and not feel as if some of herself were dead?

Now, walking there, this youthful maiden, fairest of all His works and purest, began to observe, as He has taught us, the delicacies, the pores, and glints of the grand universal footprint. Not that the girl perceived one–tenth of the things being done around her, any more than I can tell them; for observation grows from as well as begets experience; and the girlish mind (and the boyish too, at any rate for the most part) has very lax and indefinite communion with nature. How seldom do we meet a lady who knows what way the wind is! They all believe that it must freeze harder when the sky is cloudy; not one in fifty but trembles more at the thunder than at the lightning.

Yet Amy, with true woman's instinct, being alarmed for the lives of others, after her father's prediction, looked around her narrowly. And first her eyes went upwards, and they were right in doing so. Of the sky she knew less than nothing—although herself well known there; but the trees—come now, she was perfectly sure she knew something about the trees. So you do, you darling; and yet a very wee little; though more than half the ladies do. You know an elm from a wych–elm, and a hornbeam from a beech; and what more can we expect of you?

The rime upon the dark tree–boles and the forward push of the branches, the rime of white fur, newly breathen but an hour ago, when a flaw from the east came cat–like, and went through without moving anything; this delicate down from the lips of morning, silk work upon the night–fleece, was, as all most beautiful is, the first to fleet and vanish. Changing into a doubtful glister, which you must touch to be sure of it, then trickling away into beaded drops, like a tear which will have no denial, it came down the older and harder rime, and perhaps would bring that into its humour, and perhaps would get colder and freeze again into little lumps, like a tap leaking. Then the white face of the rough pillared trunks, pearled with glistening purity, was bighted into with scoops and dark bays, like the sweep of a scythe in the morning. On the bars of the gate, the silver harvest, spiked and cropping infinitely, began to sheave itself away, and then the sheaves were full ripe tears, and the tears ran down if you thought of them.

But the notable sight of all, at least to a loitering mind the most striking, was to see how the hoar–frost gradually was lifting its light wing from the grass. In little tufts and random patches—random to us who know not why—the spangles, the spears, and the crusted flakes, the fairy tinsel, the ermine of dew, the very down of moonlight, the kiss of the sky too pure for snow, and the glittering glance of stars reflected—all this loveliness, caught and fastened, by the night's halourgic, in one broad sheet of virgin white, was hovering off in tufts and patches, as if a blind angel had breathed on it, with his flight only guided by pity.

But through, and in, and between it all, the boles of the trees, and the bars of the gate, the ridge of the ruts, and dapples of lawn, one thing Amy observed which puzzled her, for even she knew that it was a thing against all usage. The thaw was not on the south side or the south–east side of anything, though the sickly sun was gazing there; but the melting came from the north, and took the frost aback. She wondered vainly about it, but the matter was simple enough, like most of the things which we wonder at, instead of at our own ignorance. A flaw of warm air from the north had set in; a lower warp which shot through and threaded the cold south–eastern woof. This is not a common occurrence. Since my vague, unguided, and weak observations began, I have only seen it thrice. And on each of those three times it has been followed by a fearful tempest. Usually, a frost breaks up with a shift of the wind to the south–east, a gradual relaxing, a fusion of warmer air, and a great effusion of damp, a blanket of clouds for the earth, and a doubt in the sky how to use them. Then the doubt ends—as many other doubts end—in precipitation. The wind chops round to the west of south; the moisture condenses outside our windows, instead of starring the inside; and then come a few spits of rain. But the rain is not often heavy at first, although it is stinging and biting,—a rain which is half ashamed of itself, as if it ought to be hail.

But, after all, these things depend on things we cannot depend upon,—moods of the air to be multiplied into humours of the earth and sea, and the product traversed, indorsed, divided, touched, and sliced at every angle by solar, lunar, and astral influences.

"Felix qui potuit rerum cognoscere causas."

Lucky the man who knows when to take out his umbrella.

That morning, the north wind crept along, sponging the rime from the grass, and hustling it rudely from the tree–sprays, on many of which the black leaves draggled, frozen while yet in verdure. Then the sky began to be slurred across with white clouds breathing out from it, as a child breathes on the blade of a knife, or on a carriage window. These blots of cloud threw feelers out, and strung themselves together, until a broad serried and serrate bar went boldly across the heavens, from south–east to north–west. It marked the point whence the gale would begin, and the quarter where it would end. From this great bar, on either side, dappled and mottled, like the wash of sepia on a drawing, little offsets straggled away, and began to wisp with a spiral motion, slow and yet perceptible.

This went on for an hour or two, darkening and deepening continually, amassing more and more of the sky, gathering vapours to it, and embodying as it got hold of them; but still there was some white wan sunshine through the mustering cloud–blots and the spattering mud of the heavens; and still the good folks who had suffered from chilblains, and found it so much milder, exclaimed, "What a beautiful day!"

Then about noon a mock sun appeared, feeble, wild, and haggard, whose mates on the crown and the east of the arc could scarcely keep him in countenance. Over all this, and over the true sun and the cirrhous outrunners, heavily drove at one o'clock the laden and leaden cumulus, blurred on the outskirts with cumulostrate, and daubed with lumps of vapour which mariners call "Noah's arks."

Then came the first sough of the wind, a long, prolonged, deep–drawn, dry sob, a hollow and mysterious sound, that shivered through the brown leaves, and moaned among the tree–boles. Away went every beast and bird that knew the fearful signal: the deer lanced away to the holm–frith; the cattle in huffs came belloking to the lew of the boughy trees; the hogs ran together, and tossed their snouts, and skittered home from the ovest; the squirrel hied to his hollow dray, the weasel slunk to his tuffet lair, and every rabbit skipped home from grass. The crows and the magpies were all in a churm; the heavy–winged heron flapped off from the brook–side; the jar–bird flicked out from the ivy–drum; the yaffingale darted across the ride with his strange discordant laugh; even the creepers that ply the trees crept into lichened fastnesses, lay flat to the bark, and listened.

Nor less the solid, heavy powers that have to stay and break the storm, no less did they, the beechen clump, the funnelled glens, the heathery breastwork, even the depths of forest night—whence common winds shrink back affrighted—even the bastions of Norman oak, scarred by many a tempest–siege, and buckled by the mighty gale of 1703,—one and all they whispered of the stress of heaven impending.

First came fitful scuds of rain, "flisky" rain they call it, loose outriders of the storm, spurning the soft ice, as they dashed by, and lashing the woodman's windows. Then a short dark pause ensued, in which the sky swirled up with clouds, and the earth lay mute with terror. Only now and then a murmur went along the uplands.

Suddenly, ere a man might say, "Good God!" or "Where are my children?" every tree was taken aback, every peat–stack reeled and staggered, every cot was stripped of its thatch, on the opposite side to that on which the blow was expected.

The first squall of that great tempest broke from the dark south–east. It burst through the sleet, and dashed it upwards like an army of archers shooting; ere a man could stay himself one way, it had caught him up from another. The leaves from the ground flew up again through the branches which had dropped them; and then a cloud of all manner of foliage, whirling, flustering, capering, flitting, soared high over the highest tree–tops, and drove through the sky like dead shooting–stars.

All that afternoon, the squalls flew faster, screaming onward to one another, furious maniacs dashing headlong, smiting themselves and everything. Then there came a lull. So sudden that the silence was more stunning than the turmoil. A pause for sunset; for brave men countless to see their last of sunlight. That evening, the sundown gun from Calshot was heard over all the forest. I remember to have expected fully that the next flaw of air would come, like a heavy sigh, from the south–west. The expectation showed how much I underrated the magnitude of that broad storm's area. If the wind had chopped then, it would have been only a hard gale, not a hurricane.

Like a wave of the sea, it came on solidly, and from the old direction; no squall, no blast, any more; but one bodily rush of phalanxed air through a chasm in the firmament. Black, and tossing stone and metal as a girl jerks up her hat–plume, it swept the breadth of land and sea, as bisons horded sweep the snow–drifts, as Niagara sweeps the weeds away.

Where the full force of that storm broke, any man must have been mad drunk who attempted to go to bed. Houses unroofed, great trees snapped off and flung into another tree, men caught like chaff from the winnowing and dropped somewhere in pond or gravel–pit, the carrier's van overthrown on the road, and three oaks come down to lie upon it,—some blown–away people brought news of these things, and fetched their breath up to tell them.

Our own staunch hearths rocked under us, and we looked for the walls to fall in upon us, as every mad rush came plunging.

Miss Eudoxia sat with Amy, near the kitchen fire; at least where the fire should have been, but the wind had quenched it long ago. Near them cowered Jemima and Jenny, begging not to be sent to bed. They had crawled up–stairs to see about it, and the floor came up to them—so they said—like the shifting plate of the oven. The parlour chimney–stack had fallen; but, in God's mercy, clear and harmless from the roof of the house. No fear of the thatch taking fire: that wind would have blown out the fire of London.

Now as they sat, or crouched and sidled, watching the cracks of the ceiling above, jumping every now and then, as big lumps of mortar fell down the chimney, and shrinking into themselves, every time the great stack groaned and laboured so, Miss Eudoxia, full of pluck, was reading aloud—to little purpose, for she scarcely could hear her own voice—the prayers which are meant to be used at sea, and the 107th Psalm. And who shall say that she was wrong, especially as the devil is supposed to be so busy in a gale of wind?

Jemima and Amy were doing their best to catch her voice at intervals. As for Jenny, she did not care much what became of her now. She knew at the last full moon that her sweetheart was thoroughly up for jilting her; and now when she had ventured out—purely of her own self–will—the wind had taken her up anyhow, and whisked her like a snow–flake against the wash–house door. She was sure to have a black eye in the morning, and then it would be all up with her; and Jemima might go sweethearting, and she could not keep her company.

The roar through the wood, the yells at the corners, the bellowing round the chimneys, the thunder of the implacable hurricane; any mortal voice was less than a whisper into a steam–whistle. Who could tell what trees were falling? A monster might be hurled on the roof, and not one of them would know it until it came sheer through the ceiling. Amy was pale as the cinders before her, but firm as the bars of iron, and even trying to smile sometimes at the shrieks and queer turns of the tempest. No candle could be kept alight, and the flame of the parlour lamp quivered like a shirt badly pinned on a washing–line. But Amy was thinking dearly of the father of the household, the father of the parish, out in the blinding wind and rain, and where the wild waves were lashing. And now and then Amy wondered whether it blew so hard in London, and hoped they had no big chimneys there.

John Rosedew had taken his little bundle, in a waterproof case, and set out on foot for Rushford, when the storm became unmistakeable. He would

no wise, nor stuck down; neither of the High nor Low Church rut, although an improvement on the old type which cared for none of these things. He did his duty by his parish; and, as follows almost of necessity, his parish loved and admired him. He never lifted a poor man's pot–lid to know what he had for dinner; he never made much of sectarian squabbles, nor tried to exorcise dissent. In a word, he kept his place, because he felt and loved it.

Only two rooms had Pell to boast of, but he was wonderfully happy in them. He could find all his property in the dark, and had only one silver spoon. And the man who can be happy with one, was born with it in his mouth. Those two rooms he rented from old Jacob Thwarthawse, or rather from Mrs. Jacob, for the old man was a pilot on the Southampton Water, and scarcely home twice in a twelvemonth. The little cot looked like a boat–house at the bottom of the bunney; so close it was to the high–water mark, that the froth of the waves and the drifting skates' eggs came almost up to the threshold when the tide ran big, and the wind blew fresh.

And in the gentle summer night—pray what is it in Theocritus? John Rosedew could tell, but not I—at least, I mean without looking—

> "Along the pinched caboose, on every side,
> With mincing murmur swam the ocean tide."
>
> *Id.* xxi. 17.

CHAPTER IV

By the time Octavius Pell had clothed, and fed, and warmed his drenched and buffeted guests, the sun was slipping out of sight, and glad to be quit of the mischief. For a minute or two, the cloud–curtain lifted over St. Alban's Head, and a narrow bar of lively green striped the lurid heavens. This was the critical period, and John Rosedew was aware of it, as well as Octave Pell. Either the wind would shift to south–west quicker than vanes could keep time with it, and then there would be a lively storm, with no very wide area; or else it would come on again with one impetuous leap and roar, and no change of direction, and work to the south–west gradually, blowing harder until it got there. The sea was not very heavy yet, when they went out to look at it; the rain had ceased altogether; there was not air enough to move the fur of a lady's boa; but, out beyond the Atlantic offing, ridges like edges of knives were jumping, as if to look over the sky–line.

"Nulla in prospectu navis," said John Rosedew, who always talked Latin, as a matter of course, when he met an Oxford man; "at least, so far as I can see with the aid of my long–rangers."

"No," replied Pell, "and I'm heartily glad that there is no ship in sight; for, unless I'm much mistaken—run, sir, run like lightning. *I've got no more dry clothes.*"

They ran for it, and were just in time before the fury came down again. Bob Garnet was ready to slip away, for he knew that his father would be wild about him; he had taken his drenched hat from the firetongs, and was tugging at the latch of the door. But now there was no help for it.

"We are in for it now," cried Mr. Rosedew; "I have not come down for nothing. It is, what I feared this morning, the heaviest storm that has broken upon us for at least a generation. And we are not yet in the worst of it. God grant there be no unfortunate ship making for the Needles. All our boats, you say, Pell, are in the Solent long ago. Bob, my boy, you must not expect to see your father to–night. I hope he will guess what has happened."

The beach, or pebble bank of Hurst, is a long and narrow spit of land, growing narrower every year, which forms a natural breakwater to the frith of the Solent. It curves away to the south of east from the straighter and more lofty coast of Barton, Hordle, and Rushford. Hurst Castle, in which it terminates, is the eastern horn of Christchurch Bay, as Hengistbury Head is the western. The Isle of Wight and the Needle Rocks protect this bay from the east wind's power, but a due south wind brings in the sea, and a south–west the Atlantic. Off this coast we see at times those strange floating or rising islands known by the name of the "Shingles;" which sometimes stay above water so long, that their surface is clad with the tender green of bladderwort and samphire; but more often they disappear after taking the air for a few short hours. For several years now they have taken no air; and a boatman told me the other day, that, from the rapid strides of the sea, he thought it impossible for the "Shingles" ever to top the waves again.

Up and down the Solent channel the tide pours at a furious speed; and the rush of the strong ebb down the narrows, flushed with the cross–tide from St. Helen's, combs and pants out into Christchurch Bay, above the floodmark of two hours since. This great eddy, or reflux, is called the "double–tide;" and an awkward power it has for any poor vessel to fall into.

All that night it blew and blew, harder and harder yet; the fishermen's boats on the beach were caught up, and flung against the gravel–cliff; the stout men, if they ventured out, were snatched up as a mother snatches a child from the wheels of a carriage; the oaks of the wood, after wailing and howling, as they had done to a thousand tempests, found that outcry go for nothing, and with it went themselves. Seven hundred towers of Nature's building showed their roots to the morning. The old moon expired at O·32; and many a gap the new moon found, where its mother threw playful shadows. The sons of Ytene are not swift–witted, nor deeply read in the calendar; yet they are apt to mark and heed the great convulsions of nature. The old men used to date their weddings from the terrible winter of 1787; the landmark of the young men's annals is the storm of 1859.

All that night, young Robert Garnet was strung by some strange tension. Of course he could not sleep, amid that fearful uproar, although he was plunged and lost from sight in Octavius Pell's great chair. The only luxury Pell possessed—and that somehow by accident—was a deep, and soft, and mighty chair, big enough for three people. After one of the windows came in, which it did, with a crash, about ten o'clock, scattering Pell's tobacco–jars, and after they had made it good with books and boxes and a rug, so that the wind was filtered through it, John Rosedew and his curate sat on a couple of hard old Windsors, watching the castle of Hurst. Thence would come the signal flash, if any hapless bark should be seen driving over the waters. There they sat, John Rosedew talking, as he could talk to a younger man, when his great heart was moved to its depth, and the multitude of his mind in march, and his soul anticipating it: talking so that Octave Pell, following his silver tones, even through that turmoil, utterly forgot the tempest, and the lapse of hours, and let fall on his lap the pipe, which John had made him smoke.

The thunder of the billows waxing, for the wind was now south–west, began to drown the roar of the gale, and a storm of foam was flying, when the faint gleam of a gun at sea was answered by artillery's flash from the walls of old Henry the Eighth. Both men saw the landward light leap up and stream to leeward; but only the younger one descried the weak appeal from the offing.

"Where is she, Pell? Have you any idea?"

"She is away, sir, here to the right: dead in the eye of the wind."

"Then may our God and Father pity our brothers and our sisters!"

Out ran both those strong good men, leaving poor Bob (as they thought) asleep in the depth of the easy–chair. The little cottage was partly sheltered by an elbow of the cliff; otherwise it would have been flying up the bunney long ago. The moment the men came out of the shelter, they were driven one against the other, and both against the cliff.

"My castle will go at high–water," said Pell, though none could hear him; "but I shall be back in time enough to get the old woman out."

Then, as far as Pell could make out in the fierce noise and the darkness, John Rosedew begged him to go back, while himself went on alone. For it was John's especial business; he had procured the lifeboat, chosen the crew, and kept the accounts; and he thought himself responsible for any wreck that happened. But what good on earth could Pell do, and all his chattels in danger?

"No good, very likely," Pell shouted, "and a good deal perhaps in–doors! Keep the sea out with a besom."

Octave had a dry way with him, not only when he sang, but when he thought he saw the right, and did not mean to argue it. So rector and curate, old man and young man, trudged along together, each bending low, and throwing his weight, like a quoit, against the wind; each stopping and crouching at every tenth yard, as the blast irresistible broke on them. Crusted with hunks of froth pell–mell, like a storm of eggs on the hustings, drenched by pelting sheets of spray, deafened by the thundering surf, and often obliged to fly with the wind from a wave that rushed up scolloping, they battled for that scoop of the bay where the ship must be flung by the indraught.

Up to the present, Christchurch Point, and St. Alban's Head beyond it, broke (as the wind was westering) some little of the wildest sea–brunt. But now they stood, or rather crouched, where the mountain rollers gathering, sweeping, towering onward, avalanche upon avalanche, burst on their destined barrier. A thousand leagues of water, swelled by the whole weight of heaven flung on it, there leaped up on the solid earth, and to the heaven that vexed it. As a strong man in his wrath accepts his wife's endorsement, so the surges took the minor passion of a fierce spring–tide, rolled it in their own, and scorned the flat land they looked down upon. Tush, the combing of their crests was bigger than any town there. On they came, too grand to be hurried even by the storm that roused them; each had a quarter of a mile to himself, and who should take it from him? The white foam fell back in the wide water valleys, and hissed and curdled away in flat loops, and the storm took the mountain ridges again and swept the leaping snow off. Anon, as it struck the shelving shore, each rolling monster tossed its crest unspeakably indignant; hung with impending volume, curling like the scroll of God; then thundered, as in judgment, down, and lashed the trembling earth.

Among them, not a mile from shore, as the breaking daylight showed it, heaved, and pitched, and wallowed hog–like in the trough of waters, a large ship, swept and naked. Swept of her masts, of her canvas naked; but clad, alas! with men and women, clustering, clinging, cowering from the great white grave beneath them. As she laboured, reeled, and staggered up to the storm–rent heavens, and then plunged down the yawning chasm, every attitude, every gesture of terror, love, despair, and madness could be descried on the object–glass of the too–faithful telescope. As a ghastly wan gleam from the east lit up all that quivering horror, all that plight of anguish, John Rosedew turned away in tears, and fell upon his knees.

But Pell caught up the clear Munich glass, blocked every now and then with foam; he wiped it with his cuff, and levelled it on a stony ledge. There he lay behind the pebbles, himself not out of danger, unable to move, or look away, spellbound by the awe of death in numbered moments coming. Round him many a sturdy boatman, gazing, listening, rubbing his eyes, wondering about the wives and children of the brave men there. The great disaster imminent was known all over the village, and all who dared to cross the gale had crept, under shelter, hitherwards. None was fool enough to talk of boat, or tug, or lifeboat; a child who had then first seen the sea must have known better than that. The best ship in the British navy could not have come out of the Needles in the teeth of such a hurricane.

Some of the tars had brought their old Dollonds, preventive glasses long cashiered, and smugglers' night–rakers cheek by jowl, and every sort of "perspective," fifty years old and upward, with the lenses cracked and rattling, and fungoid tufts in the object–glass. Nevertheless, each man would swear that his own glass was the best of the lot, and his neighbour's "not of much count." To their minds, telescopes like spectacles suit the proprietor only.

"By Jove, I believe she'll do it!" cried Pell, the chief interpreter, his glass being the only clear one.

"Do what, sir? what?" asked a dozen voices, hurriedly.

"Get her head round to windward, and swing into smoother water. They're in the undertow already. Oh, if they only knew it!"

They knew it, he saw, in a moment. They ran up a spare sail, ere he could speak, to the stump of the mizen–mast, and a score of brave men strained on the sheets until they had braced them home. They knew that it could not stand long; it would fly away to leeward most likely when once they mounted the wave–crest; but two or three minutes might save them. With eight hands jamming the helm up, and the tough canvas tugging and bellying, the ship, with the aid of the undertow, plunged heavily to windward. All knew that the ship herself was doomed, that she never could fetch off shore; but, if she could only hold her course for some half–mile to the westward, she would turn the flank of those fearful rollers, and a good stout boat might live. For there a south–western headland broke the long fury of the sea.

Every eye was intent, every bosom drew a deep breath, as the next great billow rose under the ship, and tossed her up to the tempest. They had brought her as near to the wind as they dared, so as still to have steerage way on her, and she took the whole force of the surge on her port bow, not on her beam, as the people on shore had feared. The sea broke bodily over her, and she staggered back from the blow, and shook through every timber, then leaped and lurched down the terrible valley, but still, with the good sail holding. She was under noble seamanship, that was clear to every one, and herself a noble fabric. If she could but surmount two billows more, without falling off from the wind, within three points of which her head lay, most of the crew might be rescued. Already a stout galley, manned with ten oars, was coming out of Christchurch Harbour, dancing like a cork on the waves, though sheltered by the headland.

Our ship rode over the next billow gallantly; it was a wave that had some moderation, and the lungs of the gale for the moment were panting, just as she topped the comb of it. "Hurrah!" shouted the men ashore; "By God, she'll do it yet!"

By God alone could she do it. But the Father saw not fit; the third billow was the largest of all that had yet rolled up from the ocean. Beam–end on she clomb the mountain, heeling over heavily, showing to the shore her deck–seams,—even the companion–finial, and the poor things clinging there; a wail broke from them as the great sea struck her, and swept away half a score of them.

"Now's your chance, men. D—n your eyes! She won't hang there two minutes. Out with the boats you—— lubbers. Look sharp, and be d—d to you."

The ancient pilot, Thwarthawse, dancing and stamping, his blue jacket flapping in the wind, and his face of the deepest plum colour, roared to windward his whirlwind of oaths up an old split trumpet, down which the wind came bellowing harder than his voice went up it.

"Stow that, Jacob!" cried an old Scotchman, survivor of many a wreck; "can ye nae see his reverence, mon? It's an unco thing for an auld mon like you to swear at your mates in their shrouds, chap. I ken the skipper of that there ship, and he's no lubber, no more than I be."

Sandy Macbride was known to fear God, and to have fifty pounds in the savings bank. Therefore no one flouted him.

"You're right, Mac; you're right, by George!" cried Pell. "What a glorious fellow! I can see him there holding on by the stanchion, giving his orders as coolly as if for the cabin dinner. I could die with that man."

The tear in Octavius Pell's right eye compelled him to shift the glass a bit. He was just the man who would have done even as that captain did.

"Hurrah, hurrah! they've got the launch out; only she and the gig are left. Troops on the deck, drawn up in a line, and the women hoisted in first. Give them three cheers, men, though they can't hear you! Three cheers, if you are Englishmen! Glorious, glorious! There they go; never saw such a fine thing in all my life. Oh, I wish I had been a sailor!"

The tears ran down the young parson's cheeks, and were blown into the eyes of old Macbride; or else he had some of his own.

"Shove off, shove off; now's your time, for the under–current is failing her. Both of them off, as I'm alive; and yet a third boat I could not see. What magnificent management! That man ought to command a fleet. Two of them off for Christchurch Harbour; away, away, while the wind lulls; but what is the third boat doing?" Every one was looking: no one answered. Old Mac knew what it was, though his eyes were too old to see much.

"Captain Roberts, I'll go bail, at his old tricks again. And there's none with the sense to mutiny on him, and lash his legs, as we did in the *Samphire*."

"At the side of the ship there is some dispute. The boat is laden to the water's edge, and the ship paying off to leeward, for there is no man at the wheel; there goes the sail from the bolt–ropes. If they don't push off, ere an oar's length, they will all be sucked into the rollers! Good God! now I see what it is. There is only room for one more, and not one of those three will take it. Two white–haired men and a girl. Life against honour with the old men; and what is life compared with it? Both resolved not to stir a peg; now they join to make the girl go. Her father has got her in his arms to pitch her into the boat; she clings around his neck so that both must go, or neither. He could not throw her; she falls on her knees, and clings to his legs to die with him. Smack—there, the rope is parted, and it is too late for further argument. The troops in the boat salute the officer, and he returns it as on parade."

"Name of that ship?" said Jacob, curtly, to old Sandy Macbride.

"*Aliwal*, East India trader, Captain Roberts. Calcutta to Southampton."

"Then it's all up now with the *Aliwal*, and every soul on board of her."

"Don't want a pilot to tell us that," answered old Mac, testily. "You've seed a many good craft, pilot, but never one as could last five minutes on the Shingle Bank, with this sea running."

"Ropes, ropes!" cried Octave Pell; "in five minutes she'll be ashore here."

"No, she 'ont, nor yet in ten," answered his landlord, gruffly; "she'll fetch away to the eastward first, now she is in the tide again, specially with this gale on; and she'll take the ground over yonner, and go to pieces with the next breaker."

She took her course exactly as old Jacob mapped it out for her. He knew every run and flaw of the tide, and how it gets piled in the narrows by a very heavy storm, and runs back in the eddy which had saved so many lives there. This has nothing to do with the "double tide;" that comes after high–water. As the good ship traced the track of death, doing as the waves willed (like a little boy's boat in the Serpentine), the people on shore could see those three, who had contested the right of precedence to another world.

They were all upon the quarter–deck; and three finer figures never yet came to take the air there, in the weariness of an Indian voyage. Captain Roberts, a tall, stout man, with ruddy cheeks and a broad white beard, stood with his hands in his pockets, and his feet asunder, and a sense of discipline in his face, as of a man who has done his duty, and now obeys his Maker. No sign of flinching or dismay in his weather–beaten eyes, as he watched his death roll towards him; though the gazers fancied that one tear rose, perhaps at the thought of his family just coming down–stairs at Lymington. The military man beside him faced his death quite differently; perhaps with even less of fear, but with more defiance, broken, every now and then, by anguish for his daughter. He had not learned to fear the Lord, as those men do who go down into the great deep. He looked as if he ought to be commanding–officer of the tempest. The ship, running now before wind and sea, darted along as a serpent darts over the graves in the churchyard; she did not lurch any more, or labour, but rose and fell, just showing her fore–foot or stern–post, as the billows passed under her. And so that young maiden could stand and gaze, with her father's arm thrown round her.

She was worthy to be his daughter; tall, and light of form, and calm, with eyes of wondrous brightness, she was looking at her father's face to say the last good–bye. Then she flung both arms around his neck, and fondly, sadly, kissed him. Meanwhile the ship–captain turned away, and thought of Susy Roberts. Suddenly he espied a life–belt washed into the scuppers. He ran for it in a moment, came behind the maid, and, without asking her consent, threw it over her, and fastened it. There was little chance of it helping her, but that little chance she should have.

"She'll take the ground next biller," cried the oracular Jacob; "stand by there with the ropes, boys."

On the back of a huge wave rose for the last time the unfortunate *Aliwal*. Stem on, as if with strong men steering, she rushed through the foam and the white whirl, like a hearse run away with in snow–drifts. Then she crashed on the stones, and the raging sea swept her from taffrail to bowsprit, rolled her over, pitched her across, and broke her back in two moments. The shock rang through the roar of billows, as if a nerve of the earth were thrilling. Another mountain–wave came marching to the roll of the tempest–drum. It curled disdainfully over the side, like a fog sweeping over a hedgerow; swoop—it broke the timbers away, as a giant tosses a fir–cone.

"I can't look any longer," cried Pell; "give me something to feel, men. Quick, there! I see something!"

He seized the bight of a rope, and rushed anyhow into the waters. But John Rosedew and the life–boatmen held hard upon the coil of it, and drew him with all their might back again. They hauled Octavius Pell up in the manner of a cod–fish, and he was so bruised and stupefied, that he could not tell what he had gone for. They only saw floating timber and gear, and wreck of every sort drifting, till just for one sight–flash a hoary head, whiter than driven waters, leaped out of the comb of the billow. A naval man, or a military—who knows, and to whom does it matter?

Brave men ashore, all waiting ready, dashed down the steep of death to save him, if the great wave should toss up its plaything. All Rushford strained at the cables that held them from the savage recoil. Worse than useless; the only chance of it was to make more widows. The sea leaped at those gallant strong men; there were five on either cable; it leaped at them as the fiery furnace leaped on the plain of Dura. It struck the two ropes into one with a buffet, as a lion's paw shatters a cobweb; it dashed the men's heads together, and flung them all in a pile on a ballast–heap. Lucky for them that it fought with itself, and clashed there, and made no recoil. The white–haired corpse was seen no more; and all Rushford shrunk back in terror.

The storm was now at its height; and of more than a hundred people gathered on the crown of the shore, and above the reach of the billows, not one durst stand upright. Nearer the water the wind had less power, for the wall of waves broke the full brunt of it. But there no man, unless he were most quick of eye and foot, might stand without great peril. For scarcely a single billow broke, but what, in the first rebound and toss, two churning hummocks of surf met, and flashed up the strand like a mad white horse, far in advance of the rest. Then a hissing ensued, and a roll of shingle, and the water poured huddling and lappeting back from the chine itself had crannied.

As brave men fled from a rush of this sort, and cowards on the bank were laughing at them, something white was seen in the curl of the wave which was breaking behind it. The ebb of that inrush met the wave and partly took the crash of it, then the white thing was shot on the shore like a pellet, and lay one instant motionless. There was no rope there, and the men hung back; John Rosedew cried "Shame!" and ran for it; but they joined hands across and stopped him. Before they could look round again, some one had raised the body. 'Twas young Bob Garnet, and in his arms lay the maiden senseless. She had looked at him once, and then swooned away from the whirl, and the blows, and the terror. No rope round his body, no cork, no pad; he had rushed full into the raging waves, as he woke from his sleep of heaviness. He lifted the girl, and a bending giant hung thirty feet above them.

Then a shriek, like a woman's, rang out on the wind, and two great arms were tossed to heaven. Bull Garnet stood there, and strove to rush on, strove with every muscle, but every nerve strove against it. He was balanced and hung on the wind for a moment, as the wave hung over his heart's love. Crash came the wave—what shriek should stop it, after three hundred miles of rolling?—a crash that rang in the souls of all whom youth could move or nobleness. Nothing was seen in the depth of water, the swirling, hurling whiteness, until the billow had spent its onset, and the curdle of the change was. Then Bob, swept many a fathom in–shore, but griping still that senseless thing, that should either live or die with him—Bob, who could swim as well or better than he could climb a tree, but felt that he and his load were only dolls for the wave to dandle—down he went, after showing his heels, and fought the deadly outrush. None but Nature's pet would have thought of, none but the favoured of God could have done, it. He felt the back–wave tugging at him, he felt that he was going; if another billow broke on him, it was all up with his work upon wire–worm. Holding his breath, he flung his right leg over the waist of the maiden, dug his two hands deep into the gravel, and clapped his feet together. Scarcely knowing what was up, he held on like grim death for life, and felt a barrowload of pebbles rolling down the small of his back. Presently he saw light again, and sputtered out salt water, and heard a hundred people screaming out "Hurrah!" and felt a strong arm thrown round him—not his father's, but John Rosedew's. Three senseless bodies were borne to the village—Bull Garnet's, and Bob's and the maiden's.

CHAPTER V

Meanwhile that keen engineering firm, wind, wave, and tide, had established another little business on the coast hard by. This was the general wreck and crack–up of the stout Pell–castle, a proceeding unnoticed by any one except good mother Jacob, whose attention was drawn to it forcibly, as the head of the bed fell in upon her. Thereupon the stout dame made a rush for it, taking only her cat and spectacles, and the little teapot of money. As she started at a furious pace, and presented to the elements a large superficial area, the wind could not resist the temptation, but wafted her to the top of the bunney, without her feet so much as once a–touching the blessed earth—she goes mad if any one doubts it—and planted her in a white–thorn tree, and brought an "elam" of thatch to shelter her from her own beloved roof. There, when the wind subsided, she was happily discovered by some enterprising children; the cat was sitting at her side; in one blue hand she held her specs, and in the other a teapot.

Poor Pell's easy–chair was thrown up, three miles to the westward, in the course of the next spring–tides, and, being well known all over the neighbourhood (from his lending it to sick people), was brought to him, with a round of cheers, by half a dozen fishermen. They refused the half–crown he offered them, and displayed the greatest anxiety lest his honour should believe it was them as had taken the shine off. The workmanship not being modern, the chair was little the worse for its voyage; only it took six months to dry, and had a fine smell of brine ever afterwards. Then, having been lent to an old salt's widow, it won such a reputation, all across the New Forest, as a specific for "rheumatics in the small of the back," that old women, having *no* small to their backs, walked all the way from Lyndhurst, "just to sot themselves down in it, and how much was to pay, please, for a quarter of an hour?" "A shilling," said Octave Pell, "a shilling for the new lifeboat that lives under Christchurch Head." Then they pulled out mighty silver watches, and paid the shilling at the fifteen minutes. The walk, and the thought of the miracle, and the fear of making fools of themselves, did such a deal of good, that a man got up a 'bus for it; but Pell said, "No; none who come by 'bus shall sit in my chair of ease."

The greedy sea returned brave Pell no other part of his property. His red tobacco–jar, indeed, was found by some of the dredgemen three or four years afterwards, but they did not know it was his, and sold it—crusted as it was with testacea, and ribboned with sea–weed—to the zealous secretary of—I won't say what museum. "Roman, or perhaps Samian, or possibly Phœnician ware," cried the secretary, lit with fine—though, it may be, loose—ideas; and he catalogued it: "Phœnician in the opinion of an F.A.S. There is every reason to believe it a vase for Thuricremation." "Hollo!" cried Pell, when he went there to lecture upon cricket as played by Ulysses, "why, I'm blessed if you haven't got— —" "The most undoubted Phœnician relic contained in any museum!" So he laughed with other people's cheeks, like a man of sense.

All the folk of Rushford, and many too of Nowelhurst, contributed to a secret fund for refurnishing Octavius Pell. So great were the mystery and speed, and so clever the management of the dissenting parson, that two great vans were down upon Pell before he had heard a word of it. He stood at the door of the cobbler's shop, and tried to make a speech; but the hurrahs were too many for him, and he turned away and cried. Tell me that any man in England need be anything but popular who has a heart of his own, and is not ashamed of having it!

At the Crown, where the three sick people were, a very fine trade was doing; but a finer one still upon the beach, as the sea went down and the choice contents of the *Aliwal* came up. For that terrible storm began to abate about noon on the 26th. It had blown as hard for twenty–four hours as it ever does blow in any land, except in the gaps of the Andes and during cyclones of the tropics. Now the core of the storm had no more cells in it; and the puffs that came from the west and north–west, and so on till it got to the pole–star, were violent indeed, but desultory, and seemed not to know where they were going. Finally, about midnight, the wind owned that its turn was over, and sunk (well satisfied with its work) into the arms of slumber—"placidâque ibi demum morte quievit." And its work had been done right well. No English storm since the vast typhoon of 1703—which I should like to write about some day if my little life–storm blows long enough—had wrought such glorious havoc upon that swearing beaver, man. It had routed his villages at the Land's End, and lifted like footstools his breakwater blocks; it had scared of their lives his Eddystone watchmen, and put out half his lighthouses; it had broken upon his royalty, and swept down the oaks of the New Forest; it had streaked with wrecks the Goodwin Sands, and washed ships out of harbours of refuge; it had leaped upon London as on a drain–trap, and jarred it as a man whistles upon his fingers; it had huddled pell–mell all the coal–trade;—saddest vaunt (though not the last), it had strewn with gashed and mangled bodies (like its own waves, countless) the coasts of Anglesea and Caernarvon.

On the morning now of the 27th, with the long sullen swell gold–beater–skinned by the recovering sun, the shingle–bank was full of interest to an active trader. They had picked up several bodies with a good bit of money upon them, and the beach was strewn with oranges none the worse for a little tossing. For the stout East Indiaman *Aliwal* had touched at the Western Islands, and taken on board a thousand boxes of the early orange harvest. And not only oranges were rolling among the wrack, the starfish, the shark's teeth, and the cuttle–eggs, but also many a pretty thing, once prized and petted by women. There were little boxes with gilt and paint, sucked heartily by the salt water, and porcupine–quills rasping up from panels of polished ebony, cracked mirrors inside them, and mother–of–pearl, and beading of scented wood; all the taste and the labour of man yawning like dead cockles, crimped backward, sodden and shredded, as hopeless a wreck as a drunkard.

Then there were barrels, and heavy chests, planking already like hemp in the prison–yard, bulkheads, and bulwarks, and cordage, and reeve–blocks, and ten thousand other things, well appreciated by the wreckers, who were hauling them up the bunneys; while the Admiralty droitsmen made an accurate inventory of the bungs and the blacking bottles. Some of the sailors, and most of the passengers, who had escaped in the boats to Christchurch, came over to look for anything that might turn up of their property. Hereupon several fights ensued, and many poor fellows enjoyed opportunity for a closer inspection of the Rushford stratum than the most sanguine of their number anticipated; until the police came down in force, and extinguished at once all other rights of salvage except their own.

Nevertheless there was yet one field upon which the police could not interfere; although Jack wished for nothing better than to catch the lubbers there. This was Jack's own domain, the sea, where an animated search was going on for the body of Colonel Nowell. His servant had hurried from Christchurch to Nowelhurst to report the almost certain death of Sir Cradock's only brother. He did not go first to ascertain it; for the road along the cliffs was impassable during the height of the storm. Sir Cradock received the announcement with very few signs of emotion. He had loved that Clayton in early youth, but now had almost forgotten him; and Clayton had never kept his brother at all apprised of his doings. Sir Cradock had gone into mourning for him, some three years ago; and Colonel Nowell never took the trouble to vindicate his vitality until Dr. Hutton's return. And, even though they had really known and loved one another as brothers, the loss would have been but a tap on the back to a man already stabbed through the heart. Therefore Sir Cradock's sorrow exploded (as we love to make our griefs do, and as we so often express them) in the moneyed form. "I will give 500*l*. to the man who finds my poor brother's body."

That little speech launched fourteen boats. What wrecker could hope for anything of a tenth part of the value? Men who had sworn that they never would pull in the same boat again together—might the Great Being, the Giver of life, strike them dead if they did!—forgot the solemn perjuration, and cried, "Give us your flipper, Ben; after all, there are worse fellows going than you, my lad:" and Ben responded, "Jump into the starn–sheets; you are just the hand as we want, Harry. Many's the time I've thought on you." Even the dredging smacks hauled in–shore from their stations, and began to dredge for the Colonel; till the small boats resolved on united action, tossed oars, and held solemn council. Several speeches were made, none of them very long, but all embodying that fine sentiment, "fiat justitia, ruat cœlum," in the form of "fair play, and be d—d to you." Then Sandy Mac, of the practical mind, made a suggestion which was received with three wild rounds of cheers.

"Give 'em a little ballast, boys, as they be come in–shore to dredge for it."

With one consent the fourteen boats made for the shore, like the fleet of canoes described by the great Defoe. Nor long before each shallop's nose "grated on the golden sands." The men in the dredging smacks looked at the sky to see if a squall was coming. And soon they got it, thick as hail, and as hot as pepper. The fourteen boats in battle array advanced upon them slowly, only two men rowing in each, all the rest standing up, and every man charged heavily. When they were at a nice wicket distance, old Mac gave the signal, and a flight of stones began, which, in the words of the ancient chroniclers, "well–nigh darkened the noonday sun." The bravest dredger durst not show his head above the gunwale; for the Rushford stones are close of grain, and it is sweeter to start than to stop them. As for south–westers and dreadnoughts, they were no more use than vine–leaves in a storm of electric hail.

> "Ah, little then those mellow grapes their vine–leaf shall avail, So thickly rattles on *the tiles* the pelting of the hail."
>
> *Georg.* i. 448.

The dredgers gave in, and hoisted a shirt as a signal for a parley. The Rushford men refused to hear a syllable about "snacks." What they demanded was "unconditional surrender;" and the dredgers, having no cement–stones on board, were compelled to accept it. So they took up their bags, and walked the smacks off three miles away to their station, with very faint hopes indeed that the obliging body might follow them. The boatmen celebrated their victory with three loud cheers for Sandy Mac, and a glass of grog all round. Then they returned to the likeliest spot, and dragged hard all the afternoon.

"Tarnation 'cute body," cried Ben, "as ever I come across. Who'd a thought as any perfessing Christian would have stuck to Davy Jones's locker, and refooged the parson and clerk so? Spit on your grapples, my lads of wax, and better luck the cast after."

"The Lord kens the best," replied Sandy Mac, with a long–drawn sigh, "us poor vessels canna do more than is the will of the Lord, boys. Howsomever, I brought a bit of bait, a few lug–worms, and a soft crab or two; and please the Lord I'll rig my line out, and see if the bass be moving. And likely there may be a tumbling cod on the run speering after the puir bodies. Ah, yes, the will of the Lord; we ates them, and they ates us."

The canny old Scotchman, without foregoing his share in the general venture—for he helped to throw the grapnels, or took a spell at the rudder—rigged out a hook on his own account, and fastened the line to the rowlocks.

"Fair play, my son," cried Ben, winking at his comrades; "us go snacks in what you catch, mind. And the will of the Lord be done."

"Dinna ye wish ye may get it?"—the old man glowered at him indignantly—"I'll no fish at all on that onderstanding."

"Fish away, old boy, and be blessed, then. I see he ain't been in the purwentive sarvice for nothing. But I'm blowed if he'll get much supper, Harry, if it's all to come off that darned old hook." They all laughed at old Mac, who said nothing, but regarded his line attentively.

With many a joke and many an oath, they toiled away till the evening fog came down upon the waters. Then, as they turned to go home, old Mac felt a run upon his fishing–gear. Hand over hand he began to haul in, coiling the line in the stern–sheets.

"It's a wapping big fish, as ever I feel, mates; na, na, ye'll no touch it, or ye'll be claiming to come and sup wi' me. And deil a bit—the Lord forgive me—will ye ha', for grinning at an auld mon the likes of that, I tell ye. Lord ha' mercy on me, a wake and sinful crater!"

They all fell back, except Macbride, as before them in the twilight rose the ashy grey face and the long white hair of Colonel Clayton Nowell.

Mac stuck to his haul like a Scotchman; to him the main chance was no ghost. Many a time has he told that story, and turned his quid upon it, cleverly raining between his teeth with fine art to prolong the crisis.

The line being his, and the hook being his, and the haul of his own hands only, Sandy Mac could never see why he should not have all the money. The question came close to litigation; but for that, except as a word of menace, Mac was a deal too wide awake. He compounded at last for 300*l*. and let the other four share the residue.

So poor Colonel Nowell's countenance, still looking grand and dignified, was saved from the congers and lobsters; and he sleeps close by his nephew and namesake in Nowelhurst churchyard. The body of Captain Roberts was found a long way up the Solent. He had always carried a weather helm, and shaped a good course for harbour. May they rest in peace!

I have no doubt that Captain Roberts so rests, and am fain to believe, in the mercy of God, the same of the brave old Colonel. At least, we will hope that he is not gone to that eternal punishment, whose existence our divines contend for in a manner so disinterested. He had been a harum–scarum man; and now, having drowned and buried him, we may enter upon his history with the charity due to both quick and dead, but paid to the latter only.

A soldier is, in many things, by virtue of his calling, a generous, careless man. We have always credited the sailor with these popular qualities; hornpipes, national drama, and naval novels imbuing us. I doubt if the sailor be, on the whole, so careless a man as the soldier. Jack is obliged, by force of circumstance, to bottle up his money, his rollicksomeness and sentimentality, and therefore has more to get rid of, when he comes ashore once in a twelvemonth. But spread the outburst over the year, strike the average of it, and the rainfall at Aldershot will equal that at Portsmouth.

Only by watching the Army List—which at length he was tired of doing—could the English brother tell if the Indian brother were living. Even the most careful of us begin to feel that care is too much for the nine lives of a cat, when Fahrenheit scores 110° in the very coolest corner, and the punkah is too hot to move. So, after one or two Griffin letters, full of marvels which the writer pretended not to marvel at, a silence, as of the jungle, ensued, and Sir Cradock thought of tigers. Then the slides of his own life began to move upon him; and less and less every year he thought of the boy who had laughed and cried with him.

Lieutenant Nowell was ordered suddenly to the borders of the Punjaub, and for twenty years his brother Cradock drank his health at Christmas, and wondered how about the Article against praying for the dead. The next thing he heard, though it proved his own orthodoxy, disproved it by making him swear hard. Clayton Nowell had married; married an Affghan woman, to the great disgust of his brother officers, and the furious disdain of her kinsmen. A very fine family of Affghan chiefs immediately loaded their fusils, and swore to shoot both that English dog and their own Bright Eyes of the Morning.

"To think," cried Sir Cradock Nowell, "that a brother of mine should disgrace himself, and (what matters far more) his family, by marrying a wretched low Affghan woman!"

"To think," cried Mohammed Khans, "that a sister of ours should disgrace herself, and (what matters far more) her family, by marrying a cursed low English dog!"

Which party was in the right, judge ye who understand the matter. The officers' wives got over their prejudice against Bright Eyes of the Morning, and matronised, and petted, and tried to make a Christian of her. Captain Nowell adored her; she was so elegant in every motion, so loving, and so simple. She quite reformed him for the time from his too benevolent anthropology, from the love of dice, and the vinous doings which the Prophet does not encourage.

But the poor thing died in her first confinement, while following her husband's regiment at the foot of the Himalayah, leaving her new–born babe to the care of a faithful Affghan nurse, who had kept at her dear lady's side, even among the infidels. This good nurse, being great of soul, and therefore strong of faith, could not bear that the child of her mistress, the highest blood of the Affghans, should become a low Frank idolater. So she set off with it, in the dark night, crouching past the sentinels, thieves, and other camp followers, and trusted herself to the boundless jungle, with only the stars to guide her. She put the wailing child to her breast, for her own dear babe was dead, and hushed it from the vigilant ears of the man–eating tiger. Then off again for Affghanistan, six hundred miles in the distance.

How this wonderful woman, soothing and coaxing the little stranger (obtrusively remarkable for the power of her squalls), how she got on through the thorns, the fire, the famine, the jaws of the tiger, and, worse than all, the pestilent fever, bred from the rich stagnation of that alluvial soil, is more than I, or any other unversed in woman's unity, may pretend to show. Enough that with her eyes upon the grand religious heights—heathen high places, we should call them—she struggled along through nearly three–quarters of her pilgrimage, and then she fell among robbers. A villanous hill–tribe, of mixed origin, always shifting, never working, never even fighting when they could run away, hated and despised by the nobler mountain races, the pariahs of the Himalayah, ignorant of any good, debased as any Africans—in a single word, Rakshas, or worshippers of the devil. A nice school of education for a young lady of tender years—or rather months—to commence in.

The nurse was allotted to one of their chiefs, and the babe was about to be knocked on the head, when it struck an enlightened priest that in two years' time she would make a savoury oblation to the devil; so the Affghan woman was allowed to keep her, until she began to crawl about among the dogs and babes of the station. Here she so distinguished herself by precocious skill in thieving, that her delighted owner conferred upon her the title of "Never–spot–the–dust," and even instructed her how to steal the high priest's knife of sacrifice. That last exploit saved her life. Such a genius had never appeared in any tribe of the Rakshas until this great manifestation.

So "Never–spot–the–dust" was well treated, and made much of by her owner, to whom she was quite a fortune; and soon all the band looked up to her as the future priestess of the devil. For ten years she wandered about with them, becoming every year more important, proud that none could approach her skill in stealing, lying, and perjury, utterly void of all religion, except the few snatches of Moslemism which her nurse had contrived to impart, and the vague terror of the evil spirit to whom the wild men paid their vows. But, when she was ten years old, a tall and wonderfully active child, and just about to be consecrated by the blood of inferior children, a British force drew suddenly all around the nest of robbers. Of late the scoundrels had done things that made John Bull's hair stand on end; and, when his hair is in that condition, sparks are apt to come out of it.

Seeing no chance of escape, and having very faint hopes of quarter, the robbers fought with a bravery which quite astonished themselves; but the evil spirit was against them—a rare inconsistence on his part. Their rascally camp was burnt, which they who had burned some hundreds of villages looked upon as the grossest cruelty, and more than half of their number were sent home to their patron and guardian. Then the Affghan nurse, so faithful and so unfortunate, fled from the burning camp with her charge, fell before the British colonel, and poured forth all her troubles. The Englishman knew Major Nowell, and had heard some parts of his history; so he took "Never–spot–the–dust" to her father, who was amazed at once and amused with her. She could run up the punkah, and stand on the top, and twirl around on one foot; she could cross the compound in three bounds; she could jump upon her father's shoulder, and stay there with the spring of her sole; she could glide along over the floor like a serpent, and hold on with one hand to anything. And then her most wonderful lightness of touch; she had fully earned her name, she could brush the dust without marking it. She could come behind her father's back, crawling over the table, and fasten his sword–hilt to his whiskers, without his knowing a thing of it. She could pick all his pockets, of course; but that was too rude an operation for her to take any delight in it. What she delighted to do, and what even she found difficult, was to take off his shoes and stockings without his being aware of it. It was a beautiful thing to see her: consummate skill is beautiful, in whatever way it is exercised. The shoe she could get off easily enough, but the difficulty was with the stocking; and there the chief difficulty was through the sensitiveness of the skin, unaccustomed to exposure. Though she had never heard of temperature, evaporation, or anything long, her genius told her the very first time where the tug was and how to meet it. Keeping her little cornelian lips—lips which you could see through—just at the proper distance, she would breathe so softly upon the skin that the breath could not be felt, as inch by inch she lowered down the thin elastic covering. Then she would jump up out of the ground, and shout into his ears, with a voice of argute silver—

"Faddery, will 'oo have 'oor shoe? Fear to go wiyout him?"

She began to talk English, after a bit; and the weather beaten Colonel—for now he had got that far—who had never looked upon any child, except as one rupee per month—thinking of his beloved Bright Eyes of the Morning, who might, with the will of God, have made a first–rate man of him, only she was too good for him,—thinking of her, and seeing the gleam of her glorious eyes in her child, he loved that child beyond all reason, and christened her "Eoa."

He never took to bad things again. He had something now in pledge with God; a part of himself that still would live, and love him when he was skeleton. And that, his better part, should learn how lying and stealing do not lead to the right half of the other world.

His ideas about that other world were as dormant as Eoa's; but now he began to think about it, because he wanted to see her there. So, with lots of tears, not only feminine, Eoa Nowell was sent to the best school in Calcutta, where she taught the other young ladies some very odd things indeed.

Wherever she went, she must be foremost; "second to none" was her motto. Therefore she learned with amazing quickness; but it was not so easy to unlearn.

Then arose that awful mutiny, and the Colonel at Mhow was shot through the neck, and let lie, by his own soldiers. His daughter heard of it, and screamed, and no walls ever built would hold her. All the way from Calcutta, up the dreary Ganges, she forced her passage, sometimes by boat, sometimes on her weariless feet.

She had never cared much for civilization, and loved every blade of the jungle. The old life revived within her, as she looked upon the broad waters, and the boundless yellow tangle, wherein glided no swifter thing, nothing more elegant, than herself.

She found her darling father in some rude cantonment, prostrate, helpless, clinging faintly to the verge of death. Dead long ago he must have been but for Rufus Hutton; and dead even now he would have been but for his daughter's presence. His dreamy eyes went round the hut to follow her graceful movements; she alone could tend the wounds as if with the fall of gossamer, she alone could soothe and fan the intolerable aching. They looked into each other's eyes and cried without thinking about it.

Then, as he gradually got better, and the surge of trouble passed them, Eoa showed for his amusement all her strange accomplishments. She had not forgotten one of them in the grand school at Calcutta. They had even grown with her growth, and strengthened with her strength.

She would leap over Rufus Hutton's head like a flash of light, and stand facing him, without a muscle moving, and on his back would be a land–crab; she would put his up–country hat on the floor, and walk on one foot round the crown of it; she would steal his case of instruments, and toss them in the air all open, and catch them all at once.

By her nursing and her loving, her stealing and her mockery, she won Dr. Hutton's heart so entirely that he would have proposed to her, had she only been of marriageable age, or had come to think about anything.

Then they had all to cut and run, with barely three hours' notice, for the ebb of the rebellion swept through that district mightily. Eoa went to school again, and her father came to see her daily, until he was appointed to a regiment having something more than name and shadow.

Now Eoa, having learned everything that they can teach in Calcutta, the Himalayah, or the jungle, was coming to England to receive the down and crown of accomplishments. Who could tell but what they might even teach her affectation? Youth is plastic and imitative; and she was sure to find plenty of models.

Not that the honest Colonel wished to make a sickly humbug of her. His own views were wide and grand, only too philoprogenitive. Still, like most men of that class, who, upon sudden reformation, love Truth so much that they roll upon her, having no firm rules of his own, and being ashamed to profess anything, with the bad life fresh in memory, he took the opinion of old fogeys who had been every bit as unblest as himself, but had sown with a drill their wild oats. The verdict of all was one—"Miss Nowell must go to England."

Finding his wound still troublesome, he resolved to retire from service; he had not saved half a lac of rupees, and his pension would not be a mighty one; but, between the two, there would be enough for an old man to live upon decently, and go wherever he was told that his daughter ought to go.

He had seen enough of life, and found that it only meant repentance; all that remained of it should be for the pleasure and love of his daughter. And he knew that there was a sum in England, which must have been long accumulating—a sum left on trust for him and his children, under a very old settlement. He would never touch a farthing of it; every farthing should go to Eoa. Bless her dear eyes; they had the true light of his own Bright Eyes of the Morning.

CHAPTER VI

Eoa was now sixteen years old, tall, and lithe, and graceful as the creepers of tropic woodlands. Her face was of the clearest oval, a quick concise terse oval, such as we find in the eggs of wild birds rather than of tame ones. Her eyes were of bewildering brightness, always flashing, always in motion, rarely allowing the gazer a chance of guessing what their colour was. Very likely they were of no positive colour, but a pure dark lustre, such as a clear swift river has, when overhung by palm–trees. Her complexion, beautifully soft and even, was toned with a delicate eastern tinge, like that fawn–coloured light which sometimes flushes a cloudless sky before the midsummer sunrise. And her warm oriental blood suffused it, at the slightest emotion, as the leaping sun pervades that sky with a flood of limpid rubies.

She had never been flattened by education: all her qualities and feelings, like her beauty, were in excess. You could see it in the quick rise and fall of her breath, in the sudden grace of her movements, in the infinite variety of her attitudes and aspects.

Whatever she thought, she said at once; yet none ever called her a bold girl. Her modes of thought were as widely different from those of an English maiden, as a wild honeysuckle differs in form, habit, and scent, from a rose. She cared for no one's opinion of her, any more than the wind cares how a tree swings; unless indeed it were one whom she loved, and then she would crawl to please him. For she loved with all her heart and soul, and hated with no less; and she always took care in either case to apprise the object of it. And yet, with all her depth of passion, Eoa was pure of heart and mind,—ay, as pure as our own Amy.

She soon recovered from her bruises, being perfectly healthy, and elastic as india–rubber. Nevertheless, she would not have been saved from that terrible sea but for the generosity of poor Captain Roberts, and the gallantry of Bob Garnet.

Now Bob was hurt rather seriously, and, being (as we are well aware) an uncommonly shy young fellow, he was greatly astonished, and shocked a little, when on the Friday morning a beautiful girl, very strangely dressed, ran to the side of his sofa, threw her arms round him, and kissed him till he was out of breath, and his face was wet with the dew of her tears.

"Oh, please don't," said Bob; "I am sure I don't deserve it."

"Yes, you do; and I will marry you when I am old enough. I don't know what you are like, and I don't care two straws, directly they told me what you had done. Only I must have papa's leave. Kiss me again, I like it. Now where is my darling papa?"

"What, don't you know? Haven't they told you? Oh, poor thing!"

At the tone of his voice she leaped back, like a bird at the gun–flash, and stood with her little hands clasped on her head, her eyes with their deep light quivering, and the whole of her form swinging to and fro, from the wild push of sudden terror. Then she spoke with a hollow depth, which frightened Bob more than the kissing.

"They told me that he was well, gone to his brother somewhere, and I thought it wasn't like him to leave me so, and—tell me the truth, or I'll shake you to pieces."

"No, don't," said Bob, as she leaped at him; "I have had shaking enough."

"Yes, you poor boy, and for my sake. I am a brute, I know. Tell me the truth, if you love me."

"Your dear father is dead. But they have found his body."

"Do you mean to say that God has been so wicked as to kill my father?"

"God knows best," said Bob; he could think of nothing else to say.

"No, He doesn't. No, He doesn't. No, He never knows anything. He couldn't have known who he was, and how terribly I loved him, or He wouldn't have the heart to do it. Oh, you wicked boy; oh, you wicked boy! I will never forgive you for saving me. Hya, hya, hya!"

Bob never saw such a thing before, and never will again. And he won't be much the loser; although the sight was magnificent. The screams and shrieks of the clearest voice that ever puzzled echo brought up the landlord and landlady, and our good friend Rufus Hutton, who had set forth full speed from home on hearing about the *Aliwal*. He caught Eoa in his arms, carried her back to her room, and dosed her. He gave her some Indian specific, some powder of a narcotic fungus, which he had brought on purpose.

It stupefied her for nearly three days, and even then she awoke into the dreamy state of Nirwana, that bliss of semi–consciousness, like mild annihilation, into which the Buddha is absorbed, and to which all pious Buddhists look as their eternal happiness. Then she opened her delicate tapering arms, where you could see the grand muscles moving, but never once protruding, and she called for her darling father to come. Finding that he did not come, she was satisfied with some trifling answer, and then wanted to have Bob instead; but neither was Bob forthcoming.

On the very day when Dr. Hutton came to look for Eoa, Mr. Garnet found himself getting better from that wretched low nervous fever into which his fright had thrown him. Then he asked Dr. Hutton whether there would be any danger in moving Robert, and, finding that there would be none whatever, if it were carefully managed, he ordered a carriage immediately, and with some of his ancient spirit. The Crown, which had the cross–bar of its N set up the wrong way (as is done, by–the–by, on the roof of Hampton Court chapel, and in many other places), made public claim to be regarded as a "commercial hotel and posting–house." No Rushford folk having yet been known to post anything, except a letter at rare intervals, and a bill at rarer, this claim of the Crown had never been challenged, and strangers entertained a languid theoretical faith in it. But Mr. Brown looked very blue when Bull Garnet in reviving accents ordered "a chaise and pair at the door in half an hour's time; a roomy chaise, if you please, because my son must keep his feet up."

"Yes, sir; yes, to be sure, sir; I quite understand, sir. It shall be attended to, sir."

"Then why don't you go and order it?"

"To be sure, sir; I forgot. I will speak to Mrs. Brown, sir."

Mrs. Brown, being a woman of resource, mounted the boy on her donkey, the only quadruped she possessed, but a "wonner to go," as the boy said, "when you knows the right place to prog him in," and sent him post–haste to Lymington, whence the required conveyance arrived in about an hour and a half.

Rufus Hutton, having promised to be at home that evening, left Eoa to sleep off her heavy soporific, and followed the carriage on horseback; neither did he leave its track where the Ringwood Road turns off, for he had undertaken to tell Sir Cradock how his niece was getting on. He started nearly half an hour after the Lymington chaise, for Polly would never demean herself by trotting behind the "posters." During that half–hour he drank hot brown brandy–and–water, although he could not bear it, to ingratiate him with Mrs. Brown for the sake of the poor Eoa. For Mrs. Brown had no other hot method of crowning the flowing bowl. And now, while I think of it, let me warn all gentle and simple people who deign on this tale of the New Forest, never to ask for pale brandy within the perambulations. How do you think they make it? By mixing brown brandy with villanous gin. Rufus was up to this, of course; and, as he must take something for the good of the house, and to get at the kindly kernel of the heavy–browed hostess, he took that which he thought would be least for his own evil. Then, leaving Mrs. Brown (who, of course, had taken her own glass at his sole charge and largesse, after fifty times "Oh no, sir, never! Oh Lord, how my Brown would be shocked!"), having imbued that good Mrs. Brown, who really was not a bad woman—which means that she was a good one, for women have no medium—with a strong aromatic impression that he was a pleasant gentleman, and no pride, not a bit of it, in him, no more than you nor me might,—off he trotted at a furious pace, smoking two cheroots at once.

I believe that there was and is—for I am happy to say that he still inhales the breeze of life down his cigar, and looks browner and redder than ever—I believe that, in spite of all his troubles in connexion with this story, which took a good deal out of him, there was and is no happier man in our merry England than the worthy Rufus Hutton. And, as all happiness is negative, and goes without our knowing it, and only becomes a positive past for us to look back upon, so his went before it came, and goes or e'er it comes. And yet he enjoys it none the less; he multiplies it by three for the past and by nine for the future, and he never finds it necessary to deduct for the present moment.

Happy man who never thinks beyond salutary average, who can accept, in perfect faith, the traditions of his forbears, and yet is shrewd enough to hope that his grandsons will discard at least a portion of them,—who looks upon the passing life as a thing he need not move in, a world which must improve itself, and every day is doing it. And all the while he sympathises with his fellow–men, enjoys a bit of human nature, laughs at the cross–purposes of native truth and training, loves whatever he finds to be true, and does his best to foster it, is pleased with his after–dinner story, and feels universally charitable; then smiles at his wife, and kisses his children; and goes to bed with the firm conviction that they are worth all the rest put together.

Yet this man's happiness is not sound, because it is built upon selfishness.

In Nowelhurst village Dr. Hutton met Mark Stote, the gamekeeper, who begged him to stop for a moment, just to hear a word or two. Rufus, after hearing his news, resolved to take the upper road to the Hall, past Mr.

Garnet's house; it was not so very far out of his way, and perhaps he might be of service there, and—ah, yes, Dr. Hutton, this last was the real motive, though you may not have thought so—what a fine opportunity to discover something which plagued him! Perhaps I ought to say rather, the want of which was plaguing him. Rufus took so kind an interest in his neighbours' affairs, that anything not thoroughly luculent in their dealings, mode of life or speech, or management of their households, was to him the subject–matter of continual mental scratchings. Ah, how genteel a periphrase, worthy of Bailey Kettledrum; how happily we have shown our horror of that English monosyllable, beginning with the third vowel, which must be (according to Dr. Aldrich) the correlative of scratch! Score two, and go on after Dr. Hutton.

He overtook the Garnets twain just at their front gate, whence the house could not be seen, on account of a bank of evergreens. The maid came out with her cap flying off, and all her mind perturbed. Rufus Hutton, checking his mare, for the road was very narrow, heard the entire dialogue.

"Oh, sir! oh, master! have you heard of it? Such a thing, to be sure!"

"Heard of what, Sarah? Of course I have heard of the great disaster at Rushford."

"No, no. Here, sir, here! The two big trees is down on the house. It's a mussy as Nanny and me wasn't killed. And poor Miss Pearl have been in hysterics ever since, without no dinner. There, you can hear her screeching now, worse than the mangle, ever so much."

Mr. Garnet did not say a word, but set off for the house full speed, even forgetting that Bob wanted help to get from the gate to the doorway.

Rufus Hutton jumped down from his mare, and called to the driver to come and hold her, just for a minute or two; no fear of *his* horses bolting. Then, helping Bob to limp along, he followed through the shrubbery. When they came within full view of the house, he was quite amazed at the mischief. The two oaks interlocked had fallen upon it, and, crashing as they did from the height above, the breaches they made were hideous. They had cloven the house into three ragged pieces, from the roof–ridge down to the first floor, where the solid joists had stopped them. It had happened in the afternoon of the second day of the tempest; when the heart of the storm was broken, but tremendous squalls came now and then from the bright north–west. Mr. Garnet's own bed was occupied by the tree which he detested. Pearl had screamed "Judgment, judgment!" and danced among the ruins; so the maid was telling Mr. Garnet, as he feared to enter his own door.

"Judgment for what?" asked Rufus Hutton, and Mr. Garnet seemed not to hear him.

"I am sure I don't know, sir," answered the maid, "for none of us done any harm, sir; unless it was the bottle of pickled onions, when master were away, and there was very few of them left, sir, very few, I do declare to you, and we thought they was on the turn, sir, and it seemed such a pity to waste them. And please, sir, we've all been working like horses, though frightened out of our lives 'most; and we fetched down all the things from your room, where the cupboards was broken open, for 'fraid it should come on to rain, sir; and we've taken all our meals standing, sir; and made up a bed in the meat–screen, and another upon the dresser; and Miss Pearl, what turns she have given us—— Here she comes, I do declare."

"Dr. Hutton," said Bull Garnet, hastily, "good–bye; I am much obliged to you. I shall see you, I hope, next week. Good–bye, good–bye. Excuse me."

But, before he could get him out of the way—for Rufus lingered strangely—Pearl Garnet came into the little hall, with her eyes distended fearfully. "There, there it is," she cried, "there it is, I tell you! No wonder the tree came down upon it. No wonder the house was crushed for it." And she pointed to a shattered box, tilted up endwise, among a heap of account–books, clothes, and furniture.

"Oh yes, you may look at it. To be sure you may look at it. God would not have it hidden longer. I have done my best, God knows, and my heart knows, and my—I mean that man there knows. Is there anything more I can do for you, anything more, *dear father*? You have done so much for me, you know. And I will only ask you one little thing—put me in his coffin."

"The girl is raving," cried Mr. Garnet. "Poor thing, it comes from her mother."

"No, it comes from her father," said Pearl, going boldly up to him, and fixing her large bright eyes upon his. "Do as you like with me; I don't care; but don't put it on any one else. Oh, father, father, father!"

Moaning, she turned away from him; and then sprang into his arms with shrieks. He lifted her tenderly, and forgot all about his own safety. His great tears fell on her wan, sick face; and his heavy heart throbbed for his daughter only, as he felt hers bounding perilously. He carried her off to an inner room, and left them to their own devices.

"I should like uncommonly," said Rufus Hutton, rubbing his chin, "to know what is in that box. Indeed, I feel it my duty at once to ascertain."

"No, you shan't," cried Bob, limping across in front of it; "I know no more than you do, sir. But I won't have father's things pryed into."

"You are very polite," replied the Doctor; "a chip of the old block, I perceive. But, perhaps, you will believe me, my boy, when I tell you that, if ever there was a gentleman totally devoid of improper curiosity, it is Dr. Rufus Hutton, sir."

"Oh, I am so glad," said Bob; "because you won't be disappointed, then."

Rufus grinned, in spite of his wrath; but he was not to be baffled so easily. He could not push poor Bob aside, in his present disabled state, without being guilty of cowardice. So he called in an auxiliary.

"Betsy, my dear, your young mistress wished me just to examine that box. Be kind enough to bring it to the light here, unless it is too heavy for your little hands."

Oh, if he had only said "Miss Sarah," what a difference it might have made!

"Betsy, indeed!" cried Sarah, who had followed her mistress, but, being locked out, had come back to see the end of it; "my name, sir, is nothing so low as that. My name is Sarah Mackarness, sir, very much at your service; and my mother keeps a potato–shop, the largest business in Lyndhurst, sir. Betsy, indeed! and from a stranger, not to say a strange gentleman, for fear of making a mistake. And as for my hands"—she thought he had been ironical, for her hands were above regulation size—"my hands are such as pleased God to make them, and honest hands, anyhow, and doesn't want to interfere with other people's business. Oh, what will poor Nanny say, to think of me, Sarah Mackarness, be permiscuous called Betsy?"

At this moment, when Sarah Mackarness, having recovered breath, was starting into another native discourse on prænomina, and Rufus was calling upon his resources for some constitutional measure, Bull Garnet came back, treading heavily, defiant of all that the world could do. His quick eyes, never glimpsing that way, but taking in all the room at once, espied the box unmeddled with, and Bob upon guard in front of it. He was his own man now again. What did he care for anybody, so long as he had his children?

"Dr. Hutton, I thought that you were gone."

"You see I am not," said Rufus, squaring his elbows, and looking big, for he was a plucky little fellow, "and, what's more, I don't mean to go till I know what is in that box."

"Box, box!" cried Bull Garnet, striking his enormous forehead, as if to recall something; "have we a box of yours, Dr. Hutton?"

"No, no; that box of *yours*. Your daughter told us to examine it. And, from her manner, I believe that I am bound to do so."

"Bound to examine one of my boxes!" Bull Garnet never looked once that way, and Rufus took note of the strange avoidance; "my boxes are full of confidential papers; surely, sir, you have caught my daughter's—I mean to say, you are labouring under some hallucination."

"There are no papers in that box. The contents of it are metal. I have seen one article already through the broken cover, and shall not forget its shape. Beware; there have been strange things done in this neighbourhood. If you refuse to allay my suspicions, you confirm them."

The only answer he received was a powerful hand at the back of his neck, a sensation of being lifted with no increase of facilities for placid respiration; finally, a lateral movement of great rapidity through the air, and a loud sound as of a bang. Recovering reason's prerogative, he found himself in a dahlia, whose blossoms, turned into heel–balls by the recent frost, were flapping round his countenance, and whose stake had gone through his waistcoat back, and grazed his coxendix, or something; he knows best what it was, as a medical man deeply interested.

He had also a very unpleasant reminiscence of some such words as these, to which he had no responsive power—"You won't take a hint like a gentleman; so take a hit like a blackguard."

Dr. Rufus Hutton was not the man to sit down quietly under an insult of any sort. At the moment he felt that brute force was irresistibly in the ascendant, and he was wonderfully calm about it. He shook himself, and smoothed his waistcoat, and tried the stretch of his garters; then never once looked toward the house, never shook his fist, nor frowned even. He walked off to his darling Polly as if nothing at all had happened; gave the man a shilling for holding her, after looking long for a sixpence; then mounted, and rode towards Nowelhurst Hall, showing no emotion whatever. Only Polly knew that burning tears of a brave man's sense of ignominy fell upon her glossy shoulder, and were fiercely wiped way.

At the Hall he said nothing about it; never even mentioned that he had called at Garnet's cottage; but told Sir Cradock, like a true man, of Eoa's troubles, of her poor forlorn condition, and power of heart to feel it. He even contrived to interest the bereaved man, now so listless, in the young life thrown upon his care, as if by the breath of heaven. We are never so eloquent for another as when our own hearts are moved deeply by the feeling of wrong to ourselves; unless, indeed, we are very small, and that subject excludes all others.

So it came to pass that the grand new carriage was ordered to the door, and Sir Cradock would himself have gone—only Rufus Hutton had left him, and the eloquence was oozing. The old man, therefore, turned back on the threshold, saying to himself that it would be hardly decent to appear in public yet; and Mrs. O'Gaghan was sent instead, sitting inside, and half afraid to breathe for fear of the crystal. As for her clothes, they were good enough, she knew, for the Lord Mayor's coach. "Five–and–sixpence a yard, ma'am, lave alone trimming and binding." But, knowing what she did of herbs, she could not answer for the peppermint.

Of course, they did not intend to fetch poor Eoa home yet; but Biddy had orders to stay there until the young lady was moveable. Biddy took to her at once, in her heavy, long–drawn sleep, with the soft black lashes now and then lifting from the rich brown cheek.

"An' if she isn't illigant, then," said Biddy to Mrs. Brown, "ate me wi'out a purratie. Arl coom ov' the blude, missus. Sazins, then, if me and Pat had oonly got a child this day! Belikes, ma'am, for the matter o' that, a drap o' whisky disagrays with you."

Biddy, feeling strongly moved, and burning to drink her new child's health, showed a bottle of brown potheen.

"To tell you the truth, mem," said Mrs. Brown, "I know nothing about them subjects. Spirituous liquors is a thing as has always been beyond me."

"Thin I'll clap it away again," said Biddy, "and the divvil only the wiser. I never takes it alone, marm."

"It would ill become me, mem," replied Mrs. Brown, "to be churlish in my own house, mem. I have heard of you very often, mem. Yes, I assure you I have, from the people as comes to bathe here, as a lady of great experience in diseases of the chest. If you recommend any cordial, mem, on the strength of your experience, for a female of weak witality, I should take it as a dooty, mem, strictly as a dooty to my husband and two darters."

"Arrah, then, I'm your femmale. Me witality goes crossways, like, till I has a drap o' the crather." And so they made a night of it, and Mr. Brown had some.

CHAPTER VII

Leave we now, with story pending, Biddy and Eoa, Pearl, and even Amy; thee, too, rare Bull, and thee, O Rufus, overcast with anger. It is time to track the steps of him whom Fortune, blithe at her cruel trade, shall track as far as Gades, Cantaber, and wild Syrtes, where the Moorish billow is for ever heaving. Will he exclaim with the poet, who certainly was a jolly mortal,—"I praise her while she is my guest. If she flap her nimble wings, I renounce her charities; and wrap me in my manhood robe, and woo the upright poverty, the bride without a dower." "A very fine sentiment, Master Horace; but were you not a little too fond even of Sabine and Lesbian—when the Massic juice was beyond your credit—to do anything more than *feel* it?"

As Cradock Nowell trudged that night towards the Brockenhurst Station, before he got very far from Amy, and while her tears were still on his cheek, he felt a little timid lick, a weak offering of sympathy.

Hereby black Wena made known to him that she was melted by his misfortunes, and saw that the right and most feeling course, and the one most pleasing to her dead master, was the transfer of her allegiance, and the swearing of fealty to the brother. To which conclusion the tender mode in which she was being carried conduced, perhaps, considerably; for she was wrapped in Clayton's woolly jacket, enthroned on Cradock's broad right arm, and with only her black nose exposed to the moon. So she jogged along very comfortably, until she had made up her mind, and given Cradock the kiss of seisin.

"Dear little thing," he cried, for he looked on her now as Amy's keepsake, "you shall go with me wherever I go. You are faithful enough to starve with me; but you shall not starve until after me."

Then he put her down, for he thought that a little run would do her good, and, in spite of all her misery, Amy had kept her pretty plump, plumper than she herself was; and it became no joke to carry her, with a travelling–bag, &c., after the first half mile.

Then Wena capered about, and barked, and came and licked his shoe, and offered to carry the coat for him. As he would not let her do this, she occupied her mind with the rabbits, which were out upon the feed largely, and were the last she would see for a long while, except the fat Ostenders.

When he got to London, and took small lodgings at a Mrs. Ducksacre's, "greengrocer and general fruiterer, Mortimer–street, Cavendish–square,"—I quote from the lady's bags: confound it, there! I am always saying improper things; *honi soit*—I mean, of course, her paper bags—it was not long before he made two important discoveries, valuable rather than gratifying.

The first of these discoveries was, that our university portals are a mere side–postern, and not the great *janua mundi*. He found his classical scholarship, his early fame at Oxford, his love of elegant literature, rather a disadvantage than a recommendation for business.

"Prigs, sir, prigs," said a member of an eminent City firm; "of course, I don't mean to be personal; but I have always found you Oxford men prigs, quite unfit for desk–work. You fancy you know so much; you are always discovering mare's–nests, and you won't bear to be spoken to, even if you stick to your work; which, I assure you, is quite the exception. Then you hold yourself aloof, with your stupid etiquette, from the other young men, who are quite as good as you are. I assure you, the place was too hot to hold us with the last Oxford man we took in the counting–house; he gave himself such airs, the donkey! I vowed never to do it again: and I never will, sir. Good morning, sir; Gregson, show this gentleman the way out."

Gregson did so with a grin, for Cradock's face proved that the principal had not been altogether wrong.

Is this prejudice, or, rather, perhaps, I should say, this aversion, disappearing now–a–days, or is it upon the increase? At any rate, one cause of it is being removed most rapidly; for the buckram etiquette of Oxford will soon become a tradition. We will only hope she may not run too far into the free and easy.

Cradock's other discovery was that 50*l.* is no large capital to commence in life with, especially when the owner does not find his start prepared for him; fails to prepare it for himself; and has never been used to economy. He would not apply to any of his father's friends, or of the people whom he had known in London, to help him in this emergency. He would rather starve than do that; for he had dropped all name and claim of Nowell, and cut his life in twain at manhood; and the parts should never join again. Only one feeling should be common to the two existences, to the happy and the wretched life; that one feeling was the love of Amy, and, what now seemed part of it, his gratitude to her father.

John Rosedew had given him a letter to a clergyman in London, a man of high standing and extensive influence, whom John had known at college. But the youth had not undertaken to deliver that credential, and he never did so. It would have kept him to his identity, which (so far as the world was concerned) he wished to change entirely, immediately, and irrevocably. So he called himself "Nowell" no longer—although the name is common enough in one form or another: the Nowells of Nowelhurst, however, are proud of the double *l*, and think a good deal of the *w*—and Cradock Nowell became "Charles Newman," without license of Her Majesty.

Even before his vain attempts to enter the stronghold of commerce, and before he had learned that Oxford men are not thought *"prima virorum,"* he had lifted the latch of literature, but the door would not swing back for him. The *mare magnum*—to mix metaphors, although bars are added to the Lucrine—the *mare magnum* of letters was more like his native element; and, if he once could have gotten—bare-footed as we must be—over the jagged rocks which hedge that sea, I believe he might have swum there.

In one respect he was fortunate. The publishers upon whom he called were gentlemen, and told him the truth.

"Oh, poetry!" exclaimed one and all, as their eyes fell upon his manuscript, "we cannot take it on our own account; and, if we published it at your expense, we should only be robbing you."

"Indeed!" replied Cradock, in the first surprise; "is there no chance, then, of a sale for it?"

"None whatever. Poetry, unless it be some one's whose name is well known, is a perfect drug in the market. In the course of ten or a dozen years, by advertising continually, by influence among the reviewers, by hitting some popular vein, or being taken up by some authority, you might attain an audience. Are you ready to encounter all this? Even if you are, we must decline, we are sorry to say, to have anything to do with it."

"Verse, eh? Better have cut your throat," more tersely replied an elderly gentleman, well known for his rudeness to authors. However, even that last was a friend, when compared with some whom it might have been his evil luck to consult. They advertise their patent methods of putting a work before the public, without any risk to the author, &c. &c. Disinterested gentlemen! They are to have no profit whatever, except from the sale of the work, and they know they won't sell five copies.

However, there are not many of this sort in an honourable and most important profession; and Cradock Nowell was lucky enough not to fall in with any of them. So he accepted the verdict so unanimously returned, and stored away with a heavy heart his laborious little manuscript. It was only a translation in verse of the Halieutics, and a few short original pieces—the former at any rate valuable, as having been revised by John Rosedew.

There are courts and alleys in the neighbourhood of Mortimer-street which, for misery and poverty, dirt and desperation, may vie with almost any of the more famous shames of London.

Cradock's own great trouble, the sympathy he had met with, and the comfort he received from it, had begun by this time to soften his heart, and render it more sensitive to the distress of others. At first, it had been far otherwise. The feeling of bitter injustice, resentment at, and defiance of, a blow which seemed to him so unmerited, and, worse than all, his own father's base and low mistrust of him—who could have been surprised if these things, acting upon a sad lone heart, and a bold mind beginning to think for itself, had made the owner an infidel? And very likely they would have done so, when he was removed from John Rosedew's influence, but for that scene with Amy. He loved that girl so warmly, so devotedly, so purely, that, when he found his love returned in equal quantity and quality, it renewed his faith in justice. He saw that there is a measure and law, even where all appears to be anarchy and anomaly; that the hand of God is not stretched forth upon His children wantonly; that we cannot gauge His circling survey by the three-inch space between human eyes, neither does He rest His balance on His earthly footstool. So Cradock escaped the deadly harm, which almost seems designed to poise that noblest gift of Heaven—a free and glorious intellect—he escaped it through the mercy which gave him true affection.

And now once more he looked with love upon his fellow-men, such love as the frigid atheist school shall never form nor educate—which truth alone to a great heart might be conclusive against that school—the love which few religions except our own inculcate, and no other takes for its essence.

As yet he was too young to know the blind and inhuman selfishness, the formality and truckling, and the other paltry dishonesties, which still exist and try to cheat us under the name of "Society." The cant is going by already. Every man who dares to think knows that its laws are obsolete, because they have not for their basis either of these three—truth, simplicity, charity.

Even that young man was astonished at the manner in which society ignores its broader and only true meaning—fellowship among men—and renounces all other duties, save that of shaking from its shoes its fellow-dust. He could not look upon the scenes so nigh to him, and to each other, parted often by nothing more than nine inches of brick or two inches of deal; the wealth and the want, the feast and the famine, the satiety and the ravening, the euphemy and the blasphemy—though sometimes that last got inside the door, blew its nose, and was infidelity; the prudery and the indecency, the whispered lie and the yelled one, the sale of maidens by their mothers, or of women by themselves—though here again the difference was never very perceptible; all this impious contrast, spread as if for God's approval, for the Universal Father's blessing, in the land most chiefly blessed by Him: which of His sons, not cast out for ever, could look on it without weeping?

Cradock did something more than weep. He went with his little stock of money, though he knew it could not do much; and he tried to help in little ways, though as yet he had no experience. He bought meat, and clothes, and took things out of pawn, and tried to make peace where fights were.

At first he was grossly insulted, as a meddlesome swell; but, when he had done two or three good things, and done them as a brother should, he began to be owned among them. In one thing he was right, although he had no experience; he confined his exertions to a very narrow compass. Of course he got imposed upon—of course he helped the unworthy; but after a while he began to know them, and even the unworthy—some two hundred per cent.—began to have faint ideas of trying to deserve good luck.

One man who attempted to pick Crad's pocket was knocked down by the biggest thief there. "I wish I had a heap of money," said Cradock, every day; "I must keep some for myself, I suppose. Perhaps, after all, I was wrong, in throwing up so hastily my chance of doing good."

Then he remembered that, but for his trouble, he might never have thought of the good to be done. And the good done to him was threefold as much as he could do to others. Every day he grew less selfish, less imperious, less exacting; every day he saw more clearly the good which is in the worst of us.

There is a flint of peculiar character—I know not the local name of it—which is found sometimes on the great Chissel Bank, and away towards Lyme Regis. It is as hard, and sullen, and dull a flint (with even the outside polish lost from the chafing of the waves)—a stone as grey and foggy-looking;—as ever Deucalion took the trouble to cast away over the left into an empty world. Yet it has, through the heart of it, traversing it from pole to pole (for its shape is always conical) a thread, a spindle, a siphuncle, of the richest golden hue. None but those who are used to it can see the head of the golden column, can even guess its existence. The stone is not hollow; it is quite distinct from all pudding-stones and conglomerates.

Many such flints poor Crad came across, and sought in vain for the beauty of them. He never tried to split them with a hammer, as too many do of our Boanergæ; but he was too young to see or feel the chord of the golden siphuncle. One, especially, one great fellow, was harder and rougher than any flint, like the matrix of the concentric jasper.

"Confound that fellow," said Cradock to himself; "I never shall get at the heart of him. If my pluck were up a little more. I'd fight him; though I know he would lick me. He'd be sorry for me afterwards."

Issachar Jupp could lick any two men in the court. He was a bargee, of good intentions—at least, when he took to the cuddy; but his horses had pulled crosswise ever since; and the devil knew, better than the angels, what his nature now was.

"None of your d—d Scripture–reading for me!" he cried, when Cradock came near him; though the young man had never attempted anything of the sort.

He knew that the Word of God is not bread to a blackguard's empty belly. And another thing he knew—that he was not of the age and aspect for John Bunyan's business. Moreover, Jupp was wonderfully jealous of his wife, a gentle but grimy woman, forty–five years old, whom he larruped every day; although he might be an infidel, he would ensure his wife's fidelity. Nevertheless, he had his pure vein, and Cradock at last got at it.

Mrs. and Miss Ducksacre were very good–hearted women, but, like many other women of that fibre, whose education has been neglected, of a hot and hasty order. Not that we need suppose the pepper to be neutralized by the refinement, only to be absorbed more equably, and transfused more generally.

A little thing came feeling the way into the narrow, dingy shop, one dark November evening, groping along by the sacks of potatoes (all of them "seconds," for the firm did not deal much in "Ware Regents"), feeling its way along the sacks which towered above its head, like bulky snow–giants embrowned with thaw; and then by the legs of the "tatie–bin," with the great scales hanging above it, and then by the heap of lighting–wood, piled in halfpenny bundles, with the ends against the wall; and so the little thing emerged between two mighty hills of coleworts, and under the frugal gas–burner, and congratulated itself, with a hug of the heart, upon safety.

"Take care, my dear," cried Mrs. Ducksacre, looking large behind the counter, "or you'll tumble down the coal–trap, where the black bogeys lives. Bless my heart, if it ain't little Loo! Why, Loo, I hardly knew you. You ain't looking like yourself a bit, child. And who sent you out at this time of night? What a shame, to be sure!"

Loo, the pride of Issachar Jupp, was rather a pretty little body, about three and a half years old, "going on for four," as she loved to say, if anybody asked her; and her pale but clean face would have been *very* pretty, if her mother would have let her hair alone. But it was all combed back, and tied tightly behind, like the tail of a horse at a fair, or as affording a spout to pour the little girl out by. She looked up at Mrs. Ducksacre, while her fingers played with the coleworts, for her hands were hot, and this cooled them; and then, with the instinct of nature, she stuck up for her father and mother.

"Pease, ma'am, Loo not fray much,"—though her trembling frock belied her, all over the throat and the heart of it—"and father don from home, ma'am, on the Wasintote" [Basingstoke canal], "and mother dot nobody, on'y Loo, to do thins. And she send this, 'cause Loo's poor troat be bad, ma'am."

The little child, whose throat was tied up with worn flannel from the char–bucket, with the grey edge still upon it, wriggled in and out of her shape and self, in the way only children can do; and at length drew, from some innermost shrine, a halfpenny and a farthing.

"And what am I to give you for it, Loo? Oh, you poor little thing, how very hoarse you are!"

Loo, with a confidence in human nature purely non–Londinian, had placed her cash upon the altar, upon the inside of which so many worship, while on the outside so many are sacrificed; without circumlocution, the counter. Her eyes were below the rim of it, till she stood upon tiptoe with one foot, while the other was up in the colewort roots, and then she could see the money, and she poked out her little lips at it, as if she would fain suck it back again.

"Pease, ma'am, Loo's troat so bad, mother are goin to make a 'tew, tree ha'porth of tipe and a ha'porth of 'egents, and a fardy of inons!"

"What a splendid stew, Loo!" said Mrs. Ducksacre, seeming to smell it; "and so you want a ha'porth of taties, and a farthing's worth of onions. And you shall have them, my dear, and as good a three farthings' worth as ever was put up in London. Where are you going to put them all?"

Loo opened her sore throat, and pointed down it. She had not yet lost her appetite; and that child did love tripe so.

"No, no, I don't mean that, Loo. I know you have a nice room inside; though some will be for mother, won't it, now? I mean, how are you going to carry it home?"

"In Loo's pinney," replied the child, delighted with her success; for ever so many people had told her, that the Ducksacres now were getting so high, they would soon leave off making farthings–worths; and any tradesman who does that is above the sphere of the street–child.

"My dear, your pinney won't hold them, potatoes are so cheap now"—she had just sworn they were awfully dear to a person she disliked—"I am sure you can't carry a ha'porth. Oh, Mr. Newman, you are so good–natured"—Cradock was just coming in, rather glum from another failure—"I really don't believe you would think you were bemeaning yourself by going home with this poor little atom."

"I should rather hope I would not," replied Cradock, looking grand.

"Oh, I did not know. I beg your pardon, I'm sure. I would go myself, only Sally is out, and the boy gone home ever so long ago. I beg your pardon, I'm sure, Mr. Newman; I thought you were so good–natured."

"Mrs. Ducksacre," said Cradock, "you utterly misunderstand me. I replied to the form of your sentence, perhaps, rather than to its meaning. What I meant was, that I should rather hope I would not think it below me to go home with this little dear. If I could suppose it any disgrace to me, I should deserve to be kicked by your errand–boy all round this shop, Mrs. Ducksacre; and I am surprised you misunderstand me so. Why, I know this little girl well; and her name is Louisa Jupp."

"Tiss Loo," said the little child, standing up on tiptoe, and spreading out her arms to Cradock. All the children loved him, as the little ones at Nowelhurst would run after Mr. Rosedew. Children are even better judges of character than dogs.

"Why, you poor little soul," said Crad, as he seated her on his strong right arm with her little cheek to his, and she drew a thousand straws of light through her lashes from the gas–jet, which she had never yet been so close to, "how hot and dry your lips are! I hope you are not taking the—sickness"—he was going to say "fever," but feared to frighten Loo.

"Mother fray," cried the small girl, proud of the importance accruing to her, "Loo dot wever; Irishers dot bad wever on the foor below mother. Loo det nice thins, and lay abed, if me dot the wever."

"Put the poor child's things, whatever they are, in a basket, Mrs. Ducksacre. How odd her little legs feel! And a shilling's worth of grapes, if you please, in a bag by themselves. Here's the money for them. You know I'll bring back the basket. But the bags don't come back, do they?"

"No, sir, of course not. Half–a–crown a gross for the small ones, with the name and the cross–handle basket, and the cabbage and carrots, sir. Sixpence more for cornopean–pattern with a pineapple, and grapes and oranges. But lor, sir, the cornopean" [cornucopiæ] "would frighten half our customers. The basket–pattern pays better for an advertisement than to get them back again, even if parties would bring them, which I knows well they never would, sir."

Then Cradock set forth with the child on his arm, his coat thrown over his shoulders, and the best shilling's worth of foreign grapes—Mrs. Ducksacre never bought English ones—and the best three farthing's worth of potatoes and onions that was made that day by any tradesman in any part of London, not excluding "them low costers," as the Ducksacre firm expressed it.

Little Loo Jupp's sore throat proved to be, as Cradock feared it would, the first symptom of scarlet fever; and the young man had the pleasure—one of the highest and purest pleasures which any man can have—of saving a human life. He watched that trembling flame of life, and fostered it, and sheltered it, as if "the hopes of a nation hung"—as the penny–a–liners love to say of some babe not a whit more valuable—upon its feeble flicker. He hired another room for her, where the air was purer; he made the doctor attend to the case, which at first that doctor cared little to do; he brought her many a trifling comfort; in a word, he waited upon her so that the old women of the court called him thenceforth "Nurse Newman."

"What, you here again, you white–livered young sneak!" cried Issachar Jupp, reeling in at the door, just as Cradock was coming out; "take that, then——" and he lifted a great oak bludgeon, newly cut from the towing–path of the Basingstoke Canal. If Cradock had not been as quick as lightning, and caught the stick over the bargeman's shoulder, there would have been weeping and wailing and a lifelong woe for Amy.

"Hush," he said; "don't make such a noise, man. Your child is at the point of death, in the room overhead."

Poor Crad, naturally of a bright complexion, but pale from long unhappiness, might now have retorted the compliment as to the "pallor jecoris." The bargee turned so pale, that he looked like a collier's tablecloth. Then he planted his heavy stick on the ground; else he would have lain flat on his threshold.

"My Loo, my Loo!" was all he could say; "oh my Loo! *It's a lie, sir!*"

"I wish it was," replied Cradock; "take my arm, Mr. Jupp. Don't be over–frightened. We hope with all our hearts to save her, and to–night we shall know. Already I think I perceive some change in her breathing, though her tongue is like a furnace."

He spoke with a tone and in a voice which no man ever has described, nor shall, but which every born man feels to be genuine, long ere he can think.

"[Condemn] me for a [sanguineous] fool," cried Jupp, with two enormous tears guttering down the coal–dust, and his great chest heaving and wanting to sob, only it didn't know the way; "[condemn] my eyes for swearing so, and making such a [female dog] of myself, but what the [Hades] am I to do? Oh my Loo, my Loo! If you die, I'll go to [Hades] after you."

Excuse me for washing out this speech to regulation weakness; perhaps it was entered in white on high, as the turn of a life of blackness.

Cradock turned away, and trembled. Who can see a rugged man split to the bottom of his nature, and not himself be splintered? I don't believe that any can: not even the cold iron scoundrels whom modern plays delight in.

"Now come up with me, Mr. Jupp," said Crad, taking care not to look at him, "out at this door, in at the other. Poor little soul! she has been so good. You can't think how good she has been. And she has taken her medicine so nicely."

"Pray God Almighty not to [condemn] me, for not [condemning] myself enough," said Issachar Jupp, below his breath, as he leaned on Cradock's arm.

It was his form of prayer; and it meant more than most of ours do. Though I may be discarded by turtle–dove quill–drivers for daring to record it, will he ever be worse for uttering it? Of course, it was very shocking; but far more so to men than to angels.

CHAPTER VIII

Little Loo's fever "took the turn" that night. Cradock went away, of course, now her own father was come; and the savage bargee would have gone on his knees, and crawled in that fashion—wherein all fashion crawls—down the rough stairs, every one of them, if the young man would only have let him. We are just beginning to scorn the serfdom of one mind to another. We begin to desire that no man should, without fair argument, accept our dicta as equal to his own in wisdom. And I fully believe that if fate had thrown us across Shakespeare, Bacon, or Newton, we should now refer to our own reason what they said, before admiring it. For, after all, what are we? What are our most glorious minds? Only one spark more of God.

And yet the servience, not of the mind, but of the heart to a larger one, is a fealty most honourable to the giver and the receiver. In a bold independent man, such as Issachar Jupp was, this fealty was not to be won by any of that paltry sentiment about birth, clanship, precedency, position, appearance, &c., which is our national method of circumcising the New Testament—it was only to be won by proof that the other heart was bigger than his. Prove that once, and till death it was granted.

Now, the small Loo Jupp being out of danger, and her father, grinning like a gridiron with the firelight behind it, every day at her bedside, the force of circumstances—which, in good English, means the want of money—sent Cradock Nowell once more cat's–cradling throughout London, to answer advertisements. His heart rose within him every day as he set out in the morning, and in the same relative position fell, as he came home every evening.

"Do, sir, do," cried Issachar Jupp, who never swore now, before Cradock, except under strongest pressure; "do come aboard our barge. I've a'most a–got the appointment of skipper to the *Industrious Maiden*, homeside of Nine Elms, as tight a barge as ever was built, and the name done in gold letters. Fact, I may say, and not tell no secrets; I be safe to be aboord of her, if my Loo allow me to go, and I don't swear hard at the check–house. And, perhaps, I shall be able to help it, after Loo so ill, and you such a hangel."

"Very few people does, young man; very few people indeed. Scarcely any, I may say, except Jenny and the cookshop woman; and the latter have got encumbrances as quite outweighs the business. Ain't you ever heard of the fiddle of a teaspoon, sir?"

"Oh, very well," said Cradock, tossing off his brandy–and–water to bring things to a point. It was a good thing for him that he got it, poor fellow, for he was sadly wet and weary.

"Lor, now, to see that!" cried Clinkers, opening his eyes; "I'm blowed if you mustn't be a Hoxford gent."

"To be sure, so I am," replied Cradock, laughing; "but I should not have thought that you would have known—I mean, I am surprised that you, at this distance, should know anything of Oxford men."

"Tell you about that presently. Come over again the fire, sir. Up with your heel–tap, and have another."

"No, thank you, Mr. Clinkers. You are very kind; but I shall not take one drop more."

"Then you ain't been there very long, that's certain. Now you have come about this place, I know; though it's a queer one for a Hoxford gent. 'Gent under a cloud,' thinks I, the moment I claps eyes on you. Ah, I knows the aristocraxy, sir. Now, what might be your qualifications?"

"None whatever, except such knowledge as springs from a good education."

"Whew!" whistled Mr. Clinkers, and that sound was worth fifty sentences.

"Then you conclude," said Cradock, not so greatly downcast, for he had got this speech by heart now, "that I am not fitted for the post offered in your advertisement?"

"Knows what they Hoxford gents is," continued Clinkers, reflectively; "come across a lot of them once, when I was gay and rattling. They ran into my tax–cart, coming home from Ascot, about a mile this side of Brentford. Famous good company over a glass, when they drops their aristocraxy; they runs up a tick all over town, and leaves a Skye dog to pay for it; comes home about four in the morning, and don't know the latch from the scraper. Always pays in the end, though; nearly always pays in the end—so a Hoxford tradesman told me—and interest ten per cent. Differs in that from the medicals; the fast medicals never do pay, sir."

"Most unjust," said Cradock, rising, "a most unjust thing, Mr. Clinkers; you not only judge the present by the past, but you reason from the particular to the universal—the most fruitful and womanlike of the fallacies."

"It ain't anything about fallacy, sir, that makes me refuse you," cried Clinkers, who liked this outburst; "I'll tell you just what it is. You Hoxford scholars may be very honest, *but you ain't got the grease for business*."

Sorely down at heart and heel, Cradock plodded away from the yard of the hospitable Clinkers, who came to the door and looked after him, fearing to indulge his liking for that queer young fellow. But he had taken Crad's address; for who knew but something might turn up?

"That man," said Cradock to himself, "has a kindly heart, and would have helped me if he could. He wanted to pay my fare back to town, but of course I would not let him. It was well worth while to come all this distance, and get wet through twice over, to come across a kind–hearted man, when a fellow is down so. I began with applying for grand places; what a fool I was! Places worth 150*l.* or 200*l.* a–year. No wonder I did not get them: and what a lot of boot I have wasted! Now I am come down to 50*l.* per annum, and 75*l.* would be a fortune. If I had only begun at that mark, I might have got something by this time. 'Vaulting ambition doth o'erleap itself.' And I might have emigrated—good Heavens! I might have emigrated upon the bounty of Uncle John, to some land where a man is worth more than the cattle of the field. Only Amy stopped me, only the thought of my Amy. Darling love, the sweetest angel—stop, I am so unlucky; if I begin to bless her, very likely she'll get typhus fever. After all, what does it matter what sort of life I take to? Or whether, indeed, I take the trouble to take to any at all? Only for her sake. A man who has done what I have lives no more, but drags his life. Now I'll go in for common labour, work of the hands and muscles; many a better man has done it; and it will be far wiser for me while my brain is so loose and wandering. I wonder I never thought of that. Isn't it raining, though! What we used, in the happy days, to call 'Wood Fidley rain'".

The future chironax trudged more cheerfully after this decision. But he was very sorry to get so soaked, for he had his only suit of clothes on. He had brought but one suit of his own; and all he had bought with the rector's money was six shirts at 3s. 6d., and four pairs of cotton hose. So he could not afford to get wet.

There could be no doubt that he was shabbily dressed, no rich game to an hotel–tout, no tempting fare to a cabman; but neither could there be any doubt that he was a pure and noble gentleman; that was as clear as in the heyday of finest Oxford dandyism. Only he carried his head quite differently, and the tint of his cheeks was gone. He used to walk with his broad and well–set head thrown back, and slightly inclined to one side; now he bore it flagging, drooping, as if the spring of the neck were gone.

But still the brave clear eyes met frankly all who cared to look at him; the face and gait were of a man unhappy but not unmanly. If, at the time Sir Cradock condemned his only son so cruelly, he had looked at him once, and read the sorrow so unmistakeable in his face, the old man might have repented, and wept, and saved a world of weeping. A tear in time saves ninety–nine; but who has the sense to yield it?

Soaked and tired out at last, he reached his little lodgings—quite large enough for him, though—and found Black Wena warming the chair, the only chair he had to sit on. Unluckily, he did not do what a man who cared for himself would have done. Having no change of raiment—in plain English, only one pair of trousers—he should have gone to bed at once, or at any rate have pulled his wet clothes off. Instead of doing so, he sat and sat, with the wet things clinging closer to him, and the shivers crawling deeper, until his last inch of candle was gone, and the room was cold as an icehouse, for the rain had turned to snow at nightfall, and the fire had not been lit.

Wena sat waiting and nodding upwards, on the yard and a half of brown drugget, which now was her chiefest *pulvinar*, and once or twice she nudged her master, and whined about supper and bedtime. But Cradock only patted her, and improved the turn of his sentence. He was making one last effort to save from waste and ridicule his tastes and his education. A craftsman, if he have self–respect, is worthy, valuable, admirable, nearer to the perception of simple truth than some men of high refinement. Nevertheless, it is too certain—as I, who know them well, and not unkindly, can testify—that there is scarcely one in a dozen labourers, even around the metropolis, who respects himself and his calling. Whose fault this is, I pretend not—for pretence it would be—to say. Probably, the guilt is "much of a muchness," as in all mismanaged matters. The material was as good as our own; how has it got so vitiated? It is as lowering to us as it is to themselves, that the "enlightened working–men of England" cannot go out for their holiday, cannot come home from their work, cannot even speak among their own children, and in the goodwife's presence, without words, not of manly strength, but of hoggish coarseness. In time this must be otherwise; but the evil is not cured easily. The boy believes it manly to talk as he hears his father talk; he rejoices in it the more, perhaps, because the school forbids it. He does not know what the foul words mean; and all things strange have the grandest range. Those words tell powerfully in a story, with smaller boys round him upon the green, or at the street–corner. And so he grows up engrimed with them, and his own boys follow suit.

Cradock was young and chivalrous, and knew not much of these things, which his position had kept from him; nor in his self–abandonment cared he much about them. Nevertheless, he shrank unconsciously from the lowering of his existence. And now he sat up, writing, writing, till his wet clothes made little pools on the floor, while he answered twenty advertisements, commercial, literary, promiscuous. Then he looked at his little roll of postage–stamps, and with shivering fingers affixed them. There were only fifteen; and it was too late to get any more that night; and he felt that he could not afford to use them now so rashly. So he ran out into the slushy streets, gamboged with London snow, and posted those fifteen of his letters which were the least ambitious. By this time he knew that the best chance was of something not over–gorgeous. Wena did not go with him, but howled until he came back. Then he gave the poor little thing, with some self–reproach at his tardiness, all the rest of his cottage loaf, and his ha'porth of milk, which she took with some protestations, looking up at him wistfully now and then, to see whether he was eating.

"No, Wena, I can't eat to–night; bilious from over–feeding, perhaps. But I've done a good evening's work, and we'll be very plucky for breakfast, girl, and have sixpenceworth of cold ham. No fear there of making a cannibal of you, you innocent little soul."

He was desperately afraid, as most young fellows from the country are, of having unclean animals spicily served up by the London allantopolæ. This terror is the result for the most part of rustic sham knowingness, and the British love of stale jokes. However, beyond all controversy, dark are the rites of sepulture of the measly pigs around London.

He crept, at last, beneath his scanty bedding—clean, although so patched and threadbare—and the iron cross–straps shook and rattled with the shudders that went through him.

Wena, who slept beneath the bed in a nest which she made of the drugget–scrap, jumped upon the blanket at midnight, to know pray what was the matter. Then she licked his face, and tried to warm him, in his broken slumbers. That day he had taken a virulent cold, which struck into his system, and harboured there for a fortnight, till it broke out in a raging fever.

The next day, Cradock received a letter, of doubtful classicality, and bearing the Hammersmith post–mark.

> "Respected Sir,—Was sorry after you streaked off yesterday that had not kept you longer. You was scarce gone out of the gate as one might say, when in comes a

gent, no end of a nob, beats you as one might say in some respects, and a head of hair as good. Known by the name of Hearty,—Hearty Wibraham, Esquire, but friends prefers callin' him Hearty, such bein' his character. And hearty he were with my brandy, I do assure you, and no mistake. This gent say as he want to establish a hagency for the sale of first–class Hettons to the members of the *bone tons*: was I agreeable to supply him? So I say, 'Certainly, by all means, if I see my way to my money.' And then he breaks out, in a manner as would frighten some hands, about the artlessness of the age, the suspiciousness of commercial gents, and confidence between man and man. 'Waste of time,' says I; 'coals is coals now, and none of them leaves this yard for nothing. Better keep that sort of stuff,' says I, 'for the green young gent from Hoxford as was here just now.' 'What,' says he, 'Hoxford man after a situation?' ' Yes,' I says, 'nice young gent, only under a cloud.' Says he, 'I loves a Hoxford man; hope he has got some money.' ' For what?' I says; 'have you got anything good for him to invest in?' 'Haven't I?' he says; 'take a little more brandy, old chap'—my own brandy, mind you, blow me if he ain't a hearty one. Well, I can't tell you half he said, not being a talkative man myself, since the time as I lost Mrs. Clinkers. Only the upshot of it is, I think you couldn't do no harm by callin', if he write you as he said he would.

"Yours to command, and hope you didn't get wet,

"Robert Clinkers, Jun., for Poker, Clinkers, and Co., Coal Merchants, West London Terminuss, Hammersmith.

"N.B.—Coke supplied in your own sacks, on the most moderate terms."

By the next delivery, Cradock got another letter, far more elegantly written, but not half so honest.

"Mr. Hearty Wibraham, having heard of Mr. Charles Newman from a mutual friend, Mr. Clinkers, of Hammersmith, presents his compliments to the former gentleman, and thinks it might be worth Mr. Newman's while to call upon him, Mr. H. W., at six o'clock this evening, supposing the post to do its duty, which it rarely does. Hearty Wibraham, No. 66, Aurea Themis

> Buildings, Notting Hill district. N.B.—The above is *bonâ fide*. References will be required. But perhaps they may be dispensed with.
>
> "H. W."

"Well," said Cradock to Wena, shivering as he said it, for the cold was striking into him, "you see we are in request, my dear. Not that I have any high opinion of Mr. Hearty Wibraham; as a gentleman, I mean. But for all that he may be an honest man. And beggars—as you know, Wena, dear, when you sit up so prettily—beggars must not be choosers. Do you think you could walk so far, Wena? If you could, it would do you good, my beauty; and I'll see that you are not run over."

Wena agreed, rather rashly, to go; for the London stones, to a country dog, are as bad as a mussel–bank to a bather; but she thought she might find some woodcocks—and so she did, at the game–shops, and some curlews which they sold for them—but her real object in going, was that she had made some nice acquaintances in the neighbourhood, whom she wanted to see again. She wouldn't speak to any low dog, for she meant to keep up the importance and grandeur of the Nowell family, but there were some dogs, heigho! they had such ways with them, and they were brushed so nicely, what could a poor little country dog do but fall in love with them?

Therefore Wena came after her master, and made believe not to notice them, but she lingered now and then at a scraper, and, when she snapped, her teeth had gloves on.

When Cradock and his little dog, after many a twist and turn, found Aurea Themis Buildings, the master rang at the sprightly door, newly grained and varnished. Being inducted by a young woman, with a most coquettish cap on, he told black Wena to wait outside, and she lay down upon the door–step.

Then he was shown into the "first–floor drawing–room," according to arrangement, and requested to "take a seat, sir." The smart maid, who carried a candle, lit the gas in a twinkling, but Cradock wondered why the coal–merchant had no coals in his fireplace.

Just when he had concluded, after a fit of shivering, that this defect was due perhaps to that extreme familiarity which breeds in a grocer contempt for figs, Mr. Wibraham came in, quite by accident, and was evidently amazed to see him.

"What! Ah, no, my good sir, not Mr. Charles Newman, a member of the University of Oxford!"

"Yes, sir, I am that individual," replied Cradock, very uncomfortable at the prominent use of his "alias."

"Then, allow me, sir, to shake hands with you. I am strongly prepossessed in your favour, young gentleman, from the description I received of you from our mutual friend, Mr. Clinkers. Ah, I like that Clinkers. No nonsense about Clinkers, sir."

"So I believe," said Cradock; "but, as I have only seen him once, it would perhaps be premature of me— —"

"Not a bit, my dear sir, not a bit. That is one of the mistakes we make. I always rely upon first impressions, and they never deceive me. Now I see exactly what you are, an upright honourable man, full of conscientiousness, but *not overburdened here* ."

He gave a jocular tap to his forehead, which was about half the width of Cradock's.

"Well," thought Cradock, "you are straightforward, even to the verge of rudeness. But no doubt you mean well, and perhaps you are nearer the truth than the people who have told me otherwise. Anyhow, it does not matter much." But, in spite of this conclusion, he bowed in his stately manner, and said:

"If that be the case, sir, I fear it will hardly suit your purpose to take me into your employment."

"Ah, I have hurt your feelings, I see. I am so blunt and hasty. Hearty Wibraham is my name; and hearty enough I am, God knows; and perhaps a little too hearty. 'Hasty Wibraham, you ought to be called, by Jove, you ought,' said one of my friends last night, and by Gad I think he was right, sir."

"I am sure I don't know," said Cradock; "how can I pretend to say, without myself being hasty?"

"I suppose, Mr. Newman, you can command a little capital? It is not at all essential, you know, in a *bonâ fide* case like yours."

"That's a good job," said Cradock; "for my capital, like the new one of Canada, is below contempt."

"To a man imbued, Mr. Newman, with the genuine spirit of commerce, no sum, however small, but may be the key of fortune."

"My key of fortune, then, is about twenty pounds ten shillings."

"A very, very small sum, my dear sir; but I dare say some of your friends would assist you to make it, say fifty guineas. You Oxford men are so generous; always ready to help each other. That is why I can't help liking you so. Thoroughly fine fellows," he added, in a loud aside, "thoroughly noble fellows, when a messmate is in trouble. Can't apply to his family, I see; but it would be mean in him not to let his friends help him. I do believe the highest privilege of human life is to assist a friend in difficulties."

Cradock, of course, could not reply to all this, because he was not meant to hear it; but he gazed with some admiration at the utterer of such exalted sentiments. Mr. Hearty Wibraham, now about forty–five years old, was rather tall and portly, with an aquiline face, a dark complexion, and a quick, decisive manner. His clothes were well made, and of good quality, unpretentious, neat, substantial. His only piece of adornment was a magnificent gold watch–chain, which rather shunned than courted observation.

"No," said Cradock, at last, "I have not a single friend in the world to whom I would think of applying for the loan of a sixpence."

"Well, we *are* independent," Mr. Wibraham still held discourse with himself; "but Hearty Wibraham likes and respects him the more for that. He'll get over his troubles, whatever they are. My good sir," he continued, aloud, "I will not utter any opinion, lest you should think me inclined to flatter—the last thing in the world I ever would do. Nevertheless, in all manly candour, I am bound to tell you that my prepossession in your favour induces me to make you a most advantageous offer."

"I am much obliged to you. Pray, what is it?"

"A clerkship in my counting–house, which I am just about to open, having formed a very snug little connexion to begin with."

"Oh!" cried Cradock, for, green as he was, he would rather have had to do with a business already established.

"I see you are surprised. No wonder, sir; no wonder! But you must know that I shall have at least my *quid pro quo*. My connexion is of a very peculiar character. In fact, it lies entirely in the very highest circles. To meet such customers as mine, not only a man of gentlemanly manners is required, but a man of birth and education. How could I offer such a man less than 150*l.* per annum?"

"Your terms are very liberal, very liberal, I am sure," replied Cradock, reddening warmly at the appraisement of his qualities. "I should not be comfortable without telling you frankly that I am worth about half that yearly sum; until, I mean, until I get a little up to business. I shall be quite content to begin upon 100*l.* a year.

"No! will you, though?" exclaimed Hearty Wibraham, flushed with a good heart's enthusiasm. "You are the finest young fellow I have seen since I was your age myself. Suppose, now, we split the difference. Say 125*l.*; and I shall work you pretty hard, I can tell you. For we do not confine our attention exclusively to the members of the Ministry, and the House of Lords; we also deal with the City magnates, and take a contract for Somerset House. And remember one thing; you will be in exclusive charge whenever I am away negotiating. A man deserves to be paid, you know, for high responsibility."

"And where will the"—he hardly knew what to call it—"the office, the counting–house, the headquarters be?"

"Not in any common thoroughfare," replied Mr. Wibraham, proudly; "that would never do for a business of such a character. What do you think, sir, of Howard Crescent, Park Lane? Not so bad, sir, is it, for the sale of the grimy?"

"I really do not know," said Cradock; "but it sounds very well. When do we open the books?"

"Monday morning, sir, at ten o'clock precisely. Let me see: to–day is Friday. Perhaps it would be an accommodation to you, to have your salary paid weekly, until you draw by the quarter. Now, remember, I rely upon you to promote my interest in every way consistent with honour."

"That you may do, most fully. I shall never forget your kind confidence, and your liberality."

"You will have two young gentlemen, if not three, wholly under your orders. Also a middle–aged gentleman, a sort of sleeping partner, will kindly attend *pro tem.*, and show you the work expected of you. I myself shall be engaged, perhaps, during the forenoon, in promoting the interests of the business in a most important quarter. Now, be true to me, Newman—I take liberties, you see—keep your subordinates in their place, and make them stick to work, sir. And remember that one ounce of example is worth a pound of precept. If you act truly and honestly by me, as I know you will, you may look forward to a partnership at no distant date. But don't be over–sanguine, my dear boy; there is hard work before you."

"And you will not find me shrink from it," said Cradock, throwing his shoulders back; "but we have not settled yet as to the amount of the premium, or deposit, whichever it may be."

"Thank you. To be sure. I quite forgot that incident. Thirty guineas, I think you said, was all that would be convenient to you."

"No, Mr. Wibraham; I said twenty pounds ten shillings."

"Ah, yes, my mistake. I knew that there was an odd ten shillings. Say twenty–five guineas. A mere matter of form, you know; but one which we dare not neglect. It is not a premium; simply a deposit; to be returned at the expiration of the first twelve months. Will you send it to me by cheque? That, perhaps, would be the more convenient form. It will save you from coming again."

"I am sorry to say I cannot; for now I have no banker. Neither can I by any means make it twenty–five guineas. I have stated to you the utmost figure of my present census."

"Ah, quite immaterial. I am only sorry for your sake. The sum will be invested. I shall hold it as your trustee. But, for the sake of the books, merely to look well on the books, we must say twenty guineas. How could I invest twenty pounds ten shillings?"

This appeared reasonable to Cradock, who knew nothing about investment; and, after reflecting a minute or two, he replied as follows:

"I believe, Mr. Wibraham, that I might manage to make it twenty guineas. You said, I think, that my salary would be payable weekly."

"To be sure, my dear boy, to be sure. At any rate until further arrangements."

"Then I will undertake to pay you the twenty guineas. Next Monday, I suppose, will do for it?"

"Oh yes, Monday will do. But stop, I shall not be there on that morning; and, for form's sake, it must be paid first. Let us say Saturday evening. I shall be ready with a stamped receipt. Will you meet me here at six o'clock, as you did this evening?"

Cradock agreed to this, and Mr. Hearty Wibraham shook hands with him most cordially, begging that mutual trust and amity might in no way be lessened by his own unfortunate obligation to observe certain rules and precedents.

In the highest spirits possible under such troubles as his were, Crad strode away from Aurea Themis Buildings, and whistled to black Wena, whom two of the most accomplished dog–stealers in London had been doing their best to inveigle. Failing of skill—for Wena was a deal too knowing—they at last attempted violence, putting away their chopped liver and hoof–meat, and other baits still more savoury, upon which I dare not enlarge. But, just as Black George, having lifted her boldly by the nape of the neck, was popping her into the sack tail foremost, though her short tail was under her stomach, what did she do but twist round upon him, in a way quite unknown to the faculty, and make her upper and lower canines meet through the palm of his hand? It won't do to chronicle what he said—I am too much given to strictest accuracy; enough that he let her drop, in the manner of a red–hot potato; and Blue Bill, who made a grab at her, only got a scar on the wrist. Then she retreated to her step, and fired a royal salute of howls, never ending, ever beginning, until her master came out.

"Wena, dear," he said, for he always looked on the little thing as an inferior piece of Amy, "you are very tired, my darling; the pavement has been too much for you. Sit upon my arm, pretty. We are both going to make our fortunes. And then you 'shall walk in silk attire, and siller hae to spare.'"

Wena nuzzled her nose into its usual place in Cradock's identicity, and growled if any other dog took the liberty of looking at him. And so they got home, singing snug little songs to each other upon the way; and they both made noble suppers on the strength of their rising fortunes.

CHAPTER IX

The following day was Saturday, and the young fellow spent great part of it in learning the rules, the tables, and statistics of the coal trade, so far as they could be ascertained from a sixpenny work which he bought. Not satisfied with this, he went to the Geological Museum, in Jermyn–street, and pored over the specimens, and laid in a stock of carbonic knowledge that would have astonished Clinkers and Jenny. When the building was closed at four o'clock he hurried back to Mortimer–street, paid Mrs. Ducksacre for his week's lodgings, and ran off to a pawnbroker's to raise a little money. Without doing this, he would not be able to deposit the twenty guineas. Mr. Gill's shopman knew Cradock well, from his having been there frequently to redeem some trifling articles for the poor people of the court, and felt some good–will towards him for his kindness to the little customers. It increased the activity of his trade, for most of the pledges were repledged or ever the week was out. And of course he got the money for issuing another duplicate.

"Hope there's nothing amiss, Mr. Newman," said the pawnbroker's assistant; "sorry to see you come here, sir, on your own account."

"Oh, you ought to congratulate me," returned Cradock, with a knowing smile: "I am going to pay a premium, and enter into a good position upon advantageous terms; very advantageous, I may say, seeing how little I know of the coal trade."

"Take care, sir, take care, I beg of you. People run down our line of business, and call it coining tears, &c.; but you may take my word for it, there is a deal more roguery in the coal trade, or rather in the pretence of it, than ever there is in the broking way."

"There can be none in the present case, for the simple reason that I am not in any way committed to a partnership, neither am I to be at all dependent upon the profits." And Cradock looked thankful for advice, but a deal too wise to want it.

"Well, sir, I hope it may be all right; for I am sure you deserve it. But there is a man, not far from here, I think you took some things out for him, by the name of Zakey Jupp; a shrewdish sort of fellow, though a deal too fond of fighting. He'll be up to some of the coal tricks, I expect, he's about in the yards so much; and the whippers and heavers are good uns to talk. Don't you think it beneath you, sir, to consult with Zakey Jupp, if you have the pleasure of his acquaintance."

"I am proud to say that I have at last," replied Cradock, smiling grimly; "but he went on board the *Industrious Maiden*, at Nine Elms, yesterday morning, and may not be back for a month. He wanted me to go with him; but I did not see how to be useful, and had not given my landlady notice. Now, if you please, I have not a moment to spare."

The shopman saw that he could not, without being really impertinent, press his advice any further; and, although Cradock was so communicative, as young men are apt to be, especially about their successes, he never afforded much temptation to any one for impertinence.

"And how much upon them little articles?" was the next question put to Cradock; and he did not ask any very high figure, for fear of not getting them out again.

As he set off full speed for Aurea Themis Buildings, without inviting Wena, it struck him that it would be but common prudence just to look at the place of business; so he dashed aside out of Oxford–street, at the rate of ten miles an hour—for he was very light of foot—and made his way to Howard–crescent, whose position he had learned from the map. Sure enough there it was, when he got to the number indicated. And what a noble plate! So large, indeed, that it was absolutely necessary to have it in two parts. What refulgent brass! What fine engraving, especially on the lower part! You might call it chalco–illumination, chromography, chromometallurgy; I do not know any word half grand enough to describe it. And the legend itself so simple, how could they have made so much of it? The upper plate, though beautifully bright, was comparatively plain, and only carried the words, "Wibraham, Fookes, and Co.;" the lower and far more elaborate part enabled the public to congratulate itself upon having the above as "Coal Merchants and Colliery Agents to Her Most Gracious Majesty and the Duchy of Lancaster. Hours of Business, from Ten till Four."

Cradock just took time to read this, by the light of the gas–lamp close to it; then glanced at the house (which looked clean and smart, though smaller than what he expected), and, feeling ashamed of his mean suspiciousness, darted away towards Notting Hill. When he arrived at Aurea Themis Buildings, he was kept waiting at the door so long that it made him quite uneasy, lest Hearty Wibraham should have forgotten all about his little deposit. At last the smart girl opened the door, and a short young man, whose dress more than whispered that he was not given to compromise his æsthetic views, came out with a bounce, and clapped a shilling in the hand of the smiling damsel. "There, Polly, get a peach–coloured cap–ribbon, and wear it in a true knot for my sake. I fancy I've done your governor. He's a trifle green; isn't he?" But, in spite of his conversational powers, the handmaid dismissed him summarily, when she saw Cradock waiting there.

The gas in the drawing–room was lit this time, and a good fire burning; and Mr. Wibraham, in spirits absolutely jocular, sprang forward to meet Cradock, and cried, "Hail, oh future partner!" Then he offered him a glass of "rare old Madeira;" and, producing a blank receipt form, exclaimed, "Whatever you do, my young friend, never let it be known in the counting–house that I accepted you with so ridiculous a deposit as the sum of thirty guineas."

"Twenty, sir, twenty was what you agreed to accept." Poor Cradock trembled from head to foot, lest even now, at the last moment, he should be rejected. But, to his delight, his new principal replied,

"Then, sir, twenty be it: if in a weak moment I agreed. Hearty Wibraham would rather throw up all his connexion than allow any man to say of him, sir, that he had departed from his word." His voice trembled slightly, and there was a twinkle as of tears in his eyes. Crad began to apologize, though he could not quite see what harm he had done.

"Dash it, my boy, not another word. We understand each other. There is your receipt."

In his confidence, Hearty Wibraham passed the receipt form, now filled up, to the aspiring coal–merchant, without having seen so much as the colour of his money. Then Cradock pulled out Amy's purse, in which he had put the cash, for good luck, and paid his footing bravely.

"Sir, I will not thank you," said Mr. Wibraham, as he took the money, "because the act would not be genuine. And I am proudly able to declare that I have never yet done anything, even for the sake of the common courtesies of life, which has not been thoroughly genuine. My boy, this paltry twenty guineas is the opening of your mercantile life. May that life be prosperous; as I am sure you deserve."

Cradock took another glass of Madeira, as genuine as its owner, and, after a hearty farewell, felt so rapidly on the rise, so touched, for the first time of many weeks, by the dexter wand of fortune, that he bought a quarter of an ounce of bird's–eye with an infusion of "Latakia" (grown in the footpath field at Mitcham), and actually warmed his dear brother's pipe, which had not once been incremated ever since the sacred fire of the Prytaneum had languished.

Wena was overjoyed to see him, and she loved the smell of tobacco, and had often come sniffing about on the hearth–rug (or the bit of baize that did for it) to know whether it was true that a big man—a mastiff of a man, they told her—had succeeded in abolishing it; now, seeing the blue curls quivering nicely, she jumped upon his lap; and, although she was rather heavy, he thought it would be practice towards the nursing of Amy, and possibly Amy's children. Then, when he thought of that, he grew more happy than fifty emperors.

Fortune may jump on a young fellow's heart, with both heels set together; but, the moment she takes one off, up it comes, like a bladder too big to go into the football.

On Monday morning at ten o'clock, our Crad, in a state of large excitement, appeared before the gorgeous plate, and rang the bell thereover. It was answered by an office–boy, with a grin so intensely humorous that it was worth all the guineas that could have been thrust into the great mouth he exhibited.

"Mr. Newman?" asked the boy, with a patronizing air, which a little mind would have found offensive.

"To be sure," replied Cradock; "I suppose I am expected."

"That you are," said the cheeky boy, grinning harder than ever; "the other three gents is waiting, sir. Get you a penny paper for three half–pence."

"Thank you," answered Cradock, hoping to depress that boy, "I am not come here, young man, I trust, to waste time in reading the papers."

"Oh no! oh lor no," cried the boy as he led the way in; "tip–top business this is, and all of us wears out our marrow–bones. His Ro–oyal Highness will be here bumbye. 'Spect they'll appoint you to receive him, 'cos you would look such a swell with our governor's best boots on. Don't you refoose now, mind me, don't refoose, mate, if you loves me."

"You want a little whipcord," said Cradock; "and you shall have it too, my boy, if you come much into my neighbourhood."

"There now; there now!" sighed the boy—who would have been worth something on the stage—"I have never been appreciated, and suppose I never shall. What's the odds to a jinker? Cockalocks, there go in, and let me mind your beaver."

Cradock was shown into a room furnished as philosophically as the wash–house of Cincinnatus; still, it looked like business. There was no temptation to sit down, even though one had rowing–trousers on. There were four tall desks of deal uncovered; each had four legs, and resembled a naked Punch–and–Judy box. Hales, the Norfolk giant, could not have written at either of them, while sitting on any of the stools there.

Three of these desks were appropriated by three very nice young gentlemen, all burning to begin their labours. Two of the men were unknown to Cradock; but the third, the very short one, who had taken a stool to stand upon, and was mending a pen most earnestly—him Cradock recognised at once as the disburser of the shilling, the sanguine youth, of broad views in apparel, who had cheated Mr. Wibraham so.

"Mr. Fookes, I presume," he exclaimed, with a leap from the stool, and a little run towards Cradock; "you see we are all ready, sir, to receive the junior partner. Hardly know what to be up to."

"I am sure I cannot tell you," answered Crad, with a smile; "I do not belong to the firm as yet, although I am promised a partnership at a date not very distant."

"So am I," said the little man, staring; "indeed, I came up from Cambridge principally upon the strength of it."

"The deevil you did!" cried a tall, strapping fellow, crossing suddenly from his desk; "if ye'll hearken me, my time comes first. The agrahment was signed for Candlemas, when the gloot of business allows it. And a Durham man knows what coals are."

"Agrayment, thin, is it?" exclaimed the fourth, a flourishing, red–haired Irishman; "do you think I'd a left me Oonivarsity, Thrinity College, Dooblin, wi'out having it down all black and white? By the same token, it's meself as is foremost. Christmas is the time, me boys; and the farst dividend on St. Pathrick's Day, wakely sthipend in the intherim. Divil take me sowl, but none o' ye shall git before Manus O'Toole."

"Gentlemen," said Cradock, "don't let us be in a hurry. No doubt Mr. Fookes will be here presently, and then we can settle precedence. I see there is work set out for us; and I suppose we are not all strangers here."

"Can't answer for the other gentlemen," returned the little Cambridge man, "but I was never here before, except to see the place on Saturday."

"And that's joost my own predeecament," cried the tall man from Hatfield Hall.

"Chop me up smarl," said the Irishman, when they turned to him as their senior, "but the gintleman has the advantage o' me. I niver was here at all, at all; and I hope I niver shall be."

The four young men gathered round a desk, and gazed sadly at one another. At this moment the office–boy, seeing the distance safe, for he had been watching through the keyhole, pushed his head in at the door, and shouted, "Hi! there, young coal–merchants, don't yer sell too much now! Telegram from the Exchange, gents; grimy is on the rise. But excoose me half an hour, gents; Her Majesty have commanded my presence, to put the ro–oyal harms on me. Ho–hoop! I'm after you, Molly. Don't be afraid of my splashing your legs, dear."

"Well," said Cradock, as the rising young coal–merchants seemed to look to him for counsel, and stood in silent bewilderment—"it appears to me that there is something wrong. Let us hope that it is a mistake only; at any rate, let us stop, and see the matter out. I trust that none of you gentlemen have paid a premium, as I have."

"I am sure I don't know," said the Cantab, "what the others have done; but I was allowed to enter the firm for the sum of eighty guineas, a great deal too little, considering all the advantages offered—the proper sum being a hundred; but an abatement was made in my favour."

"Ahty guineas!" cried the Durham man; "why I was admeeted for saxty, because I had no more."

"It's me blessed self, then, as bates you all," shouted the son of Dublin; "shure and I've made a clear sixty by it, for I hadn't no more than forty."

"And I," replied Cradock, with a melancholy air, "was received for the trifling sum of twenty, on account of my being an Oxford man."

"Why, gentlemen," said the little Cantab, "let us shake hands all round. We represent the four chief universities, only Scotland being omitted."

"Catch a Scotchman with salt, me frinds!" cried the red Hibernian, as they went through the ceremony. "By Jasers, but that infarnal old Jew would have had to pay the porridge–man, for the pleasure of his company."

"Now let us fall to our work, gentlemen" (Crad tried to look hopeful as he said it); "the books before us may throw some light upon this strange, and, as it seems, very roguish matter. I was told to act for our principal, during the absence of the sleeping partner; to keep you all in your places, and make you stick to your work; and especially to remember that one ounce of practice is worth a pound of precept."

"I should be most happy, sir, to obey orders," said the little Cambridge man, bowing; "only I hold the identical commission, ounce of practice and all, for your benefit, my good sir, and that of all the other juniors."

"Now that shows a want of vareaty," cried the tall Dunelmian, "for the sole charge of all of ye is commeeted to *me*."

"It's me blessed self that got it last, and that manes to kape it. What time wur you there, gintlemen, at Ory Thamis Buildings?"

It was settled that the Irishman had received his commission last, for, some whisky having been produced, he and Hearty Wibraham had kept it up until twelve o'clock on the Saturday night. So, to his intense delight, he was now appointed captain.

"An' if I don't drag him from his hole, to pay him the sixty guineas I owe him, out of your money, gintlemen, say my name isn't Manus O'Toole. Now the fust arder I give, is to have in the bhoy, and wallop him."

Easier said than done, Mr. Toole. There was no boy to be found anywhere; and the only result of a strong demonstration in the passage was a curt note from the landlord.

> "Gentlemen,—I understood as I had lett my rooms to a respectable party, rent payable weakly, and weak is up this day. Will take it a favuor to reseeve two pound ten per bearer.
>
> "John Codger."

The four university men looked wondrously blank at this—"gelidusque per ima cucurrit ossa tremor."

"Well, I *am* blowed!" cried the little Cantab, getting smaller, and with the sky–blue stripes on his trousers quivering.

"There's a cousin of mine, a soleecitor," said the young north countryman, "would take up this case for us, if we made a joint deposeet."

"Have down the landlord and fight him," proposed the Emerald Islander.

"I don't care a fig for the landlord," said Cradock, who now recalled some shavings of law from the Quarter Sessions spokeshave; "he can do nothing at all to us, until twelve o'clock, and then he can send us about our business, and no more harm done. We were not parties to the original contract, and have nothing to do with the rent. Now, gentlemen, there is only one thing I would ask you, in return for my lucid legal opinion."

"What is that?" cried all the rest; "whatever it is, you shall have it."

"That you make over to me, *vivâ voce*, your three–fourths of the brass–plate. I have taken a strange fancy to it; the engraving is so fine."

"You are perfectly welcome to it," exclaimed the other three; "but won't it belong to the landlord?"

"Not if it is merely screwed on, as probably is the case. And I have a screw–driver in my knife, which very few screws can resist."

"Then go and take it, by all means, before twelve o'clock, for afterwards we shall only be trespassers."

Crad put his hat on and went out, but returned with the wonderful screw–driver snapped up into his knife–handle, and the first flush of real British anger yet seen upon his countenance. What wonderful beings we are! He had lost nearly all his substance, and he was vexed most about the brass–plate.

"Done at every point," he said; "that glorious under–plate is gone, and only the narrow bar left with the name of the thief upon it, which of course would not suit him again."

"Oysters all round!" cried the Cambridge man, "as the landlord cannot distrain us. An oyster is a legal esculent; I see they teach law at Oxford; let us at least die jolly. And I claim the privilege of standing oysters, because I have paid the highest premium, and am the most promising partner—at any rate, the softest fellow. Gentlemen, if you refuse me, I claim our captain's decision. Captain O'Toole, how is it?"

"Arrah, thin, and I order eysters at this gintleman's expinse, London stout for the waker stomiks, and a drop o' poteen for digestion, to them as are wakest of all."

"Done," said the little Cantab, "if only to rile the landlord, and he may distrain the shells. Call four university men, by implication, unrespectable parties! We must have our action against him. Gentlemen. I am off for the grub, and see that I get in again."

"Faix, then, my honey," cried the Irishman, forgetting all university language, "and, if ye don't, 'twill be a quare job for the bones on the knuckles of Manus O'Toole."

While all four were enjoying their oysters—for Cradock, being a good–natured fellow, did not withhold his assistance—a sharp rap–rap announced the postman, and Mr. O'Toole returned from the door with a large square letter, sealed with the coat of arms of the company. "Ship–letther, and eightpence to pay, begorra. Gintlemen, will we take it?"

"How is it addressed?" asked two or three.

"Most gintaal. 'To the sanior clerk or junior partner of the firm of Wibraham, Fookes, and Co., Coal Merchants,' and that's meself, if it's nobody."

"Then it's you to pey the eightpence," cried the Durham man.

"Do yer think, then, it's me who can't do it?" answered Mr. O'Toole, angrily. And then he broke open the letter and read:

"P. & O. steamer *Will o' the Wisp*, off the Start Point.—*Sunday.*

"Respected and beloved Partners,—His Royal Highness the Pasha of Egypt, having resolved to light with gas the interior of the Pyramids, also to provide hot–water bottles for the comfort of his household–brigade, principally female, and to erect extensive gas–cooking premises, where hot crocodile may always be had, has entrusted me with the whole arrangements, and the entire supply of coal, with no restriction except that the Nile shall not be set on fire.

"Interested as you are in the success of our noble firm, you will thank, instead of blaming me, for an apparently unceremonious departure. By an extraordinary coincidence, Mr. Fookes has also been summoned peremptorily to Constantinople, to contract with the Sultan for warming the sacks of the ladies who are, from time to time, deposited in the Bosporus.

"Therefore, gentlemen, the entire interest of the London branch is left in your experienced hands. Be steady, I entreat you; be diligent, be methodical. Above all things, remember that rigid probity, and the strictest punctuality in meeting payments, are the *very soul of business*, and that an ounce of practice is worth a pound of precept. But I have the purest confidence in you. I need not appeal to the honour of four university men. From my childhood upward, I have admired those admirable institutions, and the knowledge of life imparted by them. 'Quid leges sine moribus?' Excuse me; it is all the Latin I know.

"There is a raw Irishman among you, rather of the physical order; if he is violent, expel him. Every gentleman will be entitled to his own deal desk, upon discharge of the bill, which he will find made out in his name, in the drawer thereof. And now farewell. I have been prolix in the endeavour to be precise.

"There are no funds in hand for the London branch, but our credit is unbounded. Push our united interests, for I trust you to the last farthing. I hope to find you with coffers full, and commercial honour untainted, on the 31st of February prox.

"Believe me, Gentlemen, ever your affectionate partner,

"Hearty Wibraham, D.C.L.

"P.S.—If none of my partners know the way to enter an order, the office–boy will instruct the manager of the firm.—H. W."

"Consummate scoundrel!" exclaimed the little Cantab, with the beard of an oyster in his throat.

"Detasteable heepocrite!" cried the representative of Durham.

"Raw Irishman! Oh then the powers! And the punch of the head I never giv' him, a week will be next Saturday." Mr. O'Toole danced round the room, caught up the desks like dolls, and dashed all their noses together. Then he summoned the landlord, and pelted him out of the room and up the stairs with oyster–shells, the books, and the whisky–bottle, and two pewter–pots after his legs, as he luckily got round the landing–place. The terrified man, and his wife worse frightened, locked themselves in, and then threw up a window and bawled out for the police.

Cradock, feeling ashamed of the uproar, seized O'Toole by the collar; and the Durham man, being sedate and steady, grasped him on the other side. So they lifted him off the ground, and bore him even into Hyde Park, and there they left him upon a bench, and each went his several way. The police, according to precedent, were in time to be too late.

CHAPTER X

Cradock Nowell shivered hard, partly from his cold, and partly at the thought of the bitter life before him. He had Amy's five and sixpence left, an immutable peculium. In currency his means were limited to exactly four and ninepence. With the accuracy of an upright man (even in the smallest matters), he had forced upon Mr. O'Toole his twopence, the quaternary of that letter. Also he had insisted upon standing stout, when thirst increased with oysters. Now he took the shillings four, having lost all faith in his destiny, and put one in each of his waistcoat pockets; for he had little horse–shoes upwards, as well as the straight chinks below. This being done, he disposed of his ninepence with as tight a view to security.

All that day he wandered about, and regretted Issachar Jupp. Towards nightfall, he passed a railway terminus, miserably lighted, a disgrace to any style of architecture, teeming with insolence, pretence, dirt, discomfort, fuss, and confusion. Let us call it the "Grand Junction Wasting and Screwing Line;" because among railway companies the name is generally applicable.

In a window, never cleaned since the prorogation of Parliament, the following "Notice" tried to appear; and, if you rubbed the glass, you might read it.

"Wanted immediately, a smart active young man, of good education. His duties will not be onerous. Wages one pound per week. Uniform allowed. Apply to Mr. Killquick, next door to the booking–office."

Cradock read this three times over, for his wits were dull now, and then he turned round, and felt whether all his money was safe. Yes, every blessed halfpenny, for he had eaten nothing since the oysters.

"Surely I am an active young man, of good education," said Crad to himself, "although not very smart, perhaps, especially as to my boots; but a suit, all uniform, allowed, will cure my only deficiency. I could live and keep Wena comfortably upon a pound a week. I hope, however, that they cash up. Railway companies have no honour, I know; but I suppose they pay when they can't help it."

Having meditated with himself thus much, he went, growing excited on the way—for now he was no philosopher—to the indicated whereabouts of that line's factotum, Mr. Killquick. Here he had to wait very nearly an hour, Mr. Killquick being engaged, as usual, in the company's most active department, arranging very effectually for a collision down the line. "Successfully," I would have said; but, though the accident came off quite according to the most sanguine, or sanguinary expectation, the result was a slur on that company's fame; only three people being killed, and five–and–twenty wounded.

"Now, young man," asked Mr. Killquick, when all his instructions were on the wires, "what is your business with me?"

Cradock, having stated his purpose, name, and qualifications, the traffic–manager looked at him with interest and reflection. Then he said impressively, "You can jump well, I should think?"

"I have never yet been beaten," Crad answered, "but of course there are many who *can* beat me."

"And run, no doubt? And your sight is accurate, and your nerves very good?"

"My nerves are not what they were, sir; but I can run fast and see well."

"Why do you shiver so? That will never do. And the muscles of his calf are too prominent. We lost No. 6 through that."

"It is only a little cold I have caught. It will go off in a moment with regular work."

"You have no relation, I suppose, in any way connected with the law? No friends, I mean, of litigious tendencies?"

"Oh no. I have no friends whatever; none, I mean, in London, only one family, far in the country, to care at all about me."

"No father or mother to make a fuss, eh? No wife to prevent your attending to business?"

"No, sir, nothing of the sort. I am quite alone in the world; and my life is of no importance."

"Wonderful luck," muttered Mr. Killquick; "exactly the very thing for us! And I have been so put out about that place, it has got such a reputation. Poor Morshead cannot get through the work any longer by himself. And the coroner made such nasty remarks. If we kill another man there before Easter, the *Times* will be sure to get hold of it. Young man," he continued in a louder tone, "you are in luck this time, I believe. It is a very snug situation; only you must look sharp after your legs, and be sure you never touch spirits. Not given to blue ruin, I hope?"

"Oh no. I never touch it."

"That's right. I was afraid you did, you look so down in the mouth. You can give us a reference, I suppose?"

"Yes, to my landlady, Mrs. Ducksacre, a most respectable person, in trade in Mortimer–street."

"Good," replied Mr. Killquick; "you mustn't be alarmed, by the way, by any foolish rumours you may hear as to dangers purely imaginary. Your predecessor lost his life through the very grossest carelessness. You are as safe there as in your bed, unless your nerves happen to fail you. And, when that is the case, I should like to know," asked the traffic–manager indignantly, "which of us is not in danger, even in coming down–stairs?"

"What will my duties be, then?" asked Cradock, with some surprise.

"Why, you are not afraid, are you?" Mr. Killquick looked at him contemptuously.

"No, I should rather hope not," replied Cradock, meeting him eye to eye, so that the wholesale smasher quailed at him; "there is no duty, even in a powder–mill, which I would shrink from now."

"Ah, terrible things, those powder–mills! A perfect disgrace to this age and country, their wanton waste of human life. How the Legislature lets them go on so, is more than I can conceive. Why, they think no more of murdering and maiming a dozen people— —"

"Please, sir," cried one of the clerks, coming down from the telegraph office, "no end of a collision on the Slayham and Bury Branch. Three passengers killed, and twenty–five wounded, some of them exceedingly fatally."

"Bless my heart if I didn't expect it. Told Sykes it would be so. How's the engine, Jemmy?"

"She's all right, sir; jumped over three carriages, and went a header into a sand–hill. Driver cased in glass, from vitrifaction of the sand. Stoker took the hot water—a thing he ain't much accustomed to."

"No! What a capital joke. Hell–fire–Jack (I can swear it was him), preserved in a glass case, from the results of his own imprudence! I shall be up with you in five minutes, James. Be quite ready to begin."

"Now," said Mr. Killquick, drawing out his cigar–case, "I have little more to say to you, young man, except that you can begin at eight o'clock to–morrow morning. We will dispense with the references, for I have the utmost confidence in you, and you will be searched very carefully every time you come out of the gate—which you never will be allowed to do, except when your spell is over, and your mate is in. You will go at once to our outfitters, and, upon presenting this ticket, they will fit you up, as tightly as possible, with your regimentals. And see that you don't take boots, but the very best shoes for jumping in. What they call 'Oxford shoes' are best, when tied tight over the instep, and not too thick in the sole. No nails, mind, for fear of slipping upon the flange. Good–bye, my boy; be very careful. By–the–by, you say you don't value your life?"

"Very little indeed," said Cradock, "except just for one reason."

"Then now you must add another reason; you must value it for our sake. The Company can't have another inquest for at least six months. I mean, of course, *by the same coroner*. Confound that fellow; he will not take a right view of things. At eight o'clock to–morrow morning, you will be at the gate of the Cramjam goods station. The clerk there will have his orders about you. He will supply you with a book, and map out for you your duties. Also Morshead, your mate, an invaluable man, will show you the practical part of it. Now, good–bye, my lad. Remember, you never wear any except your official dress. We allow you two suits in the twelvemonth. Your duties will be of a refined character, and the exercise exhilarating. I trust to receive a good report of you; and I hope, my boy, that you are at peace, both with God and man."

Even Mr. Killquick had been touched a little by Cradock's air of uncomplaining sorrow, and the stamp of high mind and good breeding.

"Very foolish of me," he muttered, as he lit his cigar, and went up to telegraph to the Slayham station–master—'Commit yourself to nothing; observe the strictest economy; and no bonfires of the splinter–wood, as they had last week'—"very foolish of me," he said on the stairs, "but it goes to my heart to kill that young fellow. How I should like to know his history! That face does not mean nothing."

Cradock, caring very little what his duties might be, and feeling the night–wind go through his heart, hastened to the outfitters', and there he was received with a grin by an experienced shopman, on the production of his note.

"Capital customers, sir," he said; "famous customers of ours, that Grand Junction Wasting and Screwing Line, and the best of all for the gentlemen in your way of business, sir. Must have new clothes every new hand, and they changes pretty often, sir. Pervides all the comforts of a home for you, and a gentlemanly competence, before you've been half a year with them."

The man grinned still more at his own grim wit, while Cradock stared at him in wonderment.

"Don't you see, sir, they can't pass the clothes on, after the man has been killed, even if there's a bit of them left; for they must fit you like your skin, sir. The leastest little wrinkle, sir, or the ruffle of a hinch, or so much as the fray of a hem, and there you are, sir; and they have to look for another hactive young man, sir. And hactive young men are getting shy, sir, uncommon shy of it now, except they come from the country. Hope you insured your life, sir, before taking the situation. There's no company will accept your life now, sir. What a nice young man the last were,—what a nice young man, to be sure! outrageous fond of filberts; till they cracked him, and found a shell for him."

"Well," said Cradock, whom the busy tailor had been measuring all this while, "from all that you tell me, there would be less imprudence in ordering my coffin than to–morrow's dinner. What is there so very dangerous in it?"

"Well, you'll see, sir, you'll see. I would not frighten you for the world, because it's all up in a moment, if you lose your presence of mind. Thank you, sir; all right now, except the legs of the tights, and that's the most particular part of it all. May I trouble you to turn your trousers up? It will never do to measure over them. We shall put six hands on at once at the job. The whole will be ready at eleven this evening. You must kindly call and try everything. We are ordered to insist upon that."

The next morning, Crad, in a suit of peculiar, tough, and yet most elastic cord, which fitted him as if he had been dipped in it, walked in at the open gates of the front yard, leading to the Cramjam general goods terminus. This was the only way in or out (except along "the metals"), and, as it was got up with heaps of stucco, all the porters were very proud of it, and called it a "slap–up harchway."

"Stop, stop," cried a sharp little fellow, gurgling up, like a fountain, from among the sham pilasters; "what's your business here, my man, on the premises of the Grand Junction Wasting and Screwing Company? Ah, I see by your togs. Just come this way, if you please, then."

Here let me call a little halt, for time enough to explain that the more fashionable of the railway companies have lately agreed that a station–yard is a sort of royal park, which cannot be kept too private, which no doors may rashly open upon, a pleasant rural solitude and weed–nursery for the neighbourhood, and wherein the senior porter has his private mushroom–bed. They are wise in this seclusion, and wholesome is their privacy, so long as they discard all principle—so long as they are allowed to garotte us, while they jabber about "public interests." Perhaps, ere very long, we shall have a modern Dædalus; and then the boards of directors, so ready to do collectively things which, done individually, no gentleman would own to, may abate a few jots of their arrogance, and have faint recollections of honour.

Cradock, not very deeply impressed by the "compo" arch (about half the size of the stone one at Nowelhurst Hall's chief entrance), presented himself to the sharp little fellow, and told him what he was come for.

"Glad to hear it," said the gateman, "uncommonly glad to hear it. Morshead is a wonderful fellow; there is not another man in England could have stuck to that work as he has done. He ought to have five pounds a week, that he ought, instead of a single sovereign. Screwing Co." (this was their common name) "will be sorry when they have lost him. Now your duty is to enter, in this here book, the number of every truck, jerry, trod, or blinkem, tarpaulin, or covering of any sort; also the destination chalked on it, and the nature of the goods in the truck, so far as you can ascertain them; coals, iron, chalk, packing–cases, boxes, crates, what not, so fast as they comes into the higher end, or so fast as they goes out of it. You return this book to the check office every time you come off duty. You begin work at eight in the morning, and you leave at eight in the evening. You don't pass here meanwhile, and you can't pass up the line. Hope you have brought some grub. You'll have five minutes in the afternoon, long enough to get a snack in, after the up goods for Millstone is off. Oh, you ought to have brought some grub; if you faint, you will never come to again. But perhaps Morshead can spare you a bit. He'll be glad to see you, that's certain, for he ain't slept a wink for a week. And such a considerate chap. I enter you in and out. 'Number–taker 26.' That's all right from your cap, my lad. No room for it on your sleeve. Might stick out, you know, and you must pack tighter than any of the goods is. 'Undertakers,' we call you always. Good–bye, sir; Morshead will tell you the rest, and I hope to see you all right at eight P.M. The first day is always the worst. Go in at that door by the Pickford, and ask the first porter you see for Morshead, and take care how you get at him."

Morshead was resting for a moment upon a narrow piece of planking, amid a regular Seven Dials of sidings, points, and turn–tables. Cradock could scarcely see him, for trucks and vans and boxes on wheels were gliding past in every direction, thick as the carts on London Bridge, creaking, groaning, ricketing, lurching; thumping up against one another, and then recoiling with a heavy kick, straining upon coupling–chains, butting against bulkheads, staggering and jerking into grooves and out of them, crushing flints into a shower of sparks, doing anything and everything except standing still for a moment. And among them rushed about, like dragons—ramping, and routing, and swearing fearfully, gargling their throats with a boiling riot, and then goring the ground with tusks of steam, whisking and flicking their tails, and themselves, in and out at the countless cross–webs, screaming, and leaping, and rattling, and booming—the great ponderous giant goods–engines. Every man was out–swearing his neighbour, every truck browbeating its fellow, every engine out–yelling its rival. There is nothing on earth to compare with this scene, unless it be the jostling and churning of ice–packs in Davis's Straits, when the tide runs hard, and a gale of wind is blowing, and the floes have broken up suddenly. And even that comparison fails, because, though the monsters grind and crash, and labour and leap with agony, they do not roar, and vomit steam, and swear at one another.

At the risk of his life, for as yet he knew nothing of the laws that governed their movements—a very imperfect code, by–the–by—Cradock made his way to the narrow staging where Morshead was taking a breathing–time. His fellow "number–taker" of course descried him coming; for he had acquired the art of seeing all round, as a spider is falsely supposed to do. He knew, in a moment, by Cradock's dress, what business he was meant for; and he said to himself, "Thank God!" in one breath, for the sake of his wife and family; and "Oh, poor fellow!" in the next, as he saw how green our Cradock was. Then he held up his hands for Cradock to stop and waved them for him to run; and so piloted him to the narrow knife–board, "where a man's life was his own a'most."

The highest and noblest of physical courage is that which, fully perceiving the danger, looking into the black pit of death, and seeing the night of horrors there (undivested of horror by true religion), encounters them all, treads the narrow cord daily, not for the sake of honour or fortune not because of the dash in it, and the excitement to a brave soul; not even to win the heart's maiden, that pearl of romance and mystery: but simply to supply the home, to keep in flow the springs of love—whence the geyser heat is gone—to sustain and comfort (without being comforted by them) the wife, whose beauty is passed away, and who may have taken to scold and the children, whose chief idea of daddy is that he has got a halfpenny.

This glorious inglorious courage, grander than any that ever won medal or cross for destroying, had a little home—though he knew it not and never thought about it—in the broad, well–rounded bosom of simple Stephen Morshead. None but himself knew his narrow escapes; an inch the wrong way and he was a dead man, fifty times a day. And worst of all in the night—oh, in the horrible night, and yet more in the first gleam of morning when the body was worn out, and dreams came over the eyes, but were death if they passed to the brain, and the trucks went by like nightmares—that very morning he had felt, after taking duty night and day for more than a week, since they killed his partner, he had felt that his Sally must be a widow, and his seven children orphans, if another night went over him without some relief of sleep. That every word of this is true, many a poor man would avouch (if he only had time and the money to read it, and were not afraid); but few rich men will care to swallow facts so indigestible.

Stephen Morshead was astonished at seeing that his mate was come. None of the men in the goods station would have anything to do with it. It was very well to be up in the trucks, or upon the engines, or even to act as switchman, for you had a corner inviolable, and could only do mischief to others. But to run in and out, and through and through, in that perpetual motion, to be bound to jot down every truck, the cover, and contents of it, entering or departing from that crammed and crowded terminus, to have nobody to help you therein, and nobody to cry "dead man" if you died, and the certainty that if you stood a hair's–breadth out of the perpendicular, or a single wheel had a bunion, you with the note–book in your hand must flood the narrow 'tween–ways, and find your way out underneath to heaven; all this, and the risk of the fearful jumps from one sliding train to another, sliding oppositely, and jerking, perhaps, as you jumped; and yet if you funked the jump you must be crushed, like a frog beneath a turf–beater: these considerations, after many pipes were smoked over them, had induced all the porters and stokers to dwell on the virtues of the many men killed, and to yield to their wives' entreaties, acquiesce in their sixteen shillings, nor aspire to the four shillings Charon–fare.

"Now," said Morshead, "shake hands with me," as Cradock, breathless with running wonder, leaped upon the nine–inch gangway. "I see you belongs to a different horder of society; obliged to keep my eyes open, mate; but, as long as you and I works together, I ask it as a favour of you, to shake hands night and morning."

"With the greatest pleasure," said Cradock, "if you think there's room for our funny–bones."

"Ha, ha!" laughed Morshead, "you are the right sort for it. Not a bit afeard, I see. Now I mustn't stop to talk; just follow me, and do as I do. I can put you up to it in six hours; and then if you can spare me for the other six, 'twill be the saving of the little ones. But tell the truth if you're tired. I should scorn myself if harm came to you."

"You are the bravest man I ever met," said Cradock, with his heart rising; "you cannot expect me to be like you. But you shall not find me a coward."

"I can see it by your eyes, lad. No sparkle, but a glowing like. I can always tell by the eyes of a man how long he will last at this work. Now come along o' me, and I'll show you the nine worst crushing places."

Cradock followed him through the threads—threads of Clotho and Atropos—feeling the way with his legs, like a gnat who "overs the posts" of a spider's web. In and out, with a jump here and there, when two side–boards threatened to shear them, they got to the gorge at the entrance, where the main turmoil of all was. The Symplegades were a joke to it. And all because the Screwing Company would not buy land enough to get elbow room. There are several lines of railway which do a much larger business; there is no other which attempts to do so much upon less than four times the acreage.

"I've tottled all them as are going out," Mr. Morshead informed Cradock; "now you'll see how we enters them as they enters."

Laughing at his own very miserable joke, he leaped on the chains of the passing waggons, and held up his hand for Cradock not to attempt to do the same.

"Takes a deal of practice that," he cried, after he had crossed the train; "it ain't like a passenger–train, you know; and you must larn when they are standing. I need not to have done it now, but sometimes I be forced. Bide where you are; no danger unless they comes with the flaps down."

Then he jotted down, with surprising quickness, all the necessary particulars of the train that was coming in. It happened to be an easy one; for there were no tarpaulins at all, and it was not travelling faster than about four miles an hour.

"Some drivers there is," said Morshead, as he rejoined Cradock round the tail of the train, "who really seem to want to kill a fellow, they come by at such a pace, without having any call for it. I believe they think, the low fools, that we are put as spies upon them, and they would rather kill us than not.—Hold your tongue," to a man in a truck, who was interrupting his lecture; "don't you know better than to offer *me* that stuff? Never touch what they offers you, sir. They means no harm, but you had safer take poison when you be on duty. There is not much real danger *just here,* if a fellow is careful, because the rails run parallo; there is nothing round the curve now, I see, and only two coming out, and both of they be scored; it's a rare chance to show you the figures of eight, and slide–points where the chief danger is. Show you where poor Charley was killed last week, and how he did it."

"Poor fellow! Did he leave any family?"

"Twelve in all. No man comes here, unless he be tired of his life, or be druv to it by the little ones."

"And what did the Company do for them?"

"Oh, behaved most 'andsome *for them*. Allowed 'em two bob a week for a twelvemonth to come—twopence apiece all round. But they only did it to encourage me, for fear I should funk off. I have seen out three mates now. Please God, I shan't see you out too, my lad."

"If you do, it shan't be from funk, Morshead. I rather like the danger."

"That's the worst thing of all," replied Stephen; "I beg of you not to say that, sir."

A thoroughly brave man almost always has respect for order. The bold man—which means a coward with jumps in him—generally has none. It was strange to see how Stephen Morshead, in all that crush, and crash, and rattle, that swinging and creaking as of the Hellespontic boat–bridge, mixed deference with his pity for Cradock. He saw, from his face, and air, and manner, that he was bred a gentleman. Shall we ever come—or rather the twentieth generation come—to the time when every man of England (but for his own fault) shall be bred and trained a gentleman in the true and glorious sense of it?

Cradock saw the fatal places, where the sleepers still were purple, where danger ran in converging lines, where a man must stand sideways, like a duellist, and with his arms in like a drill–sergeant's, and not shrink an inch from the driving–wheels; where his size was measured as for his coffin, and if he stirred he would want nothing more. Then, if a single truck–flap were down, if an engine rollicked upon the rail, if a broad north–country truck, overreaching, happened to be in either train, when you were caught between the two, your only chance was to cry, "Good God!" and lie upon your side, and straighten all your toes out.

And yet these were the very places where, most of all, the "number–taker" was bound to have his stand—where alone he could contrive to check two trains at once. "Could they help starting two trains at once?" poor Crad asked himself—for he had found no time to ask it before—when, weary to the last fibre with the work of the day, he fell upon his little bed, and could hardly notice Wena. Perhaps they could not; it was more than he knew; only he knew that, if they could, they were but wanton man–slaughterers.

After a deep sleep, all in his clothes, he awoke the next morning quite up for his work, and Morshead, who had been on duty all night, and whose eyes seemed cut out of card–board, only stayed for an hour with him, and then, feeling that Crad was quite up to the day–work, ran home and snored for ten hours, as loud as Phlegethon or Enceladus.

The most fearful thing, for a new hand, was, of course, the night–work; and Stephen Morshead, delighted to have such a mate at last, had begged to leave Cradock the day–spell, at least for the first three weeks; for to Stephen the moon was as good as the sun, and sweet sleep fell like wool when plucked at, and hushed the tramping steeds of the day–god. Only, for the sake of Stephen's eyes, on whose accuracy hung the life–poise, it was absolutely necessary not to dilate the pupils incessantly.

But Cradock never took night–work there; and the change came about on this wise. Wena felt that she was wronged by his going away from her every day so early in the morning, and not coming home to her again till ever so late at night, and then too tired to say a word, or perhaps he didn't care to do it. Like all females of any value—unless they are really grand ones, and, if such there be, please to keep them away—Wena grew jealous desperately. She might as well be anybody else's dog; and the baker's dog was with his master all day; and the butcher's lady dog, a nasty ill–bred thing—the idea of calling her a lady!—why, even she was allowed, though the selfish thing didn't care for it, unless there was suet on his apron, to jump up at him and taste him, all the time he was going for orders. And then look even at the Ducksacre dog, a despicable creature—his father might have been a bull–terrier, or he might have been a Pomeranian, or a quarter–bred Skye, or the Lord knows who, very likely a turnspit, and his mother, oh! the less we say of her the better;—why, that wretched, lop–eared, split–tailed thing, without an eye fit to look out of, had airs of his own; and what did it mean, she would like to know, and she who had formed some nice acquaintances, dogs that had been presented at Court, and got Eau–de–Cologne every morning, and not a blessed [run away] upon them? Why, it meant simply this: that Spot, filthy plague–spot, was allowed to go out with the baskets, and made a deal of by his owners, and might cock his tail with the best of them, while she, black Wena, who had been brought up so differently——

Here her feelings were too much for her, and she put down her soft flossy ear upon the drugget–scrap, and looked at the door despairingly, and howled until Mrs. Ducksacre was obliged to come up and comfort her. Even then she wouldn't eat the dripping.

From that day she made her mind up. She would watch her opportunity. What was the good of being endowed with such a nose as she had, unless she could smell her master out, even through the streets of London? What did he wear such outlandish clothes for? Very likely, on purpose to cheat her. Very likely he was even keeping some other dog. At any rate, she would know that, if it cost her her life to do it. What good was her life now to her, or anybody else? Heigho!

On the following Saturday, when Cradock was gone to his fifth day's work, what does Wena do, when Mrs. Ducksacre came up on purpose to coax and make much of her, but most ungratefully give her the slip, with a skill worthy of a better purpose, then scuttle down the stairs, all four legs at once, in that sort of a bone–slide which domestic dogs acquire. Miss Ducksacre ran out of the shop at the noise—for this process is not a silent one; but she could only cry, "Oh, Lord!" as Wena, with the full impact of her weight multiplied into her velocity; or, if that is wrong, with the cube of her impetus multiplied into the forty–two stairs—bang she came anyhow, back–foremost, against the young lady's—nay, you there, I said, "lower limbs"—and deposited her in a bushel of carrots, just come from Covent Garden.

"Stop her, Joe, for God's sake, stop her!" Miss Ducksacre cried to the shop–boy, as well as she could, for the tail of a carrot which had gotten between her teeth.

"Blowed if I can, miss," the boy responded, as Wena nipped his fingers for him; the next moment she was free as the wind, and round the corner in no time.

"Oh dear, oh dear," cried Polly Ducksacre, a buxom young lady, with fine black eyes, "whatever will Mr. Newman think of us? It will seem so unkind and careless; and he does love that dog so!"

Polly was beginning to entertain a tender regard for Cradock; especially since he had shown his proportions in "them beautiful buff pantaloons." What a greengrocer he would make, to be sure, so hupright and so lordly like; and she'd like to see the man in the "Garden" who would tell her she had eaten sparrow–pie, with Mr. Newman to hold the basket for her.

By this time, Mrs. Ducksacre was come down the stairs, screaming "Wena!" at the top of her voice the whole way; and out they ran, boy and all, to search for her, while three or four urchins came in, without medium of exchange, and filled cap, mouth, and pocket. One brat was caught upon their return, and tied up for the day in an empty potato–sack, and exposed, behind the counter, to universal execration; in which position he took such note of manner and custom, time and place, that it was never safe for the Ducksacre firm to dine together afterwards.

Meanwhile, that little black Wena, responsive and responsible to none except her master, pursued the even tenor of her way, nosing the ground, and asking many a question of the lamp–posts, as far as the Cramjam

Terminus, at least three miles from Mortimer–street. The sharp little gate–clerk, animated with railway love of privacy, ran out, and clapped his hands, and shouted "hoo" at Wena; but she only buttoned her tail down, and cut across the compound. As for the stone he threw at her, she caught it up in her mouth as it rolled, and carried it on to her master.

There was Cradock, in the thick of it, standing on a narrow pile of pig–iron, one of his chief fortalices; his book was in his hand, and he was entering, as fast as he could, all the needful particulars of a goods train sliding past him.

Creak, and squeak, and puff, and shriek,—Oh, what a scene, thought Wena,—and the rattle of the ghostly chains, and the rushing about, and the roaring. She lost her presence of mind in a moment,—she always had been such a nervous dog—she tightened her tail convulsively, and dropped her ears, while her eyes came forth; and, glancing at the horrors on every side, she fled for dear life from the evil to come.

The faster she fled, the more they closed round her. She had not espied her master yet; she could not find the way back again; she was terrified out of all memory; and a host of frightful genii, more sooty than Cocytus, and riding hideous monsters, were yelling at her on every side, clapping black hands, and hooting. The dog on the Derby course, when the race rushes round the corner, was in a position of glory and safety compared to poor Wena's now. Already the tip of her tail was crushed, already one pretty paw was broken; for she had bolted in and out through the trains, truck bottoms, wheels, and driving–wheels. Oh, you cowards, to yell at her! with black death grating and grinding upon her soft silky back!

At last, she gave in altogether. They had hunted her to her grave. Who may contend with destiny? She lay down under a moving coal–train, and resigned herself to die. But first she must ask for sympathy, although so unlikely to get it. She looked once more at her wounded foot, and shivered and sobbed with the agony; and then gave vent to one long low cry, to ask if no one loved a poor dog there.

Cradock heard it, and started so that it was nearly all up with him too. Thoroughly he knew the cry, wherein she had wailed for Clayton. He flung down his book, and dashed to the place, and there he saw Wena, and she saw him. She began to try to limp to him, but he held up his hand to stop her; disabled as she was, she was sure to be caught by the wheel. Could she stay there, and let the train pass her? No. At its tail was an empty horse–box, almost scraping the ground, perfectly certain to crush her. Crying, "Down,

down, my poor darling!" he ran down the train, which was travelling seven or eight miles an hour, seized the side of a truck, and leaped, at the risk of his life, upon the fender in front of the horse–box. Then he got astride of the coupling–chain, and kept his right hand low to the ground, to snatch her up ere the crusher came. Knowing where she was, he caught her by the neck the instant the truck disclosed her, and, with a strong swing, heaved her up into it. But he lost his balance in doing it, and fell sideways, with his head on the other coupling–chain. Stunned by the blow, he lay there, only clinging by his right calf to the chain he had sat astride upon. The first jerk of either chain, the first swing of either carriage, and he must be ground to powder.

Luckily for him and for Amy, Morshead was not gone home yet, seeing more to do than usual. Missing his mate from the proper place, he had run up in terror to look for him, when a man in a truck, who had vainly been shouting to stop the coal–train's engine, pointed and screamed to him where and what was doing. Morshead jumped on the heap of pig–iron, and sideways thence on the board of the truck just passing, as dangerous a leap as well could be, but luckily that truck was empty. He jumped into the truck, a shallow one, where poor Wena lay quite paralysed, and, stooping over the back with both arms, he got hold of Cradock's collar. Then, with a mighty effort, he jerked him upon the tail–board, and lugged him in, and bent over him.

Wounded Wena crawled up, and begged to have her poor foot looked at, then, obtaining no notice at all, she felt that Cradock must be killed and dead, just as Clayton had been. Upon this conclusion, she fetched such a howl, though it shook her sore tail to do it, that the engine–driver actually looked round, and the train was stopped.

Hereupon, let me offer a suggestion—everybody now is allowed to do so, though nobody ever takes it. My suggestion is, that no man should be allowed to drive an engine without having served a twelvemonth's apprenticeship as an omnibus conductor. I don't mean to say it would improve his morals—probably rather otherwise; but it would teach him the habit of looking round; it would let him know that there really is more than one quarter of the heavens. At present, all engine–drivers seem afraid of being turned into pillars of salt. So they fix themselves, like pillars of stone, and stare, *ἀχηνίαις ὀμμάτων*, through their square glass spectacles.

When one of the railway bajuli—who are, on the whole, very good sort of fellows, and deserve their Christmas–boxes—came home in the cab with Cradock and Wena at the expense of the Company (which was boasted of next board–day)—when one of them came home with Crad—for Morshead had double work again—Polly Ducksacre went into strong hysterics, and it required two married men and a boy to get her out of the potato–bin.

It was all up with our Crad that night. The overwork of brain and muscle, the presence of mind required all the time when his mind was especially absent, the impossibility of thinking out any of his trains of ideas when a train of trucks was upon him, the native indignation of a man at knowing that his blood is meant to ebb down a railway sewer, and a new broom will sweep him clean—all these worries and wraths together, cogging into the mill–wheel of cares already grinding, had made such a mill–clack in his head near the left temple, where the thump was, that he could only roll on his narrow bed at imminent risk of a floor–bump.

Then the cold, long harbouring, struck into his heart and reins; and he knew not that Dr. Tink came, and was learned and diagnostic upon him; nor even that Polly Ducksacre took his feet out of bed, and rubbed them until her wrists gave way; and then, half ashamed of her womanhood, sneaked away, and cried over Wena.

Wena's foot was put into splinters, Wena's tail was stypticised; but no skill could save her master from a furious brain–fever.

CHAPTER XI

Leaving the son on his narrow hard pallet, to toss and toss, and turn and turn, and probably get bed–sores, let us see how the father was speeding.

Sir Cradock Nowell sat all alone in his little breakfast–room, soon after the funeral of his brother, and before Eoa came to him. For the simple, hot–hearted girl fell so ill after she heard of her loss, and recovered from the narcotic, that Biddy O'Gaghan, who got on famously with the people at the Crown, would not hear of her being moved yet, and drove Dr. Hutton all down the stairs, "with a word of sinse on the top of him," when he claimed his right of attending upon the girl he had known in India.

That little breakfast–room adjoined Sir Cradock's favourite study, and was as pretty a little room as he could have wished to sit in. He had made pretence of breakfasting, but perhaps he looked forward to lunch–time, for not more than an ounce of food had he swallowed altogether.

There he sat nervously, trying vainly to bring his mind to bear on the newspaper. Fine gush of irony, serried antithesis, placid assumption of the point at issue, then logic as terse and tight as the turns of a three–inch screw–jack, withering indignation at those who won't think exactly as we do, the sunrise glow of metaphor, the moonlight gleam of simile, the sparkling stars of wit, and the playful Aurora of humour—alas, all these are like water on a duck's back when the heart won't let the brain go. If we cannot appreciate their beauty, because our opinions are different, how can we hope to do so when we don't care what any opinions are?

It is all very well, very easy, to talk about objectivity; but a really objective man the Creator has never shown us, save once; and even He rebuked the fig–tree, to show sympathy with our impatience.

And I doubt but it is lest we deify the grand incarnations of intellect—the Platos and the Aristotles, the Bacons and the Shakespeares—that it has pleased the Maker of great and small to leave us small tales of the great ones, mean anecdotes, low traditions; lest at any time we should be dazzled, and forget that they were but sparkles from the dross which heaven hammers on. Oh vast and soaring intellects, was it that your minds flew higher because they had shaken the soul off; or was it that your souls grew sullen at the mind's preponderance?

Fash we not ourselves about it, though we pay the consequences. If we have not those great minds in the lump, we have a deal more, taking the average, and we make it go a deal further, having learned the art of economy and the division of labour. Nevertheless, Sir Cradock Nowell, being not at all an objective man, lay deep in the pot of despondency; and, even worse than that, hung, jerked thereout every now and then, by the flesh–hook of terror and nervousness. How could he go kindly with his writer when his breakfast would not so with him?

He was expecting Bull Garnet. Let alone all his other wearing troubles, he never could be comfortable when he expected Bull Garnet. At every step in the passage, every bang of a door, the proud old gentleman trembled and flushed, and was wroth with himself for doing so.

Then Hogstaff came in, and fussed about, and Sir Cradock was fain to find fault with him.

"How careless you are getting about the letters, Hogstaff. Later and later every morning! What is the reason that you never now bring me the bag at the proper time?"

It was very strange, no doubt, of Job Hogstaff, but he could not bear to be found fault with; and now he saw his way to a little triumph, and resolved to make the most of it.

"Yes, Sir Cradock; to be sure, Sir Cradock; how my old head is failing me! Very neglectful of me never to have brought the bag to–day." Then he turned round suddenly at the door, to which he had been hobbling. "Perhaps you'd look at the date, Sir Cradock, of the paper in your hand, sir."

"Yesterday's paper, of course, Hogstaff. What has that to do with it?"

"Oh, nothing, sir, nothing, of course. Only I thought it might have comed in the letter–bag. Perhaps it never does, Sir Cradock; you knows best, as you takes it out." Here old Job gave a quiet chuckle, and added, as if to himself, "No, of course, it couldn't have come in the letter–bag this morning, or master would never have blowed me up for not bringing him the bag, as nobody else got a key to it!"

"How stupid of me, to be sure, how excessively stupid!" exclaimed Sir Cradock, with a sigh; "of course I had the bag, a full hour ago; and there was nothing in it but this paper. Job, I beg your pardon."

"And I hope it's good news you've got there, Sir Cradock, and no cases of starvation; no one found dead in the streets, I hopes, or drownded in the Serpentine. Anyhow, there's a many births, I see, and a deal too many. Children be now such a plenty nobody care about them."

"Job, you quite forget yourself," said his master, very grandly; but there came a long sigh after it, and Job was not daunted easily.

"And, if I do, Sir Cradock Nowell, I'd sooner forget myself than my children."

Sir Cradock was very angry, or was trying to feel that he ought to be so, when a heavy tread, quite unmistakable, and yet not so firm as it used to be, shook the Minton tiles of the passage. That step used to cry to the echoes, "Make way; a man of vigour and force is coming." Now all it said was, "Here I go, and am not in a mood to be meddled with."

"Come in," said Sir Cradock, fidgeting, and pretending to be up for an egg, as Mr. Garnet gave two great thumps on the panel of the door. Small as the room was, Job Hogstaff managed to be too late to let him in.

Bull Garnet first flung his great eyes on the butler; he had no idea of fellows skulking their duty. Old Hogstaff, who looked upon Garnet as no more than an upper servant, gazed back with especial obtuseness, and waved his napkin cleverly.

"Please to put that mat straight again, Mr. Garnet. You kicked it askew, as you came in. And our master can't abide things set crooked."

To Job's disappointment and wonder, Bull Garnet stepped back very quietly, stooped down, and replaced the sheepskin.

"Hogstaff, leave the room this moment," shouted Sir Cradock, wrathfully; and Job hobbled away to brag how he had pulled Muster Garnet down a peg.

"Now, Garnet, take my easy–chair. Will you have a cup of coffee after your early walk?"

"No, thank you. I have breakfasted three hours and a half ago. In our position of life, we must be up early, Sir Cradock Nowell."

There was something in the tone of that last remark, common–place as it was, without the key to it, which the hearer disliked particularly.

"I have requested the favour of your attendance here, Mr. Garnet, that I might have the benefit of your opinion upon a subject which causes me the very deepest anxiety—at least, I mean, which interests me deeply."

"Ah!" exclaimed Mr. Garnet: he could say "ah!" in such a manner that it held three volumes uncut.

"Yes. I wish to ask your opinion about my poor son, Cradock."

Bull Garnet said not a word, but conveyed to the ceiling his astonishment that the housemaid had left such cobwebs there.

"I fear, Garnet, you cannot sympathize with me. You are so especially fortunate in your own domestic circumstances."

"Oh," said Mr. Garnet, still contemplating the cornice. "*Oh exclamantis est*," beautifully observes the Eton grammar.

"Yes, your son is a perfect pattern. So gentle and gentlemanly; so amiable and poetical. I had no idea he was so brave. Shall I ever see him to thank him for saving the life of my niece?"

"He is a fine fellow, a noble fellow, Sir Cradock. The dearest and the best boy in the whole wide world."

The old man long had known that the flaw in Bull Garnet's armour was the thought of his dear boy, Bob.

"And can you not fancy, Garnet, that my son, whatever he is, may also be dear to me?"

"I should have said so, I must have thought so, but for the way you have treated him."

Bull Garnet knew well enough that he was a hot and hasty man; but he seldom had felt that truth more sharply than now, when he saw the result of his words. Nevertheless, he faltered not. He had made up his mind to deliver its thoughts, and he was not the man to care for faces.

"Sir Cradock Nowell, I am a violent, hot, and passionate man. I have done many things in my fury which I would give my life to undo; but I would rather have them all on my soul than such cold-blooded, calm, unnatural cruelty as you have shown to your only—I mean to your own—son. I suppose you never cared for him; *suppose!* I mean of course you did not."

He looked at Sir Cradock Nowell, with thunder and hail in his eyes. The old man could not glance it back; neither did he seem to be greatly indignant at it.

"Then—then—I suppose you don't think—you don't believe, I mean, Garnet—that he did it *on purpose* ?"

Mr. Garnet turned pale as a winding–sheet, and could not speak for a moment. Then he looked away from Sir Cradock's eyes, and asked, "Is it possible that *you* have ever thought so?"

"I have tried not," answered Sir Cradock, with his wasted bosom heaving. "God knows that I have struggled against it. Garnet, have pity upon me. If you have any of our blood in you, tell me the truth, what you think."

"I not only think, but know, that the devil only could have suggested such an idea to you. Man, for the sake of the God that made you, and made me as well as your brother, and every one of us brethren, rather put a pistol to your heart than that damned idea. In cold blood! in cold blood! And for the sake of gain! A brother to—do away with—a brother so! Oh, what things have come upon me! Where is my God, and where is yours?"

"I am sure I don't know," replied the old man, gazing round in wonderment, as if he expected to see Him—for the scene had quite unnerved him—"I suppose He is—is somewhere in the usual place, Mr. Garnet."

"Then that's not in this neighbourhood," replied Bull Garnet, heavily; "He is gone from me, from all of us. And His curse is on my children. Poor innocents, poor helpless lambs! The curse of God is on them."

He went away to the window; and, through his tears, and among the trees, tried to find his cottage–roof.

Sir Cradock Nowell was lost to thought, and heard nothing of those woeful words, although from the depth of that labouring chest they came like the distant sea–roar.

Bull Garnet returned with his fierce eyes softened to a woman's fondness, and saw, with pity as well as joy, that his last words had not been heeded. "Ever hot and ever hasty, until it comes to my own death," he muttered, still in recklessness; "perhaps then I shall be tardy. For my son's sake, for my Bob and Pearl, I must not make such a child of myself. Nevertheless, I cannot stay here."

"Garnet," said Sir Cradock Nowell, slowly recovering from his stupor, a slight cerebral paralysis, "say nothing of what has passed between us—nothing, I entreat you; and not another word to me now. I only understand that you assert emphatically my son Cradock's innocence."

"With every fibre of my heart. With every tissue of my brain."

"Then I love you very much for it; although you have done it so rudely."

"Don't say that. Never say it again. I can't bear it now, Sir Cradock."

"Very well, then, I won't, Garnet. Though I think you might be proud of my gratitude; for I never bestow it rashly."

"I am very thankful to you. Gratitude is an admirable and exceedingly scarce thing. I am come to give you notice—as well as to answer your summons—notice of my intention to quit your service shortly."

"Nonsense!" replied Sir Cradock, gasping; "nonsense, Garnet! You never mean that—that even you would desert me?"

Bull Garnet was touched by the old man's tone—the helplessness, the misery. "Well," he answered, "I'll try to bear with it for a little longer, in spite of the daily agony. I owe you everything; all I can do. I'll get things all into first–rate order, and then I hope, most truly, your son will be back again, sir."

"It isn't only the stewardship, Garnet; it isn't only that. You are now as one of the family, and there are so few of us left. Your daughter Pearl; I begin to love her as of my own flesh and blood. Who knows but what, if my Cradock comes back, he may take a liking to her? Amy Rosedew has not behaved well lately, any more than her father has."

"Do you mean to say that you, Sir Cradock, with all your prejudices of birth, legitimacy, and station, would ever sanction—supposing it possible—any affection of a child of yours for a child of mine?"

"To be sure—if it were a true one. A short time ago I thought very differently. But oh! what does it matter? I am not what I was, Garnet."

"Neither am I," thought Mr. Garnet; "but I might have been, if only I could ever have dreamed this. God has left me, for ever left me."

"Why don't you answer me, Garnet? Why do you shut your Pearl up so? Let her come to me soon; she would do me good; and I, as you know have a young lady coming, who knows little of English society. Pearl would do her a great deal of good. Pearl is a thorough specimen of a well–bred English maiden. I think I like her better than Amy—since Amy has been so cold to me."

To Sir Cradock's intense astonishment, Bull Garnet, instead of replying rushed straight away out of the room, and, not content with that, he rushed out of the house as well, and strode fiercely away to the nearest trees, and was lost to sight among them.

"Well," said the old man, "he always was the oddest fellow I ever did know; and I suppose he always will be. And yet what a man for business!"

That same forenoon, Mrs. Brown's boy and donkey came with a very long message from a lady who had tucked him on the head because he could not make out her meaning. He believed her name was Mrs. Jogging, and he was to say that Miss Oh Ah was fit to come home to–day, please, if they'd please to send the shay for her. And they must please to get ready Satan's room, where the daffodil curtains was, because the young woman loved to look at the yeast, and to have a good fire burning. And please they must send the eel–skin cloak, and the foot–tub in the shay, because the young woman was silly.

"Chilly, you stupid," replied Mrs. Toaster. "She shall have the foot–warmer and the seal–skin cloak; but what Satan's room with the daffodil curtains is, only the Lord in heaven knows; and how she is to see any yeast there! Are you certain that was the message?"

"Sartin, ma'am. I said it to myself ever so many times; more often than I stuck the Neddy."

Sir Cradock Nowell, upon appeal, speedily decided that the satin room was meant—the room with the rose–coloured curtains, and the windows facing the east; but the boy stuck out for the daffodil; leastways he was certain it was *some* flower.

It was nearly dark when the carriage returned; and Sir Cradock came down to the great entrance–hall to meet his brother's child. He was trembling with anxiety; for his nerves were rapidly failing him; and, from Dr. Hutton's account, he feared to see in his probable heiress—for now he had no heir—something very outlandish and savage. Therefore he was surprised and delighted when a graceful and beautiful girl, with high birth and elegance in every movement, flung off her cloak, and skipped up to him with the lightness of a gazelle, and threw her arms round his neck, and kissed him.

"Oh, uncle, I shall love you so! You are so like my darling—you have got his nose exactly, and just the same shaped legs. Oh, to think he should ever have left me!" And she burst into tears then and there before half a dozen servants. "Oh, Uncle Cradock, you have got a fine house; but I never shall get over it."

"Hush, my dear; come with me, my child!" Sir Cradock was always wide awake upon the subject of proprieties.

"I am not your child; and I won't be your child, if you try to stop me like that. I must cry when I want to cry, and it is so stupid to stop me."

"What a pretty dear you are!" said Sir Cradock, scarcely knowing what to say, but having trust in feminine vanity.

"Am I indeed? I don't think so at all. I was very pretty, I know, until I began to cry so. But now my cheeks are come out, and my eyes gone in; but, oh dear! what does it matter, and my father never, never to take me on his lap again? Hya! Hya! Hya!"

"Faix, thin, me darlin'," cried Mrs. O'Gaghan, stroking her down in a shampoo manner, "it's meself as knows how to dale with you. Lave her to me; Sir Crayduck; she's pure and parfict, every bit on her. I knows how to bring her out, and she'll come to your room like a lamb, now jist.—Git out of the way, the lot on you"—to several officious maidens—"me honey, put your hand in my neck, your blissed leetle dove of a hand, and fale how me heart goes pat for you. Sir Crayduck, me duty to you, but you might 'ave knowed how to git out of the way, and lave the ladies to the ladies."

Sir Cradock Nowell marched away, thinking what a blessing it was that he had not had much to do with women. Then he reproached himself for the thought, as he remembered his darling Violet, the mother of his children. But, before he had brooded very long in the only room he liked to use now, his study just off from the library, a gentle knock came *to* the door—as Biddy always expressed it—and Eoa, dressed in deepest mourning (made at Lymington, from her own frock, while she lay ill at the Crown), came up to him steadily, and kissed him, and sat on a stool at his feet.

"Oh, uncle, I am so sorry," she said, with her glorious hair falling over his knees, and her deep eyes looking up at him, "I am so sorry, Uncle Cradock, that I vexed you so, just now."

"You did not vex me, my pretty. I was only vexed for you. Now, remember one thing, my darling—for I shall love you as my own daughter—I have been very harsh and stern where, perhaps, I had no right to be so: if I am ever unkind to you, my dear, if I ever say anything hard, only say 'Clayton Nowell' to me, and I will forgive you directly."

"You mean I must forgive *you*, uncle. I suppose that's what you mean. If you are unkind to me, what will you want to forgive me for? But I couldn't do it. I couldn't say it, even if I had done any harm. Please to remember that I either love or I hate people. I know that I shall love you. But you must not contradict me. I never could endure it, and I never will."

"Well," said Sir Cradock, laughing; "I will try to remember that, my dear. Though, in that respect, you differ but little from our English young ladies."

"If you please, Uncle Cradock, I must go to–night to see where you have put my father. There, I won't cry any more, because he told me never to vex you, and I see that my crying vexes you. Did you cry, yourself, Uncle Cradock, when you heard of it first?"

She looked at him, as she asked this question, with such wild intensity, as if her entire opinion of him would hang upon his reply, that the old man felt himself almost compelled to tell "a corker."

"Well, my dear, I am not ashamed to confess— —"

"Ashamed to confess, indeed! I should rather hope not. But you ought to be ashamed, I know, if you hadn't cried, Uncle Crad. But now I shall love you very much, now I know you did cry. And how much have you got a year, Uncle Crad?"

"How much what, my dear? What beautiful eyes you have, Eoa; finer than any of the Nowells!"

"Yes, I know. But that won't do, Uncle Crad; you don't want to answer my question. What I want to know is a very simple thing. How much money have you got a year? You must have got a good deal. I know, because everybody says so, and because this is such a great place, as big as the palaces in Calcutta."

"Really, Eoa, it is not usual for young people, especially young ladies, to ask such very point–blank questions."

"Oh, I did not know that, and I can't see any harm in it. I know the English girls at Calcutta used to think of nothing else. But I am not a bit like them; it isn't that I care for the money a quarter so much as tamarinds; but I have a particular reason; and I'll find out in spite of you. Just you see if I don't, now."

"A very particular reason, Eoa, for inquiring into my income! Why, what reason can you have?"

"Is it usual for old people, especially old gentlemen, to ask such very point–blank questions?"

Sir Cradock would have been very angry with any other person in the world for such a piece of impertinence; but Eoa gave such a smile of triumph at having caught him in his own net (as she thought), and looked so exquisite in her beauty, as she rose, and the firelight flashed on her; then she tossed her black hair over her shoulders, and gave him such a kiss (with all the spices of India in it) that the old man was at her mercy quite, and she could do exactly what she liked with him.

Oh, Mrs. Nowell Corklemore—so proud of having obtained at last an invitation to Nowelhurst, so confident that, once let in, you can wedge out all before you, like Alexander's phalanx—call a halt, and shape your wiles, and look to belt and buckler, have every lance fresh set and burnished, every sword like a razor; for verily the fight is hard, when art does battle with nature.

CHAPTER XII

Previous to the matters chronicled in the preceding chapter, Mr. Garnet had received a note, of which the following is a copy:—

> "Sir,—My friend, Major Blazeater, late of the Hon. East India Company's 59th Regiment of Native Infantry, has kindly consented to see you, on my behalf, to request a reference to any gentleman whom you may be pleased to name, for the purpose of concerting measures for affording me that satisfaction which, as a man and a gentleman, I am entitled to expect for your cowardly and most ruffianly violence on the 28th ultimo.

"I beg you to accept my sincere apologies for the delay which has occurred, and my assurance that it has been the result of circumstances entirely beyond my own control.

"I have the honour to be, Sir,

"Your most obedient Servant,

"Rufus Hutton.

"Geopharmacy Lodge, Nov. 1st, 1859."

The circumstances beyond the fiery little doctor's control were that he could not find any one who would undertake to carry his message.

When Bull Garnet read this letter—handed to him, with three great bows of the Chinese pattern, by the pompous Major Blazeater—his face flushed to a deep amethyst tinge, which subsided to the colour of cork. Then he rolled his great eyes, and placed one strong finger across the deep channels of his forehead, and said, "Let me think, sir!"

"Hurrah," said the Major to himself, "now we shall have something to redeem the honour of the age. It is a disgrace for a fellow to live in a country where he can never get satisfaction, although he gets plenty of insult."

"Major Blazeater, you will make allowances for me," resumed Mr. Garnet; "but I have never had much opportunity of becoming acquainted with the laws—the code, perhaps, I should say—which govern the honourable practice of duelling at the present day."

"No matter, my dear sir; no matter at all, I assure you. Your second, when I have the honour of meeting him, will settle all those little points, which are beside the general issue; we shall settle them together, sir, with the strictest regard to punctilio, and to your entire satisfaction."

"Capital fellow!" pursued the Major, in his own reflection–room; "knew he couldn't be a coward: just look at his forehead. No doubt he was perfectly justified in kicking out Rue Hutton; Rue is such an impudent beggar. Ah! referring to his pocket–book to find his military friend's address; now we shall do it in style. Glorious fellow this Garnet—shall have the very best powder. Wish I was on his side." And the Major rubbed his long brown hands upon his lanky knees.

"Will it be according to rule," asked Mr. Garnet, looking steadily ("What an eye for a pistol!" said the Major to himself), "quite according to rule and order, if I write down for you, Major Blazeater, the name of the friend to whom I refer; also the time and place at which he will be ready to discuss this little matter with you?"

"To be sure, to be sure, my dear sir; nothing could be better. Your conduct, Mr. Garnet, does you the very highest honour."

"Nothing, you think, can be objected to my course in this?—nothing against the high chivalric code of modern duelling?"

"No, my dear sir, nothing at all. Please to hand me the assignation; ha, ha, it is so pleasant—I mean the rendezvous."

Mr. Garnet handed to him a card, whereon was written: "Town Hall, Lymington, Wednesday, November 2nd. Before Admiral Reale, Col. Fale, and C. Durant, Esq. Application will be made at 12 o'clock for a warrant against Rufus Hutton and Major Blazeater—Christian name unknown—for conspiring together to procure one Bull Garnet to fight a duel, against the peace of Her Majesty, and the spirit of the age."

Major Blazeater fell back in his chair; and all his blood ran to his head. As he told his daughter afterwards, he had never had such a turn in his life. The fairest prospect blasted, the sunrise of murder quenched; what good was it to live in a world where people won't shoot one another? Bull Garnet bent his large eyes upon him, and the Major could not answer them.

"Now, Major Blazeater," said Mr. Garnet, "I shall bind you over to keep the peace, and your principal as well, and expose you to the ridicule of every sensible man in England, unless I receive by to morrow morning's post at 10.15 A.M. an apology for this piece of infantile bravado. What a man does in hot passion, God knows, and God will forgive him for, if he truly strive to amend it—at least—at least, I hope so."

Here Mr. Garnet turned away, and looked out of the window, and perhaps it was the view of Bob that made his eyes so glistening.

"But, sir," he resumed—while the Major was wondering where on earth he should find any sureties for keeping Her Majesty's peace, which he could not keep with his wife—"sir, I look at things of this sort from a point of view diametrically opposed to yours. Perhaps you have the breadth to admit that my view *may* be right, and yours *may* be wrong."

"Nothing, nothing at all, sir, will I admit to a man who actually appoints the magistrates the custodians of his honour."

"Honour, sir, as we now regard it, is nothing more than fool's varnish. Justice, sir, and truth are things we can feel and decide about. Honour is the feminine of them, and, therefore, apt to confuse a man. Major Blazeater, the only honour I have is to wish you good morning."

"Hang it all," said the Major to himself, as he was shown out honourably, "I have put my foot in it this time; and won't Mrs. Blazeater give it to me! That woman finds out everything. This is now the third time I've tried to get up a snug little meeting, and the fates are all against me. Dash it, now, if I've got to pay costs, O Boadicea Blazeater, you won't mend my gloves for a fortnight."

Major Blazeater wore very tight doeskin gloves, and was always wearing them out. Hence, his appeal to the female Penates took this constricted form. The household god of the Phœnicians, and the one whose image they affixed to the bows of their galleys, hoping to steer homewards, was (as we know from many sources) nothing but a lamb; a very rude figure, certainly,—square, thick–set, inelegant; but I doubt not that some grand home–truth clung to their Agna Dea. Major Blazeater was a lamb, whose wits only went to the shearing the moment you got him upon his own hearth, and Boadicea bleated at him. He would crumple his neck up, and draw back his head, and look pleadingly at any one, as a house–lamb does on Good Friday, and feel that his father had done it before him, and he, too, must suffer for sheepishness.

Meditating sadly thus, he heard a great voice coming after him down the gravel–walk, and, turning round, was once more under Mr. Garnet's eyes. "One more word with you, if you please, sir. It will be necessary that you two warlike gentlemen should appoint a legal second. Mine will be Mr. Brockwood, who will be prepared to show that your principal was grossly inquisitive and impertinent, before I removed him from my premises."

"Oh!" cried the Major, delighted to find any loophole for escape, "that puts a new aspect upon the matter, if he gave you provocation, sir."

"He gave me as strong provocation as one man can well give another, by prying into my—domestic affairs, in the presence of my son and daughter, and even tampering with my servants. He left me no other course, except to remove him from my house."

"Which you did rather summarily. My dear sir, I should have done the same. Had I been aware of these facts, I would have declined to bear his cartel. You shall receive my apology by to-morrow morning's post. I trust this unwise proceeding—may—may not proceed any further. Your behaviour, sir, does you credit, and requires no vindication at law."

Thus spoke Major Blazeater, bowing and smiling elaborately under a combination of terrors—the law, public ridicule, expenses; worst of all, Mrs. Blazeater. The next morning, Mr. Garnet received from him a letter, not only apologetic, but highly eulogistic, at which Bull Garnet smiled grimly, as he tossed it into the fire. By the same post came a letter from Rufus, to the following effect:—

> "Sir,—I regret to find that your courage consists in mere brute force and power. I regard you as no longer worthy of the notice of a gentleman. The cowardly advantage you took of your superior animal strength, and your still more cowardly refusal to redress the brutal outrage, as is the manner of gentlemen, stamp you as no more than a navvy, of low mechanical brutishness. Do not think that, because I cannot meet you physically, and you will not meet me fairly, you are beyond my reach. I will have you yet, Bull Garnet; and I know how to do it. Your last ferocious outrage has set me thinking, and I see things which I must have been blind not to see before. I shall see you, some day, in the felon's dock, an object of scorn to the lowest of the low, so sure as my name is
>
> "Rufus Hutton.
>
> "P.S.—I shall be at Lymington to-morrow, ready to meet you, if you dare initiate the inquiry."

Mr. Garnet did not burn this letter, but twice read it through very carefully, and then stowed it away securely. Who could tell but it might be useful as a proof of animus? During these several operations his eyes had not much of triumph in them.

Rufus Hutton rode to Lymington, carrying a life-preserver: he appeared in the Town Hall, at the petty sessions; but there was no charge made against him. Being a pugnacious little fellow, and no lover of a peaceful issue, he had a great mind then to apply for a warrant against Garnet for assaulting him. But he felt that he had given some provocation, and could not at present justify it; and he had in the background larger measures, which might be foiled by precipitancy. So that lively broil, being unfought out and unforgiven—at least on one side—passed into as rank a feud as ever the sun went down upon. Not that Mr. Garnet felt much bitterness about it; only he knew that he must guard against a powerful enemy.

Amy had told her father, long ago, what Cradock had said to her in the churchyard, and how she had replied to him. In fact, she could not keep it to herself until she went to bed that night; but mingled her bright, flowing hair with his grey locks, while her heart was still pit–a–patting, and leaned on his shoulder for comfort, and didn't cry much before she got it. "My own dearest, life of my life," cried John, forgetting both Greek and Latin, but remembering how he loved her mother, "my own and only child—now you do look so like your mother, darling—may the God who has made you my blessing bless your dear heart in this!"

The very next day John Rosedew fell into a pit of meditation. He forgot all about Pelethronian Lapiths, the trimming of Gruter's lamp (which had long engaged him; for he knew the flame of learning there unsnuffed by any Smelfungus): even the Sabellian elements were but as *sabellicus sus* to him. It was one of his peculiarities, that he never became so deeply abstracted as when he had to take in hand any practical question. He could take in hand any glorious thesis, such as the traces still existing of a middle voice in Latin, or the indications of very early civilization in Eubœa, and the question whether the Ionians came not mainly westward—any of these things he could think of, dwell upon, and eat his dinner without knowing salt from mustard. But he could not make a treatise of Amy, nor could he get at her etymology. He began to think that his education had been neglected in some points. And then he thought about Socrates, and his symposiastic drolleries, and most philosophic reply when impeached of Xanthippic weakness.

Nevertheless, he could not make up his mind upon one point—whether or not it was his duty to go and inform Sir Cradock Nowell of his son's attachment. If the ancient friend had been as of old, or had only changed towards John Rosedew, continuing true all the while to the son, the parson would have felt no doubt as to how his duty lay. And the more straightforward and honest course was ever the first to open upon him. But, when he remembered how sadly bitter the father already was to the son, how he had even dared in his wrath to charge him with wilful fratricide, how he had wandered far and wide from the sanity of affection, and was, indeed, no longer worthy to be called a father, John Rosedew felt himself absolved from all parental communion.

Then how was it as to expediency? Why, just at present, this knowledge would be the very thing to set Sir Cradock yet more against the outcast. For, in the days of old confidence and friendly interfusion, he had often expressed to John his hope that Clayton might love Amy; and now he would at once conclude that Cradock had been throughout the rival of his darling, and perhaps an unsuccessful one, till the other was got rid of. Therefore John Rosedew resolved, at last, to hold his peace in the matter; to which conclusion Aunt Doxy's advice and Amy's entreaties contributed. But these two ladies, although unanimous in their rapid conclusion, based it upon premises as different as could be.

"Inform him, indeed!" cried Miss Eudoxia, swelling grandly, and twitching her shawl upon the slope of her shoulders, of which, by–the–by, she was very proud—she had heard it showed high breeding—"inform him, brother John; as if his son had disgraced him by meditating an alliance with the great–granddaughter of the Earl of Driddledrum and Dromore! Upon such occasions, as I have always understood, though perhaps I know nothing about it, and you understand it better, John, it is the gentleman's place to secure the acquiescence of his family. Acquiescence, indeed! What has our family ever thought of a baronetcy? There is better blood in Amy Rosedew, Brian O'Lynn, and Cadwallader, than any Cradock Nowell ever had, or ever will have, unless it is her son. Inform him, indeed! as if our Amy was nobody!"

"Pa, don't speak of it," said Amy, "until dear Cradock wishes it. We have no right to add to his dreadfully bad luck; and he is the proper judge. He is sure to do what is right. And, after all that he has been through, oh, don't treat him like a baby, father."

CHAPTER XIII

Mrs. Nowell Corklemore by this time was well established at the Hall, and did not mean in her kind rich heart to quit the place prematurely. Almost every day, however, she made some feint of departure, which rendered every one more alive to the value of her presence.

"How could her dear Nowell exist without her? She felt quite sure he would come that day—yes, that very day—to fetch her, in their little simple carriage, that did shake her poor back so dreadfully"—back thrown into prominence here, being an uncommonly pretty one—"but oh, how thankful she ought to be for having a carriage at all, and so many poor things—quite as good, quite as refined, and delicate—could scarcely afford a perambulator! But she hoped for dear Sir Cradock's sake, and that sweet simple–minded Eoa—who really did require some little cultivation—that, now she understood them both, and could do her little of ministering, Mr. Corklemore would let her stay, if it were only two days longer. And then her Flore, her sweet little Flore! An angel of light among them."

Georgie had been married twice; and she was just the sort of woman who would have been married a dozen times, if a dozen, save one, of husbands were so unfortunate as to leave her. Her first lord, or rather vassal, had been the Count de Vance—"a beggarly upstart Frenchman," in the language of his successor, who, by–the–by, had never seen, but heard of him too often; but, according to better authority, "a man one could truly look up to; so warm–hearted, so agreeable; and never for a moment tired, dear, of his poor little simple wife."

Perhaps it is needless to state that Mr. Corklemore long had been so scientifically henpecked that he loved the operation. Only he was half afraid to say "Haw," when his wife was there to cry "Pshaw."

Sir Cradock Nowell, of course, had seen a good deal of what is called the world; but his knowledge of women was only enough to teach him the extent of that subject. He never was surprised much at anything they did; but he could not pretend to tell the reason of their doing it, even when they had any, of which he did not often suspect them. He believed that they would have their way, whenever they could, wherever, and by whatever means; that very few of them meant what they said, and none of them knew what they meant; that the primal elements, in the entire body feminine, were jealousy, impulsiveness, vanity, and contrariety.

Georgie Corklemore soon found out that he had adopted this, the popular male opinion; and she did not once attempt to remove it, knowing, as she did, that nothing could be more favourable to her purposes. So she took up the part—which suited her as well as any, and enabled her to say many things which else would have given offence—the part of the soft, impulsive, warm–hearted, foolish woman, who is apt among men to become a great pet, if she happens to be good–looking.

Eoa would gladly have yielded her prerogatives to Georgie, but Mrs. Corklemore was too wide awake to accept any one of them. "No, darling," she replied, "for your own sake I will not. It is true that Uncle Cradock wishes it, and so, no doubt, do you; but you are bound to acquire all this social knowledge of which you have now so little; and how can you do so except by instruction and practice?"

"Oh," cried Eoa, firing up, "if Uncle Cradock wishes it, I am sure I'll leave it to you, and not be laughed at any longer. I'll go to him at once, and tell him so. And, as for being bound, I *won't* be bound to learn any nonsense I don't like. My papa was as wise as any of you, and a great deal better; and he never made such a fuss about rubbish as you do here."

"Stop, sweet child, stop a moment——"

"I am not a sweet child, and I won't stop. And another thing I'll tell you. I had made up my mind to it before this, mind—before you tried to turn me out of my place—and it's this. You may call me what you like, but I don't mean to call you 'Cousin Georgie' any longer. In the first place, I don't like you, and never shall as long as I live; for I never half believe you: and, in the next place, you are no cousin of mine; and social usage (or whatever it is you are always bothering me about) may require me to tell some stories, but not that one, I should fancy. Or, at any rate, I won't do it."

"Very well," replied Mrs. Corklemore, looking up from the softest of fancy–work, with the very sweetest of smiles; "then I shall be obliged, in self–defence, to address you as 'Miss Nowell.'"

"To be sure. Why shouldn't you?"

"Well, it can be shown, perhaps, that you are entitled to the name. Only at first it will seem absurd when applied to a baby like you."

"A baby like me, indeed!" This was Eoa's sore point; and Georgie, who delighted in making her outrageous, was always harping upon it. "Mrs. Corklemore, how dare you call me, at my age, a baby?"

Eoa looked down at Georgie, with great eyes flashing fire, and her clear, bright forehead wrinkling, and her light form poised like an antelope's on the edge of a cliff. Mrs. Corklemore, not thinking it worth while to look up at her, carelessly threw back a curl, and went on with her rug–work.

"Because you are a baby, and nothing more, Eoa."

In a moment she was tossed through the air, and sitting on Eoa's head, low satin chair and all. She had not time to shriek, so rapid was her elation. Little Flore, running in at the moment, clapped her hands and shouted, "Oh, ma, have a yide, a nice yide, same as me have yesterday. Me next, me next. Oh, ah!"

Eoa, with the greatest ease, her figure as straight as a poplar–tree, bore the curule chair and its occupant to the end of the room, and there deposited them carefully on a semi–grand piano.

"That's how we nurse the babies in India," she cried, with a smile of sweet temper, "but it takes a big baby to do it, and some practice, I can tell you. Now, I'll not let you down, Mrs. Corklemore,—and if visitors come in, what will they think of our social usages? Down you don't come, till you have promised solemnly never to call me a baby again."

"My dear," began Georgie, trying hard not to look ridiculous—though the position was so unfavourable—"my dear child——"

"No, not my dear child, even! *Miss Nowell,* if you please, and nothing else."

"Miss Nowell, if you will only lift me down—oh, it is polished so nastily, I am slipping off already—I will promise solemnly to call you only what you like, all the rest of my life."

Eoa lifted her off in an instant. "But mind, I will be even with you," cried Georgie, through her terror, when safe on the floor once more.

"I don't care *that* for you," answered Eoa, snapping her fingers like a copper–cap; "only I will have proper respect shown to me by people I particularly dislike. People I love may call me what, or do with me what, they please. My father was just the same; and I don't want to be any better than he was; and I don't believe God wants it."

"He must be easily contented, then."

Georgie, with all her deliciousness, could never pass a chance of sarcasm.

"Now I'll go and have it out with Uncle Cradock, about having you for my ayah."

Mrs. Corklemore trembled far more at those words than at finding herself on the piano. This strange girl—whom she had so despised—was baffling all her tactics, and with no other sword and shield but those of truth and candour.

"I've been a fool," said Georgie to herself, for about the first time in her life; "I have strangely underrated this girl, and shall have hard work now to get round her. But it must be done. Come, though I have been so rash, I have two to one in my favour, now I see the way to handle it. But she must not tell the old noodle; that will never do."

"I thought, Miss Nowell," she continued aloud, "that it would not be considered honourable, even among East Indians, to repeat to a third person what was said familiarly and in confidence."

"Of course not. What makes you speak of it? Do you mean to say I would do such a thing?"

"No, I am sure you would not, knowingly. But if you think for a moment, you will see that what I said just now, especially as to Sir Cradock's opinions, was told to you in pure confidence, and meant to go no further."

"Oh," answered Eoa, "then please not to tell me anything in pure confidence again, because I can't keep secrets, and you have no right to load me with them, without ever asking my leave even. But I'll try not to let it out, unless you provoke me before him."

With this half promise Georgie was obliged to be content. She knew well enough that, if Eoa brought the question before her uncle, the truth would come out that Sir Cradock had never dreamed for a moment of substituting Georgie, the daughter of his cousin, for Eoa, the only daughter of his only brother Clayton. He knew, of course, that the Eastern maiden had no artificial polish; but he saw that she had an inborn truth, a delicacy of feeling, and a native sympathy, which wanted only experience to be better than any polish.

From that day forth, Mrs. Corklemore (aided perhaps by physical terror) formed a higher estimate of Eoa's powers. So she changed her tactics altogether, and employed her daughter, that sharp little Flore, to cover the next advance. Flore was a little beauty; so far as anything artificial can be really beautiful. Dressed, as she was, in the height of French fashion, and herself nine–tenths of a Frenchwoman—for there is no such thing as a French *girl*, as we Englishmen understand girlhood—she always looked like a butterfly, just born in and just about to pop out of a bower; for little Flore was "divinely beautiful."

This angel was now nearly four years old, and would look at you with the loveliest eyes that ever appealed from the cradle to heaven, and throw her exaggerated little figure back, and tell you the biggest lie that an angel ever wiped her mouth over. Oh, you lovely child! I would rather have Loo Jupp, who knows a number of bad words, which you would faint to hear of. But Loo won't tell a lie. Her father beat her out of it the very first time she tried.

CHAPTER XIV

"Dear Uncle Cradock," said Georgie next day, for she had obtained permission long ago to address her father's cousin so, "what a very sweet girl our Eoa is!"

"I am very glad that you think so, Georgie; she reminds me very often of what my brother was at her age."

"Oh, I do love her so. She has so much variety, and she does seem so straightforward."

"Not only seems but is so, Georgie; at times, indeed, a little too much of it."

"Well, I doubt if there can be too much of it," cried Georgie, in the rapture of her own heart's truth and simplicity, "especially among relations, uncle. Just see now how all the misunderstandings which arose between ourselves, for instance, might have been saved by a little straightforward explanation. In my opinion, our Eoa would be absolutely perfect, if we could only put a little polish, a little finish, upon her. I suppose that was what her poor father intended, in bringing her to England."

"Ah, perhaps it was. I never thought of that. But I have thought, often enough, my dear Georgie, of my own duty towards her; and I wish to consult you about it; you are so discreet and sensible."

"Yes," replied Mrs. Corklemore, with a facetious curtsey, "to be sure I am, a perfect Queen of Sheba."

As this implied, by the manner of it, that Sir Cradock was a perfect Solomon, he accepted the chaff very graciously, and said to himself, "What magnificent eyes my niece Georgie has, and what a sweet complexion, and a most exquisite figure! I wonder what Corklemore is about, in leaving her here so long! But then he has such confidence in her. Women of sense and liveliness, who have an answer for everybody, are so much more trustworthy than the sly things who drop their eyes, and think all sorts of evil."

Meanwhile Georgie saw all this passing through his mind—more clearly, perhaps, than she would have seen it, if it had been passing through her own.

"To be sure. How thoughtful of you! You mean your duty, Uncle Cradock, as to making her your heiress, now?"

Mrs. Corklemore knew well enough that he meant nothing of the sort; but the opportunity for the suggestion was too fine to be lost.

"Oh," said Sir Cradock, with a grim smile, "you consider that my duty, do you? No, it was not on that subject I was anxious for your opinion, but as to sending the child to school, or taking some other means to finish her education."

"She won't go," replied Mrs. Corklemore, seeing some chance of a quarrel here; "of course it would be the best thing for her; but I am quite certain the sweet creature never will go."

"The sweet creature must, if I make her."

"To be sure, Uncle Cradock; but I don't believe you can. Has she not favoured you with her intentions as to settling in life, rather—well, perhaps rather prematurely?"

"Yes," replied the old man, laughing, "she has informed me, with all due ceremony, of her intention to marry Bob Garnet, the moment she is out of mourning for her dearest father."

"Master Garnet has not asked her yet. And I have reason to believe"— — here Georgie softly hesitated.

"What?" asked Sir Cradock, anxiously, for he was very fond of Eoa; she was such a novelty to him.

"That Master Bob Garnet, just come from school, loves Amy Rosedew above Eoa, toffee, rock, or peppermint."

"Amy Rosedew is a minx," answered the old man, hotly. "I offered to shake hands with her, when I met her on Wednesday, and was even going to kiss her, because she is my god–daughter, and—and—an uncommonly pretty girl, you know, and what do you think she said?"

"Oh don't tell me, Uncle Cradock, if it was anything impudent. You know I could not stand it, thinking what I do of those Rosedews."

"She threw herself back with her great eyes flashing, and the colour in her cheeks dark crimson, and she said, 'No, thank you. No contact for me with unnatural injustice!' And she drew her frock around her, and swept away as if the road was not wide enough for both of us. Nice behaviour, was not it? And I fear her father endorses it."

"I know he does," answered Georgie, whose face during that description had been a perfect study of horror contending with humour;

"I know that Mr. Rosedew, one of the best men in the world, if, indeed, he is sincere—which others may doubt, but not I—he, poor man, having little perception, except of his own interest, has taken a most unfavourable view of everything we do here. Oh, I am so sorry. It almost makes one feel as if we must be in the wrong." Beautiful Georgie sighed heavily, like a fair woman at a confessional.

"His own interest, Georgie! Ourselves in the wrong! I don't quite understand you."

"As if we were harsh, you know, Uncle Cradock; when, Heaven be thanked, we have not concluded, as too, too many—— But, not to talk of that absurdity, and not to pain you, darling uncle, you must know what I meant about Mr. Rosedew's interest."

"No, indeed, I don't, Georgie. I don't see how John—I mean Mr. Rosedew's interest is at all involved in the matter."

"He had a daughter passing fair," sang Mrs. Corklemore, without thinking. "Oh, uncle, I forgot; I am so light-headed and foolish, I forget everything now. It is Nowell's fault for worrying me, as he does every week, about income."

She passed her hand across her forehead, and swept the soft dark hair back, as if worldly matters were too many for her poor childish brain. Who could look at her without wishing that she really cared for herself, just a little?

"I insist upon knowing what you mean, Georgie," said Sir Cradock, frowning heavily, for he was not at all sentimental; "John Rosedew's daughter is Amy; and Amy, I know, is perfectly honest, though as obstinate as the dev'—hem, I beg your pardon; I mean that Amy is very obstinate, as well as exceedingly bigoted, and I might almost say insolent."

"Oh no; I can never believe that, Uncle Cradock, even upon your authority." In the heat of truth, Mrs. Corklemore stood up and faced Sir Cradock.

"But I tell you she is, Georgie. Don't try to defend her. No young woman of eighteen ought to have spoken as she did to me when I met her last Wednesday. 'Outrageous' is the mildest word I can use to describe her manner."

"Very likely you thought so, dearest Uncle Cradock; and so very likely I might have thought, or any of the old-school people. But we must make allowances—you know we are bound to do so—for young people brought up to look at things from a different point of view."

"No—by—George I won't. I have heard that stuff too often. Spirit of the age, and all that balderdash. Because a set of young jackanapes are blessed with impudence enough to throw to the dogs all the teachings of ages, just when it doesn't suit them, is it likely that we, who are old enough to see the beauty of what they despise, are to venerate and bow down to infantile inspiration, which itself bows down to nothing? Georgie, you are too soft, too mild. Your forbearance quite provokes me. Leave me, if you please, to form my own opinions, especially about people whom I know so much better than you do."

"I am sure, Uncle Cradock," answered Georgie, pouting, "I never presume in any way to interfere with your opinions. Your judgment is proverbial; whereas I have none whatever. Only it was natural that I should wish you to think well of one who is likely to be so nearly related to you. What! why you look surprised, uncle? Ah, you think me wrong in alluding to it. What a simple silly I am, to be sure! But please not to be angry, uncle. I never dreamed that you wished it kept secret, dear, when all the parish is talking of it."

"Georgie Corklemore, have the goodness to tell me what you mean."

"Oh, don't look at me so, uncle. I never could bear a cross look. I mean no mystery whatever, only Amy Rosedew's engagement to your unlucky—I mean your unhappy son. Of course it has your sanction."

"Amy engaged to my—to that crafty Cradock! I cannot believe it. I will not believe it; and at a time like this!"

"Well, I thought the time ill–chosen. But I am no judge of propriety. And they say that the poor—poor darling who is gone, was himself attached—let us hope that it was not so; however, I cannot believe, Uncle Cradock, that you have not even been told of it."

"But I tell you, Georgie, that it is so. Perhaps you disbelieve me in your anxiety to screen them?"

"You know better than that, dear uncle. I believe *you*, before all the world. And I will screen them no longer, for I think it bad and ungrateful of them. And after all you have done for them! Why, surely, you gave them the living! It makes me feel quite ill. Ingratitude always does." Georgie pressed her hand to her heart, and was obliged to get up and walk about. Presently she came back again, with great tears in her eyes, and her face full of anger and pity.

"Oh, uncle dear, I cannot tell you how grieved I am for your sake. It does seem so hard–hearted of them. How I feel my own helplessness that I cannot comfort you! What a passion my Nowell will be in, when I tell him this! His nature is so warm and generous, so upright and confiding, and he looks up to you with such devotion, and such deep respect. I must not tell him at night, poor fellow, or he would not sleep a wink. And the most contumelious thing of all: that pompous old maid, Miss Eudoxia Rosedew, to be going about and boasting of it—the title and the property—before any one had the manners even to inform so kind a friend, and so affectionate a father! The title and the property! How I hate such worldliness. I never could understand how people could scheme and plot for such things. And to make so little of you, uncle, because they relied upon the entail!"

This was quite a shot in the dark, for she knew not whether any entail subsisted; and, as it was a most essential point to discover this, Georgie fixed her swimming eyes—swimming with love and sympathy—full upon poor Sir Cradock's. He started a little, but she scarcely knew what to augur thence. She must have another shot at it; but not on the present occasion.

It is scarcely needful, perhaps, to say, knowing Mrs. Corklemore and Miss Rosedew as we do, that there was not a syllable of truth in what the former said of the latter. Sir Cradock himself would have doubted it, if he had been any judge of women; for Miss Eudoxia Rosedew thought very little of baronets. How could she help it, she of the illustrious grandmother? Oh her indignation, if she only could have dreamed of being charged with making vaunt over such a title! Neither was it like her, even if she had thought great things of any pledged alliance, to go about and share her sentiments with the "common people." The truth of the matter was this: Georgie, with her natural craft—no, no! skill I mean; how a clumsy pen will stumble—and ten more years of life to drill it, had elicited Amy's sentiments; as one who, having stropped a razor, carves his lady's pincushion, or one who blowing on bright gimlet tempts the spigot of bonded wine, or varlet who with a knowing worm giveth taste of Stilton. Or even,

> "As when a man, a sluice–captain, adown from a backwater headspring, All through his plants and garden a waterflow is pioneering, Holding a shovel in hand, from the carrier casting the sods out; Then as it goes flowing forward, the pebbles below in a bevy Swirl about, and it rapidly wimpling down paterooneth, In a spot where a jump of the ground is, and overgets even the guideman."
>
> *Il.* xxi. 257.

So sweet Amy, being under–drawn of her native crystal by many a sly innuendo and many an Artesian auger, gushed out, like liquid diamonds, upon the skilful Georgie, and piled upon her a flood of truth, a Scamander upon Achilles. Oh water upon a duck's back, because Georgie always swam in truth; please not to say that Castalia, *rore puro*, wets not the kerchief of a lady thrice dipped in Styx.

And so it came to pass that young Amy let out everything, having a natural love of candour and a natural hatred of Georgie, and expecting to overwhelm her with the rolling seventh billow of truth. Mrs. Corklemore, softly smiling, reared her honest head out of the waters, sleeked her soft luxuriant locks, and the only thing likely to overwhelm her was sympathy unfathomable. Amy did not wish for that, and begged her, very dryly, by no means to exhaust herself; for Amy had moral scent of a liar, even as her father had.

Now that father—the finest fellow, take him for all in all, whom one need wish to look upon—was (according to a good man's luck) in fearful tribulation. Fearful, at least, to any man except John Rosedew himself; but John, though fully alive to the stigmotype of his position, allowed his epidermis to quill toward the operator, and abstracted all his too sensitive parts into a Sophistic apory.

John, sitting in his book–room, had got an apron tucked well under his rosy chin—an apron with two pockets in it, and the strings in a bow at the back of his neck; and he trembled for his ear–lobes, whenever he forgot his subject. Around him, with perpetual clatter, snip and snap and stirabout, hovered, like a Jewish maiden fingering the mill–stone, who but his Eudoxia?

In her strong right hand was a pair of shears, keen as those of Atropos, padded at the handles, lest to hurt the thumb, but the blades, the trenchant edges—oh what should keep their bright love asunder? No human ear, for a moment; nay, nor the nose of a mortal. Neither was this risk and tug, and frequent fullers'–teaseling, the whole or even the half of the agony John was undergoing. For though he sat with a pile of books heaped in fair disorder round him—though three were pushing about on his lap, dusting themselves on his well–worn kersey, like sparrows on a genial highway—though one was even perched on his right hand and another on his left, yet he had no more fruition of them (save in the cud of memory) than had Prometheus of his fire–glow in the frost of Strobilus, or than the son of Jove and Pluto, whom Ulysses saw, had of his dessert.

> "Nay, then I looked at Tantalus having a rough tribulation, Standing fast in a lake, and it came quite home to his chin–beard; Nevertheless he stood thirsting, and had not to seize and to quaff it; For every time when the old man would stoop in his longing to quaff it, Then

> every time the water died, swallowed back, and at his ancles Earth shone black in a moment, because a divinity parched it. Trees as well, leafing loftily, over his head poured fruitage, Pear–trees, and pomegranates, and apple–trees glittering–fruited, Fig–trees of the luscious, and olive–trees of the luxuriant; Whereat whenever the old man shot out his hands to grasp them, Away the wind would toss them into the shadowy cloudland."
>
> *Od.* xi. 581.

"Now, John, you are worse than ever, I do declare you are; why, you won't even hold your neck straight. I try to make you look decent: I try so *very hard*, John; and you haven't even the gratitude to keep your chin up from the apron. You had much better go to a barber, and get half your hair pulled out by the roots, and the other half poisoned with a leaden comb, and then you'll appreciate *me*, perhaps."

"We read," said John Rosedew, complacently gazing at his white locks as they tumbled and took little jumps on the apron, "that when the Argives lost Thyrea, they pledged themselves to a law and a solemn imprecation, that none of the men should encourage his hair, and none of the ladies wear gold."

"And pray what gold do *I* wear? Brother John, you are so personal; you never can let me alone. I do believe you have never forgiven me my poor dear grandmother's ring, and watch, and Aunt Diana's brooch and locket; no, nor even my own dear mother's diamond ring with the sapphires round it. And perhaps you don't hate even my bracelet, a mere twist of gold with cat's eyes! Oh, John, John, how can you be my brother, and show such a little mind, John?"

"Whence we may infer," continued John, quite unruffled; for he knew that it would be worse than useless to assure Miss Doxy that he was not even aware of the existence of the things he was impeached with; "or at least we have some grounds for supposing that the Greeks, a very sensitive and highly perceptive race, did not like to have their hair cut. Compare with this another statement——"

"No, indeed I won't, John. I should rather hope I would not. You can't hold your tongue for a moment, however solemn the occasion is. There, that's the third cut you've got, and I won't take another snip at you. But you have quoted less Greek than usual; that's one comfort, at any rate, and I will put you on some gold–beater's skin, for being so very good, John. Only don't tell Amy; she does make such a fuss about it. But there, I need not tell you, for you won't know how you got them in half an hour's time. Now, don't make a fuss, John; one would think you were killed"—poor John had dared to put his hand up—"as if you cared indeed even if you had three great stripes of red all down your collar, or even upon your white neckerchief. You wouldn't be at all ashamed of yourself. Have you the face to say that you would, now?"

"Well, dear Doxy, I am not convinced that you are reasonable in expecting me to be ashamed of bleeding when you have been cutting me."

"Oh, of course not. I never *am* reasonable, according to your ideas. But one thing you may be convinced of, and that is, that I never will toil and degrade myself by cutting your hair again, John, after this outrageous conduct."

John had been visited so often with this tremendous menace, that he received it with no satisfaction. Well he knew that on that day four weeks he must don the blue apron again, unless something happened worse even than Aunt Doxy's tonsorial flourishes.

"Now, you are not done yet, John. You are in a great hurry, are you not, to get the apron off and scatter the hair all about? What's the good of my taking the trouble to spread Jemima's shawl down? Can you imagine you are done, when I haven't rubbed you up with the rosemary even?"

"'Coronari marino rore!' No wonder good Flaccus puts it after 'multâ cæde bidentium.' Oh, Doxy, you are inexorable. O averse Penates! By the way, that stanza is to my mind the most obscure (with one exception) in all the Odes. Either Horace had too much of the 'lene tormentum' applied just then 'ingenio non sæpe duro,' or else——"

"Please, miss"—all the girls called her miss—"Dr. Hutton, miss!"

Bang went Miss Doxy, quicker than thought, left an exclamation, semi–profane, far behind on the light air, slammed the door on the poor girl's chilblains, bolted and locked it, and pulled out the key, and put the scutcheon over the keyhole.

"Well, why, *διὰ τί; πόθεν*; unde terrarum? Women are not allowed to say 'mehercle,' neither men 'mecastor;' 'ædepol' is common to both, but only 'inscitiâ antiquitatis;' for the most ancient men abstained from that even, and I dare say were none the worse for it——"

"I have no patience with you, John," cried Miss Doxy, snatching up brush, comb, scissors, extract of the sea–dew, the blue apron, Jemima's shawl of grey hair, and we know not how many other things, and huddling all into a cupboard, and longing to lock herself in with them.

"Great truths come out," answered John, quite placidly, "at periods of mental commotion. But why, oh Doxy, and whence this inopine hurry–scurry? There is no classic expression—except perhaps in Aristophanes—of prosody quick enough; and, doubtless, for very good reason, because the people were too wise to hurry so. 'Rumpe moras,' for instance, is rather suggestive of— —"

"Oh, John! oh, John! even at such a moment, John! I believe you'll die in Latin or Greek—and I don't know which Amen is, only I don't believe it's English—there, I am as bad as you are to discuss such a question now. And I am quite sure Jenny can't tell a good story soundly. And he has got such ferret eyes! Thank Heaven, the key was inside, John."

Poor Miss Doxy was panting so, that her brother was quite frightened for her; and the more so because he had no idea what there was to be frightened at.

"Why, Doxy," he said, "my darling, he need never see that you have cut me."

"As if I cared for that! Oh, John, my dearest brother, he'll see *that I've cut your hair*!"

The idea struck John Rosedew as so gloriously novel—that man who knew the world so!—to him it appeared such a mountain of wonder that a sister should want to sink through the floor, for having saved her brother from barberism, that he laughed as hard as any man of real humour ever laughs. Miss Doxy stole on the opportunity, when he sat down to have his laugh out, to dust all the white hair with her handkerchief from his coat–collar.

Suddenly John Rosedew got up, and his laugh went away in gravity. He walked to the door more heavily than was natural to him (lest he should seem to go falsely), unlocked and unbolted it, and in his most stately manner marched into the hall. Jenny was telling a "jolly lie"—jollity down below, I suppose—to Mr. Rufus Hutton; she was doing it very clumsily, not "oculo irretorto."

"Please, sir, yes, my master is gone round the parish, sir; and the rest, they be at the school, sir. How sorry they will be, to be sure, to hear that you have called, sir, and all of them out of the way so!"

"No, they won't," said Mr. Rosedew, looking over her head; "the only thing I am sorry for, Jenny, is that you can tell a falsehood so. But the fault is not yours only. I will talk to you by–and–by. Dr. Hutton, come in, if you please. I was having my hair cut by my sister, Miss Rosedew. You have met her before. Eudoxia, Dr. Hutton is kind enough to come and see us. I have told him how good and how sisterly you have been to me, and I am sure that he must wish to have a sister so capable—that is to say if he has not," added John, who was very particular about his modal and temporal prefix.

Miss Rosedew came forward, with a few white hairs still on her dark "reps" bell–sleeve, and, being put upon her mettle, was worthy of her brother. Oh dear, that such a grand expression should be needful, even over the shell of the roasted egg of snobbery! Rufus Hutton, of course, not being quite a fool, respected, and trusted, and loved them both, more than he would have done after fifty formal dinners. And he knew quite well that there was on his own part something akin to intrusion; for he had called in the forenoon, when visits from none but an intimate friend are expected; and he had pushed his advance rather vigorously, not towards the drawing–room, but to John's favourite book–room, where the lady Licinus plied her calling. But for this he had good reason, as he wished to see Mr. Rosedew alone, and the cause of his visit was urgent.

It was not long before the lady, feeling rather unhappy because she was not arrayed much better than the lilies of the field are, withdrew in a very noble manner, earning gratitude of Rufus. Then the doctor drew his chair close home to the parson's, looked all round the room, and coughed to try how big the echo was. Finding no response returned by that prolific goddess, who loves not calf or sheep–skin, and seeing that no other lady was dangerously acoustic, Rufus inclined his little red head towards John's great and black and slightly liparous waistcoat, and spake these winged words:

"Ever see a thing like that, sir?"

"No, I don't think I ever did. Dear me, how odd it smells! Why, how grave you are, Dr. Hutton!"

"So will you be, when I have told you what I have to tell. My discovery is for your ears only; I have been to London about it, and there found out its meaning. Now I will act upon your advice. Nothing in all my experience—though I have seen a great deal of the world—nothing has ever surprised me more than what I have told you."

"But you forget, Dr. Hutton," cried John, imbibing excitement, "that as yet you have told me nothing at all, only shown me something which I cannot in the least make out. A cylinder, hollow, and blocked at one end; of a substance resembling book–binding, and of a most unsavoury odour!"

"Ha!" replied Rue Hutton, "ha, my dear sir, you little guess the importance of that thing no bigger than a good cigar. Ah, indeed! Ah, yes!"

"Do you mean to tell me, or not, Dr. Hutton? Your behaviour is most unusual. I am greatly surprised by your manner."

"Ah, no doubt; no doubt of that. Very odd if you were not. I also am astonished at your apparent indifference."

Hereupon Rufus looked so intensely knowing, so loaded with marvel and mystery, too big to be discharged even, that John Rosedew himself, so calm and large, and worthy to be called a philosopher, very nearly grew wroth with longing to know what all the matter was.

Then Dr. Hutton, having bound him by a solemn promise that he would not for the present even hint of that matter to any one, poured out the hissing contents of his mind under the white curls which still overhung the elder man's porch of memory. And what he told him was indeed a thing not to be forgotten.

The spectator is said to see more of the game than any of the players see, and the reader of a story knows a great deal more than the actors do, or the writer either, for that matter; marry, therefore, I will not insult any candid intelligence, neither betray Rue Hutton's faith, for he is an awkward enemy.

The very next day there came a letter, with coal enough on it to make some gas, and directed in a wandering manner to "Rev. Mr. Rosedew, Nowelhouse, somewhere in England." Much as we abuse the Post–office people, they generally manage to find us out more cleverly than we do them; and so this letter had not been to more than six wrong places. As our good journalists love to say, "it was couched in the following terms:"—

> "Honoured and Reverend Sir,—Takes the liberty of stating price of inland coals, as per margin, delivered free within six miles of Charing–cross. N.B. Weighed as the Act directs, whether required or otherwise, which mostly is not, and the dust come back if required. Excuse me the liberty of adding that a nice young gent and uncommon respectable, only not a good business address—no blame to him, being a Oxford gent—lie here very ill, and not much expect to get over to–morrow night. Our junior, Mr. Clinkers, with full commission to take all orders and sign receipts for the firm, have been up with him all night, and hear him talk quite agreeable about some place or business called Amery, supposed in the hardware line by mistake for emery. This young gent were called Mr. Newman, by the name of Charles Newman, but Mrs.

Ducksacre half believe clandastical and temporal only, and no doubt good reason for it, because he always pay his lodging. Rev. sir, found your direction as per endorsement very simple in the inside pocket of the young gent's coat, and he only have one to look in. But for fear to be misunderstood this firm think none the less of him by the same reason, having been both of us in trouble when we was married. Also as per left–hand cover a foreign–looking play–book, something queer and then 'Opera,' which the undersigned understand at once, having been to that same theayter when our gracious Queen was married, and not yet gone into the coal–trade. Requests to excuse the liberty, but if endorsed correctly and agreeable to see the young gent's funeral performed most reasonably, at sole expense of this firm, and no claim made on any survivors because Robert Clinkers like him, must come by express day after to–morrow at latest.

"Signed for the firm of Poker and Clinkers, West London Depôt, Hammersmith. Weighed as the Act directs. Per Robert Clinkers, jun.

"At Mrs. and Miss Ducksacre's, greengrocer and general fruiterer, Mortimer–street, Cavendish–square."

CHAPTER XV

Cradock Nowell had written from London to the Parsonage once, and once only. He told them how he had changed his name, because his father had cast him off; and (as he bitterly added), according to filial promise, he felt himself bound to be Nowell no longer. But he did not say what name he had taken, neither did he give any address; only he would write again when he had found some good situation. Of course he longed to hear from Amy—his own loving Amy, who begged that poor letter and bore it in her own pure bosom long after the Queen's head came off—but his young pride still lay hot upon him, and for Amy's sake he nursed it.

A young man is never so proud of his honour, so prompt to deny himself anything, so strong in another's lifehold, and careless about his own living, as when he has won a true love's worth, and sees it abiding for ever. Few are the good who have such luck—for the success is not of merit, any more than it is in other things; more often indeed some fish–tailed coxcomb is a woman's Dagon, doubly worshipped for crushing her—but when that luck does fall to the lot of a simple and honest young fellow, he piles his triple mountains up to the everlasting heaven, but makes no Babel of them. A man who chatters about his love soon exhausts himself or his subject.

John Rosedew, after receiving that letter, shut every book on his table, chairs, and desk, and chimney–piece. He must think what to do, and how: and he never could think hard on the flints of daily life, while the green pastures of the dead were tempting his wayward steps away. Of course he would go to London at once, by the very next train; but whether or no should he tell his people the reason of his going? He felt so strongly inclined to tell, even at risk of domestic hysterics and parochial convulsions, that he resolved at last not to tell; for he thought of the great philosopher's maxim (not perhaps irrefragable), that when the right hangs dubious, we may safely conclude that it rides in the scale swinging opposite to our own wishes. To most of us (not having a quarter of John Rosedew's ability, and therefore likely to be a hundred times less hesitant) it seems that the maxim holds good with ourselves, or any other common mortal, but makes Truth actually cut her own throat when applied to a mind like his—a mind already too timorously and humorously self–conscious.

Let 99,000 angels get on the top of John Rosedew's pen—which generally had a great hair in it—and dance a *faux pas* over that question, if it was laid the wrong way; for we, whose consciences must work in corduroys and highlows, roughly conclude that right and wrong are but as button and button–hole when it comes to a question of hair–splitting. Blest are they whose conscience–edge, like the sword of Thor, can halve every wisp of wool afloat upon the brook of life.

After breakfast John mounted Coræbus, leaving a short farewell, and set off hastily with the old–fashioned valise behind the saddle, wherein he was wont to bear wine and confections upon his parochial tours. The high–mettled steed was again amazed at the pace that could be pumped out of him; neither did he long continue ingloriously mute, but woke the echoes of Ytene with many a noble roar and shriek, so that consternation shook the heart of deer and pig and cow. But the parson did not exult as usual in these proofs of velocity, because his soul within him was sad; nevertheless he preserved cohesion, or at least coincidence, in an admirable manner, with his feet thrust strenuously into the stirrups, his bridle–hand thrown in great emergencies upon the peak of the saddle, and whip–hand reposing on the leathern outwork, which guarded and burnished his rear. Anchored thus by both strong arms—for the sake of his mission and family—he felt capable of jumping a gate, if Coræbus had equal confidence.

That evening he entered the Ducksacre shop, and found no one there but the mistress.

"Pray excuse me, but I have been told, ma'am," said John Rosedew, lifting his hat—as he always did to a matron—and bowing his silvery head, "that you have a lodger here who is very ill."

"Yes, sir," replied Mrs. Ducksacre, fetching her breath very quickly, "and dead, too, for all I know. Oh Lord, I am so put upon!"

The soft–hearted parson was shocked at this apparent apathy; and thought her no true woman. Who is not wrong sometimes? It was a very rare thing for John Rosedew to judge man or woman harshly. But only half an hour ago that poor woman had been up–stairs, neglecting till, present and future, estranging some excellent customers, leaving a wanton shop–boy to play marbles with Spanish chestnuts, while she did her most misguided best to administer to sick Cradock soup wildly beyond her own economy, and furiously beyond his powers of deglutition.

John Rosedew, with his stout legs shaking, and his stockings expressing excitement, went up three pairs (ill–assorted) of stairs into Cradock's sick room. Then he started back from the Aristophanic climax—even the rags of Telephus; though after all, Polly Ducksacre had done her best to make the room comely. Why, there were three potato–sacks on the bed, with the names of Fulham growers done in red letters upon them, and giving the room quite a bright appearance, as if newly–marked sheep were in it. Nay, and I could almost swear there were two bast mats from Covent Garden, gloriously fixed as bed curtains, mats from that noble market where a rat prays heaven vainly to grant him the coat of a water–rat.

There, by Cradock Nowell's bed, sat the faithful untiring nurse, the woman who had absorbed such a quantity of strap, and had so kindly assimilated it. Meek–spirited Rachel Jupp waited and watched by the bed of him through whom she had been enfranchised. Since Issachar Jupp became a Christian she had not tasted the buckle–end once, and scarcely twice the tongue–end.

She had been employed some years ago as a nurse in the Middlesex Hospital; so she knew her duties thoroughly. But here she had exceeding small chance of practising that knowledge; because scarcely anything which she wanted, and would have rung for, if there had been any bell, was ever to be found in the house. Even hot water, which the doctor had ordered, was cold again ere it came to her, and had taken an hour before it started; for there was no fireplace in the little room, nor even on the floor below it.

Uncle John could scarcely keep from crying, as he looked at poor Craddy propped up in the bed there, with his lips so pale and bloodless, cheeks sunken in and shining like dry oyster–shells, but with a round red spot in the centre, large eyes glaringly bright and starting, and red hot temples and shorn head swathed with dripping bandages; while now and then he raised his weak hands towards the surging tumult, and dropped them helpless on the sun–blind, tucked round him as part of his counterpane.

"Ah, that's the way, sir," said Rachel, after she had risen and curtseyed, "that's the way he go on now, all the day and all the night; and he have left off talking now altogether, only to moan and to wamble. He used to jump up in the bed at first, and shut his left eye, and put his arms like this, as if he was shooting at something; and it pleased him so when I give him the hair–broom. He would put the flat of it to his shoulder, and smile as if he see some game, and shoot at the door fifty times a day; and then scream and fall back and cover his eyes up. But he haven't done that these three days now; too weak, I'm afeard, too weak for it."

John Rosedew sighed heavily for the bright young mind, so tried above what it was able to bear; then, as he kissed the flaming forehead—sometimes flaming and sometimes icy—he thought that it might be the Father's mercy to obliterate sense of the evil. For the mind of the insane, or at least its precious part, is with Him, who showers afar both pain and pleasure, but keeps at home the happiness.

"Can you send for the doctor at once, ma'am, or tell me where to find him?" The parson still kept to the ancient fashion, and addressed every woman past thirty as "ma'am," whatever her rank or condition. As he spoke, a heavy man entered on tiptoe, and quietly moved them aside. A raw–boned, hulking fellow he was, with a slouch and a squint, made more impressive by a black eye in the third and most picturesque stage, when mauve, and lilac, and orange intone and soften sweetly off from the purple nucleus outward; as a boy's taw is, or used to be, shaded, with keen artistic feeling, in many a ring concentric, from the equator to the poles. Mr. Jupp's face was a villainous one; as even the softest philanthropist would have been forced to acknowledge. The enormous jaws, the narrow forehead, the grisly, porkish eyebrows, the high cheek–bones, and the cunning skance gleam from the black, deep–ambushed squinters—all these were enough to warn any man who wished to get good out of Zakey Jupp that he must try to put it there first, and give it time to go to the devil and back, as we say that parsley–seed does.

Mr. Jupp was a man of remarkable strength,—not active elastic Achillean vigour, nor even stalwart Ajacian bulk, but the sort of strength which sometimes vanquishes both of those, by outlasting,—a slouching, slow–to–come, long–to–go heft, that had scarcely found its proper wind when better–built men were exhausted.

Men of this stamp are usually long–armed, big in the lungs and shoulders, small in the loins, knock–kneed, and splay–footed; in a word, shaped like a John Dory, or a miller's thumb, or a banjo. They are not very "strong on their pins," nor active; they generally get thrown in the first bout of wrestling before ever their muscles get warm; they cannot even run fast, and in jumping they spring from the heel; nevertheless, unless they are stricken quite senseless at the outset—and their heads for the most part are a deal too thick for that—the chances are that they make an example of the antagonist ere he is done with. And so, in Mr. Jupp's recent duello with an Irish bully, who scoffed at Cradock, and said something low of his illness, the Englishman got the worst of it in the first round, the second, the third, and the fourth; but, just as Dan Sullivan's pals and backers were wild with delight and screeching, the brave bargee settled down on his marrow, and the real business began. After twenty–five rounds, the Tipperary Slasher had three men to carry him home, and looked fit for an inquest to sit upon, without making him any flatter.

Now, Issachar being a very slow man, there was no chance that he would hurry over his present inspection of Cradock. For a very long time he looked at him from various points of view; then, at last, he shook his head, and poked his long black chin out.

"Now this here wunna do, ye know. I'll fetch the doctor to ye, master, as ye seem to care for the pore young charp."

And Zakey Jupp, requiring no answer, went slowly down the stairs, with a great hand on either wall to save noise; then at a long trot, rolling over all who came in his way, and rounding the corners, like a ship whose rudder–bands are broken, he followed the doctor from street to street, keeping up the same pace till he found him. Dr. Tink was coming out of a court not far from Marylebone–lane, where the small–pox always lay festering.

"Ye'll just corm street 'long wi' me to the poor charp as saved our Looey," said Mr. Jupp, coolly getting into the brougham, and sitting in the place of honour, while he dragged Dr. Tink in by the collar, and set him upon the front seat. "Fire awa' now for Martimer–straat," he yelled to the wondering coachman, "and if ye dunna laither the narg, mind, I'll laither ye when we gits there."

The nag was leathered to Mr. Jupp's satisfaction, and far beyond his own, and they arrived at the coal and cabbage shop before John Rosedew had finished reading a paper which Mrs. Jupp had shown him, thinking that it was a prescription.

"He wrote it in his sleep, sir, without knowing a thing about it; in his sleep, or in his brain–wandering; I came in and found him at it, in the middle of the night; and my, how cold his fingers was, and his head so hot! We took it to three great chemists' shops, but they could not make it up. They hadn't got all the drugs, they said, and they couldn't make out the quantities."

"Neither can I," said John; "but it rings well, considering that the poor boy wrote it when his brain was weak with fever. The dialects are somewhat muddled, moreover; but we must not be hypercritical."

"No, sir, to be sure not. I am sure I meant no hypocrisy. Only you see it ain't Christian writing; and Mr. Clinkers shake his head at it, and say it come straight from the devil, and his hoof in every line of it."

"Mrs. Jupp, the Greek characters are beautiful, though some of the lines are not up to the mark. But, for my part, I wonder how any man can write mixed Greek in London. Nevertheless, I shall have great pleasure in talking it over with him, please God that he ever gets well. To think that his poor weary brain should still be hankering after his classics!"

It was the dirge in Cymbeline put into Greek choral metre, and John Rosedew's tears flowed over the words, as Polydore's had done, and Cadwal's.

Unhappy Cradock! His misty brain had vapoured off in that sweet wild dirge, which hovers above, as if the freed soul lingered, for the clogged one to shake its wings to it.

The parson was pondering and closing his wet eyes to recover his faith in God—whom best we see with the eyes shut, except when His stars are shining—while Issachar Jupp came up the stairs, poking Dr. Tink before him, because he still thought it likely that the son of medicine would evaporate. The doctor, who knew his tricks and put up with them, lest anything worse might come of it, solaced his sense of dignity, when he got to the top, by a grand bow to Mr. Rosedew. John gave him the change in a kind one; then offered his hand, as he always did, being a man of the ancient fashion.

While they were both looking sadly at Cradock, he sat up suddenly in the bed, and stretching forth his naked arms (wherein was little nourishment), laughed as an aged man does, and then nodded at them solemnly. His glazed eyes were so prominent, that their whites reflected the tint of the rings around them.

"Ladies and gentlemen, stop him if you please, and give him a pen and ink, and my best hat to write on. Oh, don't let him go by."

"Stop whom, my dear sir?" asked the doctor, putting out his arms as if to do it. "Now I've stopped him. What's his name?"

"The golden lad. Oh, don't you know? You can't have got him, if you don't. The golden lad that came from heaven to tell me I did not do it, that I didn't do it, do it, sir—all a mistake altogether. It makes me laugh, I declare it does; it makes me laugh for an hour, every time he comes, because they were all so wise. All but my Amy, my Amy; she was such a foolish little thing, she never would hear a word of it. And now I call you all to witness, obtestor, antestor, one, two, three, four, five; let him put it down on a sheet of foolscap, with room enough for the names below it; all the ladies and gentlemen put their names in double column, and get Mr. Clinkers, if you can, and Jenny, to go at the bottom; only be particular about the double column, ladies one side, gentlemen the other, like a country dance, you know, or the 'carmen sæculare,' and at the bottom, right across, Miss Amy Rosedew's name."

The contemplation of that last beatitude was too much for the poor fellow; he fell back, faint on the pillow, and the shop–blind, untucked by his blissful emotions, rattled its rings on the floor.

"Blow me if I can stand it," cried Issachar Jupp, going down three stairs at a step; and when he came back his face looked clearer, and he said something about a noggin. Mrs. Ducksacre bolted after him, for business must be attended to.

"Will he ever be right again, poor fellow? Dr. Tink, I implore you to tell me your opinion sincerely."

"Then I cannot say that *I think* he will. Still, I have some hopes of it. Much will depend upon the original strength of the cerebellum, and the regularity of his previous habits. If he has led a wild, loose life, he has no chance whatever of sanity."

"No, he has led a most healthy life—temperate, gentle, and equable. His brain has always been clear and vigorous, without being too creative. He was one of the soundest scholars for his age I have ever met with."

"But he had some terrible blow, eh?"

"Oh yes, a most terrible blow."

John thought what a terrible blow it would be to his own life's life, if the issue went against him, and for tears he could ask no more.

CHAPTER XVI

The good people assembled in Nowelhurst church were agreeably surprised, on the following Sunday, by the announcement from Mr. Pell—in that loud sonorous voice of his, which had frightened spinsters out of their wits, lest he were forbidding, instead of asking their banns of matrimony—that there would be no sermon that morning, inasmuch as he, the Rev. Octavius, was forced to hurry away, at full speed, to assuage the rampant desire of Rushford for the performance of divine service.

Mrs. Nowell Corklemore, who had the great curtained pew of the Hall entirely to herself and child—for Eoa never would go to church, because they defy the devil there—Georgie, who appeased her active mind by counting the brass–headed nails, and then multiplying them into each other, and subtracting the ones that were broken, lifted her indescribable eyes, and said, "Thank God," almost audibly.

Octavius Pell, hurrying out of the porch, ascended Coræbus, as had been arranged; but he did it so rapidly, and with such an air of decision, that Amy, standing at the churchyard gate, full of beautiful misgivings, could not help exclaiming,

"Oh please, Mr. Pell, whatever you do, leave your stick here till Monday. We will take such care of it."

"Indeed, I fear I must not, Miss Rosedew," Octavius answered, gravely, looking first at his stick, and then at the flanks of Ræby, who was full of interesting tricks; "I have so far to go, you know, and I must try to keep time with them.—Whoa, you little villain!"

"Oh dear, I am so sorry. At any rate please not to strike him, only *stroke* him with it. He is so *very* high–spirited. And he has never had a weal upon him, at least since he came to papa. And I could not bear to see it. And I know you won't, Mr. Pell."

Octavius looked at the soft–hearted girl, blushing so in her new drawn bonnet—mauve with black, for the sake of poor Clayton. He looked at her out of his knowing dry eyes in that sort of response–to–the–Litany style which a curate adopts to his rector's daughter.

"Can you suppose, Miss Rosedew, that I would have the heart to beat him now?—Ah, you will, will you then?" Ræbus thought better of it.

"No, I hope you would not," said Amy, in pure good faith, with a glance, however, at the thick bamboo, "because it would be *so cruel*. It is hollow, I hope; but it has such knots, and it looks so very hard!"

"Hollow, and thin as a piece of pie–crust; and you know how this wood splits."

"Oh, I am so glad, because you can't hurt him so very much. Please not to go, if you can hold him, more than three miles and a half an hour. Papa says that is the pace that always suits his health best. And please to take the saddle off, and keep it at your house, that the Rushford boy may not ride him back. And please to choose a steady boy from the head–class in your Sunday school, and, if possible, a communicant. But I'm sadly afraid there's no trusting the boys."

"Indeed, I fear not," said Octavius, gravely; and adding to himself, "at any rate when you are concerned, you darling. What a love you are! But there's no chance for me, I know; and it's a good job for me that I knew it. Oh you little angel, I wonder who the lucky fellow is!" Aunt Eudoxia had dropped him a hint, quite in a casual way, when she saw that the stout young bachelor was going in, over head and ears.

Sweet Amy watched Mr. Pell, or rather his steed, with fond interest, until they turned the corner; and certainly the pace, so far, was very sedate indeed. Octavius was an upright man—you could see that by his seat in the saddle—as well as a kind and good–natured one; and on no account would he have vexed that gentle and beautiful girl. Nevertheless he grew impatient, as Coræbus pricked his ears pretentiously, and snorted so as to defy the winds, and was fain to travel sidewise, as if the distance was not enough for him; and all the time he was swallowing the earth at the rate of no more than four miles an hour. Then the young parson pulled out his watch, and saw that it wanted but half an hour of the time himself had fixed for the morning service at Rushford. And he could not bear the thought of keeping the poor folk waiting about the cross, as they always did and would wait, till the parson appeared among them. As Mr. Wise has well observed, "the peasant of the New Forest is too full of veneration."

And here let me acknowledge, as behoveth a man to do, not in a scambling preface, which nobody ever would read, but in the body of my work, great and loving obligation to the labours of Mr. John R. Wise. His book is perfectly beautiful, written in admirable English, full of observation, taste, and gentle learning; and the descriptions of scenery are such that they make the heart yearn to verify them. I know the New Forest pretty well, from my own perambulations and perequitations—one barbarism is no worse than the other—but I never should have loved it as I do but for his loving guidance.

The Rev. Mr. Pell, as some people put when they write to a parson,—hoping still to keep faith with Amy, because her eyes were so lovely,—pulled the snaffle, and turned Coræbus into a short cut, through beeches and hazels. Then compromise came soon to an end, and the big bamboo was compelled to fall upon the fat flank of Coræbus, because he would not go without it. He showed sense of that first attention only by a little buck-jump, and a sprightly wag of his tail; then, hoping that the situation need not be looked in the face, shambled along at five miles an hour, with a mild responsibility.

"Five miles more," said Octave Pell, "and only twenty minutes to do it in! It's an unlucky thing for you, Coræbus, that your mistress is engaged." Whack, came the yellow bamboo again, and this time in solid earnest; Ræbus went off as if he meant to go mad. He had never known such a blow since the age wherein he belonged to the innkeeper. Oh, could a horse with four feeds a day be expected to put up with tyranny?

But, to the naggy's great amazement, Octave Pell did not tumble off; more than that, he seemed to stick closer, with a most unpleasant embrace, and a pressure that told upon the wind—not of heaven but of horse—till the following symptoms appeared:—First a wheeze, and creak internal, a slow creak, like leather chafing, or a pair of bellows out of order; then a louder remonstrance, like the ironwork of a roller, or the gudgeons of a wheelbarrow; then, faster and faster, a sucking noise, like the bucket of an old pump, when the gardener works by the job; finally, puff, and roar, and shriek, with notes of passing sadness, like the neap-tide wailing up a cavern, or the lament of the Berkshire Blowing Stone.

In forest glades, where hollow hoofs fell on the sod quite mutely, that roar was enough to try masculine courage, though never unnerved by a heart-shock. How then could poor Pearl Garnet, sitting all alone, in a lonely spot, wherein she had pledged herself to her dead love, sitting there to indulge her tears, the only luxury left her—how could she help being frightened to death as the unearthly sound approached her?

The terror was mutual. Coræbus, turning the corner sharply, stopped short, in a mode that must have sent his true master over his withers, to explore the nature of the evil. Then he shook all through, and would have bolted, if the bamboo had not fallen heavily.

In the niche of a hollow oak was crouching, falling backward with terror, and clutching at the brave old bark, yet trying to hide behind it—only the snowy arms would come outwards—a beautiful girl, clad in summer white on that foggy day of December. The brown cloak, which had protected her from sylvan curiosity, lay on the ground, a few yards away, on the spot so sad and sacred. Pearl Garnet's grief, if we knew the whole of it, or perhaps because we cannot, was greater than any girl could bear. A lovely, young, and loving maid, with stores of imagination, yet a practical power of stowing it; of building castles, yet keeping them all within compass of the kitchen–range; quite different from our Amy, yet a better wife for *some* men—according to what the trumps are, and Amy must have hearts, or she dies;—that very nice girl, we have let her go weep, and never once cared to follow her. There is never any justice in this world; therefore who cares to apologise? It would take up all our business–time, if we did it properly.

Now, as she stretched her white arms forth, and her delicate form shrunk back into the black embrace of the oak–tree; while her rich hair was streaming all down her breast, and her dark eyes still full of tear–drops; the rider no less than the horse was amazed, and seemed to behold a vision. Then as she shrunk away into the tree–bole, with a shriek of deadly terror—for what love casteth out fear?—and she saw not through the ivy–screen, and Coræbus groaned sepulchrally, Pell came down with a dash on one foot, and went, quick jump, to help her.

In a fainting fit,—for the heart so firm and defiant in days of happiness was fluxed now and frail with misery—she was cowering away in the dark tree–nook, like the pearls of mistletoe fallen, with her head thrown back (such an elegant head, a woman's greatest beauty), and the round arms hanging helpless.

Hereupon Mr. Pell was abroad. He had never experienced any sisters, nor much mother consciously—being the eighth son, as of course we know, of a jolly Yorkshire baronet; at any rate he had lost his mother at the birth of Nonus Pell; and I am sorry there are not ninety of them, if of equal merit.

So Octavius stood like a fish out of water, with both hands in his pocket, as it is so generally the habit of fishes to stand.

Then, meaning no especial harm, nor perhaps great good, for that matter, he said to himself—

"Confound it all. What the deuce am I to do?"

His sermon upon the Third Commandment, about to be preached at Rushford, where the fishermen swore like St. Peter,—that sermon went crack in his pocket at such a shocking ejaculation. Never heeding that, he went on to do what a stout fellow and a gentleman must have done in this emergency. He lifted the drooping figure forth into the open air, touching it only with his hands, timidly and reverently, as if every fair curve were sacred. Then he fetched water in his best Sunday hat—the only chimney-pot he possessed—from the stream trickling through the spire-bed; and he sprinkled it on the broad, white forehead, as if he were christening a baby.

The moment he saw that her life was returning, and her deep grey eyes, quiet havens of sorrow, opened and asked where their owner was, and her breast rose like a billow in a place where two tides meet, that moment Octave laid her back against the rugged trunk, in the thick brown cloak which he had fetched when he went for the water; and wrapped it around her, delicately, as if she were taking a nap there.

Oh, man of short pipes and hard, bachelor fare, for this thou deservest as good a wife as ever basted a leg of mutton!

At last the young lady looked up at him with a deep-drawn sigh, and said—

"I am afraid I have been very silly."

"No, indeed, you have not. But I am very sorry for you, because I am dreadfully clumsy."

She glanced at his snowy choker—which he never wore but on Sundays—and, being a very quick-witted young woman, she guessed at once who he was.

"Oh, please to tell me—I hope the service is not over at Nowelhurst church."

"The service has been over for a quarter of an hour; because there was no sermon."

"Oh, what shall I do, then? What can I do? I had better never go home again."

This was said to herself in anguish, and Pell saw that he was not meant to hear it.

"Can I go, please, to the Rectory? Mr. Rosedew is from home; but I'm sure they will give me shelter until my—until I am sent for. I have lost my way in the wood here."

This statement was none of the truest.

"To be sure," said the hasty parson, forgetting about the Rushford bells, the rheumatic clerk, and the quid-chewing pilots—let them turn their quids a bit longer—"to be sure, I will take you there at once. Allow me to introduce myself. How very stupid of me! Octavius Pell, Mr. Rosedew's curate at Rushford."

Hereupon "Pello, pepuli, pulsum" (as his friends loved to call him from his driving powers at cricket, and to show that they knew some Latin) executed a noble salaam—quite of the modern school, however, and without the old reduplication (like the load on the back of Christian)—till the duckweed came out of his hat in a body, and fell into the flounce tucket of the beautiful Pearl's white skirt.

She never looked, though she knew it was there—that girl understood her business—but curtseyed to him prettily, having recovered strength by this time; and there was something in his dry, manly tone, curt modesty, and breeding, without any flourish about it, which led the young maid to trust him, as if she had known him since tops and bottoms.

"I am Pearl Garnet," said she, imitating his style unconsciously, "the daughter—I mean I live at Nowelhurst Dell Cottage."

Coræbus had cut off for stable long ago, with three long weals from bamboo upon him, which he vowed he would show to Amy.

"Please to take my arm, Miss Garnet. You are not very strong yet. I know your brother well; and a braver or more straightforward young gentleman never thought small things of himself after doing great ones."

Pearl was delighted to hear Bob's praises; and Mr. Pell treated that subject so cleverly, from every possible point of view, that she was quite astonished when she saw the Rectory side–gate, and Octavius, in the most light–hearted manner, made a sudden and warm farewell, and darted away for Rushford. How good it is for a sad, heavy heart to exchange with a gay and light one!

"Hang it! after that let me have a burster!" was his clerical ejaculation, "or else it is all up with me. I hope we haven't spilt the sermon, though, or got any duckweed down it. Duckweed, indeed; what a duck she is! And oh, what splendid eyes!"

He ran all the way to Rushford, at a pace unknown to Coræbus; and his governor–coat flew away behind him, with the sermon banging about, and the text peeping out under the pocket–lap. "Swear not at all," were the words, I believe; and a rare good sermon it must have been, if it stuck to the text under the circumstances.

The jolly old tars, after waiting an hour, orally refreshing their grandmothers' epitaphs, and close–hauling on many a tight yarn, were just setting up stun'sails to take grog on board at the "Lugger's Locker," hard by, as the banyan time was over. Let them ship their grog, and their old women might keep gravy hot, and be blessed to them. They had come there for sarvice, and shiver their timbers if they'd make sail till the chaplain came.

Good faith, and they got their service at last, but an uncommonly short–winded one, a sermon, moreover, which each man felt coming admirably home—to his shipmate.

Meanwhile, Mr. Pell had left behind no small excitement at Nowelhurst. For a rumour took wing after morning service—when the wings of fame are briskest in all country parishes—that parson John was gone to London to complain to the Queen that Sir Cradock Nowell never came to church now, nor even sent his agent thither, to manage matters for him. For Mr. Garnet still retained his stewardship among them, though longing to be quit of it, and discharging his duties silently, and not with his old pronouncement, because his health was weaker. The vivid power of vital force seemed to be failing the man who had stamped his character upon all people around him; because he never said a thing which he did not think, and scarcely ever thought a thing with any fear of saying it.

Hitherto we have had of Bull Garnet by far the worse side uppermost. I will offer no excuses now for his too ready indulgence of his far too savage temper. In sooth, we meet with scarce any case in which excuses are undiscoverable. God and the angels find them always; our best earthly friends can see them, when properly pointed out; our enemies, when they want to make accusation of them.

All I will say for Bull Garnet is (to invert the historian's sentence) "Hæc tanta viri vitia ingentes virtutes exæquabant"—"These blemishes, however dark, had grand qualities to redress them." Strong affection, great scorn of falsehood, tenderness almost too womanly, liberality both of mind and heart, a real depth of sympathy—would all these co–exist with, or be lost in, one great vice? It appears to me that we are so toothed in, spliced and mortised, dovetailed, double–budded, and inarched, both of good and evil, that the wrong, instead of poisoning the right, often serves as guano to it. Nevertheless we had better be perfect—when we have found the way out.

CHAPTER XVII

It must not be forgotten that Rufus Hutton all this time was very hard at work, and so was Mrs. Corklemore. Between that lady and Eoa pleasant little passes gave a zest to daily intercourse, Georgie's boundless sympathies being circumscribed only by terror. Nevertheless, although Sir Cradock laughed (when his spirits were good, and his mind was clear) at their fundamental difference, Georgie began to gain upon him, and Eoa to lose ground. How could it be otherwise, even if their skill had been equal—and Eoa not only had no skill, but scorned sweet Georgie for having any—how could Mrs. Corklemore fail of doing her blessed duty, when she was in the house all day, and Eoa out, jumping the river, or looking about for Bob Garnet? Whatever the weather was, out went Eoa, peering around for the tracks of Bob, which, like those of a mole, were self–evident; and then hiding behind a great tree when she found him; and hoping, with flutter of heart about it, that Bob had not happened to see her. Yet, if he happened not to see, she would go up and be cross with him, and ask whether Amy Rosedew had turned to the right or left there, or had stopped in a hollow tree. And did Bob think she looked well that morning? Then he had no right to think so. And perhaps her own new hat, with black ostrich, was a hideously ugly thing. Oh, she only wished there were tigers!

Leave the little dear to do exactly as she likes—for nothing else she wil do; and now, in looking through the forest, grey and white with winter scorn we not the grand old trunk, in our gay love of the mistletoe.

There is a very ancient tree, an oak well known and good of fame even at the first perambulation of our legislator king. It stands upon th bend and brow under which two valleys meet, where a horse–shoe of th wood has chanced, and water takes advantage. In the scoop below th tree, two covered brooks fetch round high places into one another, prattl satisfaction, and steal away for their honeymoon, without a breeze upo them. This "mark–oak," last of seven stout brothers, dwells upon a surge c upland, and commands three valleys, two of which unite below it, and th other leads them off, welcoming their waters. The grand tree lifts its prove column, channeled, ramped, and crocketed, flaked with brown on lines of grey, and bulked with cloudlike ganglions. Then from the maintop, where is room for fifty archers to draw the bow, limbs of rugged might arise, spread flat, or straggle downwards. But the two great limbs of all, the power and main glory, the arms that reared their pride to heaven, are stricken, riven, and blasted. Gaping with great holes and rotten, heavily twisted in and out, and ending in four long scraggy horns, ghastly white in the winter sun; where the squirrel durst not build, nor the honey–buzzard watch for prey; this shattered hope of a noble life records the wrath of Heaven.

The legend is that a turf–cutter having murdered a waylost pedlar, for the sake of his pack, buried the corpse in this hollow tree, and sat down on the grave to count his booty. Here, while he was bending over the gewgaws and the trinkets, which he had taken for gold upon the poor huckster's word, and which gleamed and flashed in the August twilight, the vengeance of God fell upon him. In bodily form God's lightning crashed through the dome of oak above him, leaped on the murderer's head, and drove him through the cloven earth, breast to breast on his victim's corpse. You may be sure that the sons of Ytene, a timid and superstitious race, find small attractions in that tree, when the shades of night are around it.

John Rosedew did not return on the Monday, nor yet on the Tuesday, &c. Not even until the last down–train roared through the Forest on Saturday. Then, as it rushed through the dark night of winter, throwing its white breath (more strong than our own, and very little more fleeting) in bracelets on the brown–armed trees, and in chains on the shoulders of heather, the parson leaned back on the filthy panels of a second–class carriage, and thought of the scene he had left.

He had written from London to Miss Rosedew, insisting, so far as he ever cared to insist on a little matter, that none at home should stay up for him, that no one should come to the station to meet him, and that Pell should be begged to hold himself ready for the Sunday's duty, because Mr. Rosedew would not go home, if any change should that day befall unlucky Cradock Nowell. Lucky Cradock, one ought to say, inasmuch as for a fortnight now he had lost all sense of trouble.

Finding from Dr. Tink that no rapid change was impending, John Rosedew determined to see his home, and allay his child's anxiety. Moreover, he felt that his "cure of souls" must need their Sunday salting. Now walking away from the wooded station that cloudy Christmas Eve—

for Christmas that year fell on Sunday—how grand he found the difference from the dirty coop of London.

The new moon was set, but the clouds began to lift above the tree–tops, and a faint Aurora flushed and flickered in the far north–west. Then out came several stars rejoicing, singing in twinkles their Maker's praise; and some of the sounds that breathe through a forest, even in the hush of a winter's night, began to whisper peace and death.

John, who feared not his Master's works, and was happiest often in solitude, trudged along with the leathern valise, and three paper parcels strapped comfortably upon his ample back. Presently he began to think of home and his parish cares, and the breadth of God spread around him; and then from thinking rose unawares into higher communion, for surely it is a grander thing to feel than to think of greatness.

And in this humour quietly he plodded his proper course for the first four miles or so, until he had passed the Dame Slough, near the Blackwater stream, and was over against Vinney Ridge. But here he must needs try a short cut, through the Government Woods, to Nowelhurst, though even in the broad daylight he could scarcely have found his way there. He thought that, in spite of his orders, Amy would be sure to stay up for him, and so he must hurry homeward.

At a fine brisk pace, for a man of his years, he plunged into the deep wood, and in five minutes' time he had very little hope of getting out before daylight. Have you ever been lost in a great wood at night, alone, and laden, and weary, where the frithings have not been cut for ten years, when there is no moon or wind to guide a man, and the stars glimpse so deceitfully? How the stubs, even if you are so quick–footed as not to be doubled back by them, or thrown down with nostrils patulous—how they catch you at the knee with three prongs apiece, and make you think of white swelling! Then the slip, where the wet has dribbled from some officious branch, or sow, or cow, summer–pasturing, has kept her volutabre. Down you plump, and your heels alone have chance of going to heaven, because (unless you are a wonder) you employ such powerful language.

Rising with some difficulty, after doubting if it be worth the while, and rubbing spitefully ever so long at "the case of the part affected," you have nothing for it but to start again, and fall into worse disasters. Going very carefully then you jump from the goading repulse of a holly into the heart of a hazel–bush—one which has numberless clefts and tongs, and is hospitable to a bramble. Tumbling out of it, full of thorns, recalling your Farnaby epigram, and wishing they had pelted the hazel harder, away you go, quite desperate now, knowing well that the wood is full of swamps, some of which will petrify you, under sun–dew and blue campanula, when the summer comes again.

Through all these pleasing incidents and animating encounters John Rosedew went ahead, and, too often, a "header," until he was desperately tired, and sat down to think about it. Then he heard two tawny owls hooting to one another, across at least a mile of trees; and every forest sound grew clearer in the stillness of the night; the sharp, sad cry of the marten–cat, the bark of the fox so impatient, the rustle of the dry leaves as a weasel or rat skirred over them, the wing–flap of some sliding bird roused from his roost by danger, the scratching of claws upon trunks now and then, and the rubbing of horns against underwood: these and other stranger noises, stirring the "down of darkness," moving the sense of lonesome mystery and of fear indefinite, were abroad on the air (in spite of Shakespeare) on that Christmas Eve.

John Rosedew laid his burden by, and began to think, or wonder, what was best to do. Long as he had lived amid the woods, he knew much more of classic sylvulæ and poetical arundines, than of the natural greenwood, and the tasseling of morasses.

Bob Garnet would have found his way there, or in any other English forest, with little hesitation. From his knowledge of all the epiphytes and their different aspects, the bent of the winter grasses, the sense which even a bramble has of sun and wind and rain, he would soon have established his compass, with allowance for slope and exposure.

The parson sat upon an ants' nest, which had done its work, and feeling discharged, collapsed with him—a big nest of the largest British ant, which is mostly found near fir–trees. That nest alone would have told poor Bob something of his whereabouts; for there are not many firs in that part of the forest, and only one clump, high up on a hill, in the wood where John Rosedew had lost himself. But the man of great learning was none the wiser, only he felt that his smallclothes were done for, and Mr. Channing's fashionable cut gone almost as prematurely as the critic who had condemned it.

"Let me now consider," said Mr. Rosedew to himself, for about the fiftieth time; "it strikes me at the first sight—though I declare I can't see anything—would that I could not feel! for I confess that these legs are grievous; but putting aside that view or purview of the question, it strikes me that, having no Antigone to lead me from this, which certainly is the grove of the Eumenides—there is another ant gone up my leg—'ingentis formica laboris.' I wish he wouldn't work so hard, though, and I always have had the impression that they stayed in–doors in the winter. Mem. To consult Theophrastus, and compare him, as usual, with Pliny. Also look at the Geoponika, full of valuable hints—why there he is again, biting very hard or stinging. What says Aristophanes about the music of the gnats? Indelicate, I fear, as he too often is. Nay, nay, good ant, if indeed thou art an ant—— Why, what is that over yonder?"

It was a dim light in the great hollow oak, "the Murderer's Tree," as they called it, not a hundred yards from John Rosedew.

The parson approached it cautiously, for he knew that desperate men, and criminals under a ban, still harboured sometimes in the Forest. As he drew nearer, the feeble light, glimmering through the entrance, showed him at once what tree it was, because the rays glanced through two dark holes under the bulging and beetling brow, which peasants call "the eyes of God."

John Rosedew was as brave a man as ever wept for another's grief, or with the word of God assuaged it. No man could have less superstition, unless (as some would have us believe) all religion is that. Upon this point we will not be persuaded, until we have seen them live the better, and die the more calmly for holding it. Yet John Rosedew, so firmly set, so full of faith in his Maker, so far above childish fears (which spring from the absence of our Father),—he, who having injured none had no dread of any, yet drew back and trembled greatly at the sight before him.

A small reflector–lamp, with the wick overhung with fungus, stood upon a knotted niche in the hollow of the tree. By it, and with his face and eyes set towards the earth, a tall and powerful man, stripped to the waist, was leaning, with one great arm beneath his forehead, and bloody stripes across his back. The drooping of his figure, the woe in every vein of it, the deep and everlasting despair in every bone—it was an extremity of our human nature, which neither chisel nor pen may approach, nor even the mind of man conceive, until it has been through it.

Presently the man upraised his massive head, and scorned himself for being so effeminate. He had nearly fainted with the pain; what right had he to feel it? Why should his paltry body quail at a flea–bite lash or so, when body and soul were damned for ever?

But if his form had told of sorrow, great God, what did his face tell? He never sighed, nor groaned, nor moaned; his woe was beyond such trumpery; he simply took the heavy scourge from the murderer's grave, upon which it had dropped when the swoon came over him, and, standing well forth in the black hollow's centre, to gain full swing for his scorpion thongs, he lashed himself over back and round breast, with the utmost strength of his mighty arms, with every corded muscle leaping, but not a sign of pain on his face, nor a nerve of his body flinching. Then, at last, he fell away, and allowed himself to moan a little.

John Rosedew would have leaped forward at once, in his horror at such self–cruelty, but that he saw who it was, and knew how his meddling would be taken. He knew that Bull Garnet's religious views were very strange and peculiar, and never must be meddled with, except at his own request, and at seasonable moments. Yet he had never dreamed that self–chastisement was part of them.

"Garnet a wild flagellant!" said the parson to himself; "well, I knew that he was an enthusiast, but never dreamed that he was a fanatic. And how shockingly hard he hits himself! Strong as Dr. Mastix at Sherborne; but the doctor took good care never to hit himself. Upon my word, I must run away. It is too sad to laugh at. What resolution that man must have! He scarcely feels the blows in the agony of his mind. I must reason with him about it, if I ever can find occasion. With such violation of His image, God cannot be well pleased."

Meditating deeply upon this strange affair, the parson plodded homewards, for now he knew his way, with the Murderer's Oak for his landmark. At last he saw his quiet home, and gave a very gentle knock, because it was so late.

The door was opened by Amy herself, pale, excited, and jumping.

"Oh, daddy, daddy!" Chock—chock—chock—such a lot of kisses, and both arms round his neck.

"Corculum, voluptas, glycymelon, anima mea——"

"Oh, papa, say 'Amy dear,' and then I shall know it is you."

Then she laughed, and then she cried, and presently fell to at kissing again. I am afraid she proved herself a fool; but allowance must be made for her, because she had never learned before how to get on without her father.

"Oh, you beautiful love of a daddy! I was quite sure you would come, you know; that you could not leave me any longer; so I would not listen to a single word any one of them said. And I kept the kitchen fire up, and a good fire in your pet room, dear; and I have got such a supper for you! Now, off with your coat in a minute, darling. Oh, how poorly you look, my own father! But we will soon put you to rights again. Aunt Doxy is gone to bed, hurrah! and so are Jemima and Jenny. And she won't have the impudence to come down, with all her hair in the jelly–bags, so I shall have you all to myself, dada; and if any one can deserve you, I do."

"My own pet child, my warm–hearted dear," said John, with the tears in his eyes; "I had not the least idea that your mind was so ill–regulated. We must have a course of choriambics together, or the heavy trimacrine dimeter, as I have ventured to name it, about which— —"

"About which not another short syllable, till you have had a light tri–mackerel supper, and not a quasi–cæsura left even."

"Why, Amy, you are getting quite witty!" And John, with one arm still in his overcoat, looked at her bright eyes wonderingly.

"Of course I am, dad, when you come home. My learning sparkles at sight of you. Come, quick now, for fear of my eating you before you begin your supper. You'll have it in the kitchen, you know, dear, because it will be so much nicer; and then a pipe by the book–room fire, and a chat with your good little daughter. O father, father, mind you never go away from me such a long, long time again."

John thought to himself that, ere many years, he must go away from his Amy for much more than a fortnight; but of course he would not damp her young joy with any such troubles now.

"If you please, my meritorious father, you will come to the door, and just smell them; and then you will have five minutes allowed you to put on your dear old dressing–gown, and the slippers worked by the Vestal virgins; five minutes by the kitchen clock, and not a book to be touched, mind. Now, don't they smell lovely? I put them on when I knew your knock. The first mackerel of the season, only caught this afternoon. I sent word to Mr. Pell for them. He can do what he likes with the fishermen. And you know as well as I do, papa, you can never resist a mackerel."

When John came down, half the table was covered with some of his favourite authors—not that she meant to let him read, but only because he would miss his books a great deal more than the salt–cellar—and the other half she was bleaching, and smoothing, and stroking with a snowy cloth, soft and sleek as her own bare arms, setting all things in lovely order, and looking at her father every moment, with the skirt of her frock pinned up, and her glossy hair dancing jigs on the velvet slope of her shoulders. And she made him hungrier every moment by savoury word and choice innuendo.

"Worcester sauce, pa, darling, and a little of the very best butter, not mixed up with flour, you know, but melting on them, like their native element. Just see how they are browning, and not a bit of the skin come off. What is it about the rhombus, pa, and when am I to read Juvenal?"

"Never, my child."

"Very well, pa, dear, you know best, of course; but I thought it was very nice about weighing Hannibal, in the Excerpta. Father, put that book down; I can't allow any reading. And after supper I shall expect you to spin me such a yarn, dear, to wind up the thread of your adventures."

"Τολυπεύειν," said John, calmly, although he was so hungry; "the very word poor Cradock used in his rendering of that dirge—

> *"'Μόχθον οὕνεκα τὸν κατ' ἦμαρ*
> *Ἐκτολυπέσας οἴκαδε,*
> *Μισθὸν φερων, ἤνυσας.'*

Oh, I forgot; ah yes, to be sure. A word, I mean, which expresses in a figurative and yet homely manner——"

"Cradock, papa! Oh, father, have you been with him in London? Oh, how Aunt Doxy has cheated me! You know very well, my own father, that you cannot tell me a story. Did you go to London because poor Cradock was very, very ill?"

"Yes," said her father, those soft bright eyes beamed into his so appealingly; "my own child, your Cradock is very ill indeed."

"Not dead, father? Oh, not dead?"

"No, my child; nor in any great danger, I sincerely believe, just at present."

"Then eat your supper, pa, while it is hot. I am so glad you have seen him. I am quite content with that."

She believed, or she would not have said it. And yet how far from the truth it was!

"You shall tell me all after supper, my father. Thank God for His mercies to me. I am never in a hurry, dear."

Yet Amy, in dishing up the mackerel, had the greatest difficulty (for her breath came short, and her breast heaved fast) in holding back the tide of hysterics, which would have spoiled her father's supper.

"My amulet, I cannot eat a morsel while I see your hand shake. Darling, I must tell you all; I cannot bear your anxiety."

The second mackerel, a fish of no manners, instead of curling his tail at the frying, had glued it to the pan, until a tear of Amy's fried, and then he let go in a moment. John Rosedew caught his darling child, and drew her to his knees, with the frying–pan in her hand; and then he made her look at him, and she tried to have her eyes dry. Do what she might she could not speak, only to let her neck rise, and her drooping eyelids tremble.

"My own life's love, I have told you the worst. God is very good to us. Cradock has been at the point of death, but now he is better a little. Only his mind is in danger. And it must come home very slowly, if it comes at all. Now, darling, you know everything."

She took his magnificent silvery head between her little white hands, and kissed him twice on either brow, but not a word she said.

"My own sweet child," cried her father, slowly passing one arm around her, and swindling his heart of a smile; "I am apt to make the worst of things. Let us try to be braver, or at least to have more faith."

She leaped up at that very word, with the dawn of a glorious smile in her eyes, and she took the frying–pan once again, and eased out, with a white–handled knife, mackerel No. 3. But, upon second thoughts, she let him slide into the frizzle again, to keep him warm and comfortable. Her heart was down very deep just now, but for all that, her father must have and must enjoy his supper.

"Father, I am all right now. Only eat your supper, dear. What a selfish thing I am!"

"Have a bit, my darling heart."

"Yes, I will have a bit of tail, pa, just to test my cookery. That's what I call frying! Look at the blue upon him, and the crisp brown shooting over it! Come, daddy, no nonsense, if you please. I could have eaten all three of them if I had only been out on the warren. And you to come starving from London! Now No. 3, papa, if you please." But she kept her face away from him, and bent her neck peculiarly.

"How beautifully fresh this ale is! Oh, the stuff they sell in London! I am almost inclined to consider the result of taking another half glass."

Her quick feet went pat on the cellar–steps, while her father was yet perpending; and she came back not a whit out of breath, but sweetly fresh and excited.

"Such a race, pa; because I know of one family of cockroaches, and half suspect another. They are so very imprudent. Robert Garnet says that they stay at home, and keep their Christmas domestically, and I need not run for fear of them, at least till the end of April. And perhaps he is right, because he knows and studies everything nasty. Only I can't believe what he says about ants, because it contradicts Solomon, who was so very much older. Now, you paternal darling, let me froth it up for you."

"Thank the Lord for as good a meal as ever one of His children was blessed with."

The parson stood up as he said these words, and put his thick but not large hands together, among the crumbs on the tablecloth.

"Now, if you please, the leastest—double superlative, pa, you know, like *πρώτιστος*, and something else—oh, they will pluck me at Oxford!—the very leastest little drop of the old French cognac we bought for parochial rheumatism, with one thin slice of lemon, an ebullition of water, and half a knob of sugar."

Before John could remonstrate, there it was, all winking at him, and begging to be sniffed before sipping.

"My pet, you are so premature. How can I trust your future? You never give me time to consider a subject, even in the first of its bearings."

"To be sure not, father. You know quite well you would take at least eight different views of the matter, and multiply them into eight others of people I never heard of. Now the pipe, dear. You shall have it here, because it is so much warmer. You know you can't fill it properly."

So the parson, happy in having a child who could fill a pipe better than he could, leaned back in his favourite chair, which Amy had wheeled in for him, and held his long clay in his left hand, while his right played with her hair, as she sat at his feet, and coaxed him.

"Sermon all ready, dear?"

"Well, you know best about that, Amy; I always trust you to arrange them."

"Never fear, papa; leave it to me. What would you do without me? I have put you out such a beauty, because it is Christmas Day: one that always makes me cry, because I have heard it so often. But you must have confidence in me."

"Implicit confidence, my pet. Still I like to run my eyes over them, for I cannot see as I did. My eyes are getting so old."

"I'll kiss them till you can't see one bit, if you dare to say that again, papa. Old, indeed! They are better than mine. And I can see the pattern of a lady–bird, all across the room. There was a lady–bird on the window to–day. At this time of year, only think! That was good luck, wasn't it? And a dear little robin flew in, and perched upon the hat–pegs; and then I *knew* that you must come home."

"Oh, you superstitious pet! I must reason with you to–morrow."